spontaneous

Also by Diana Wagman

Skin Deep

spontaneous

Diana Wagman

An LA Weekly Book for St. Martin's Press 📖 New York

www.stmartins.com

Design by Heidi D. Eriksen

Library of Congress Cataloging-in-Publication Data

Wagman, Diana.
    Spontaneous / Diana Wagman. — 1st ed.
      p. cm.
    ISBN 0-312-26234-5
    1. Combustion, Spontaneous human—Fiction. 2. Inheritance and succession—Fiction. 3. Los Angeles (Calif.)—Fiction. 4. Sisters—Fiction. I. Title

PS3573.A359 S68 2000
813'.54—dc21
                                      00-040251

First Edition: October 2000

10 9 8 7 6 5 4 3 2 1

For Tod and my sisters—Sally, Nicole, Alex, and Alisa

Spontaneous

Chapter One

Auntie Ned burped up the warm taste of blood, of the red rare, rib-eye steak she had had for dinner. Her long fingers, knuckles enlarged with arthritis, slid along her yellow Formica tabletop, cleaning up the final nonexistent crumbs. Another evening dripped shadow by shadow into night. She would move soon, from the table to the green sofa in her living room, turn on a light, turn on the TV, pass the time until she went to bed. She felt a bubbling in her intestines, tasted the sour starts and stops of regurgitation in the back of her throat. Heartburn.

Her hand, this crone's liver-spotted and twisted hand, had once caressed the curve of a perfect flank, stroked the rump of her deepest desire, traced the swoop of each rib. These old fingers had tangled with hair and buttons, had worshiped, wiggling into orifices, touching, praying, adoring.

Another burp. A harder, hot pinch in her bowels, then down to her thighs, around to the small of her back. She shifted in her yellow vinyl chair. She wanted to scream, but screaming wouldn't help. Get up, she told herself, pick up the phone, write a letter. No one on the other end. Her throat was swelling, scarlet and inflamed. Her flattened breasts, her thighs sagging like old curtains were hers alone for the rest of time. She banged the table with both hands. And again. She smelled her own bitter perspiration, felt the sweat bubble up in the wrinkles on her forehead, slide into the creases of her neck, boil in the folds under her arms.

She looked down. Steam escaped between the buttons of her flowered blouse. She opened her shirt. Her skin was crimson red, the pores blistering, oozing an odd yellow pus. She had the liquid feeling of a fever. Get up, she said to herself again, drink some water. Her feet had melted, fused with the floor. She wasn't going anywhere.

The heat inside Auntie Ned expanded, the burning pain dropped between her legs. She tried to see the face she had loved, to feel the chilled hands on her sweltering body, the icy strands of blond hair in her mouth. She panted with the pain. She was crackling now. She could hear her bones turn into kindling, her blood stewing, simmering. Her heart. Her hands clawed and scratched for the past. Remembering. Remembering. She was not sorry. Not sorry. Her heart detonated, a final shuddering explosion of surrender.

The smoke alarm woke the young thief in the duplex next door, startled him out of a heavy sleep. He looked out his window. He didn't see smoke, but there was a smell in the air, sweet and greasy. He knew his old lady neighbor was in trouble. He pulled on his pants and called 911 from one of his stolen cellular phones. Then he left. He had three good televisions and a collection of car stereos in his closet. He didn't want to answer any questions.

The fireman who broke down Auntie Ned's front door had never seen anything like it, but the fire chief ran his finger through the yellow oil coating the walls and knew what some people would think. He was a trim man, still young, only three weeks and three days away from his gold watch. He didn't want to open that can of worms. Not now. He called the coroner, told him it was a kitchen accident.

Nine days later, Roosevelt James Montgomery parked his old green panel truck in front of the small clapboard house. There was no exterior evidence of a fire. He admired the bright yellow paint in the dreary neighborhood; the roses, pink, peach, and red, lining the front walk. An orange and black plastic bird perched in a pot by the front door. Its nylon wings hung limp, waiting for a breeze.

Roosevelt set his toolbox on the porch and looked for the bell. She opened the door before he could ring. His hand froze over the ivory button, one freckled finger slightly extended as he looked at her. A woman with long blond hair, not smiling, wearing tight lavender pedal pushers over slim schoolgirl thighs and eating a mint-green ice cream cone. Eight-fifteen in the morning and she was licking ice cream. He watched her pink tongue move in slow laps around the green playing field. He dropped his hand.

"I'm here about the floor," he said.

"I know," she answered and smiled. Her perfect teeth were surrounded by green milk.

He looked away, squinted up the sunny street. It was a run-down neighborhood, Echo Park, between east LA and downtown. Quiet this early in the morning. He figured at night it would really hop with tire squeals, Latin music, the more than occasional gunshot.

"Come on in," she said.

He followed her into the house, watching her bare golden calves and brand-new pink Keds sneakers.

They went into the kitchen. It was bright orange and flowered, filled with the knickknacks and fussiness of old age. There were handwritten notes taped to the cabinets, above the sink, on the fridge. The handwriting was narrow and slanted and from where he stood impossible to read. Inspirational messages, he supposed.

He could still smell smoke, the faint memento of something burnt.

"You should've seen the mess," she said. "Everything was covered in this ash—soot, sort of. Only it was yellow—and slimy—like pig fat."

"Gross," he said.

"Exactly."

What was she, he thought, thirty? Older? Her hair was long and shiny blond. Her eyes were bountiful and brown. Her cheeks were smooth, but she had that confidence, that ease of an older woman. Experience could do that too. He looked away. He was thirty-one. He was good-looking. Okay, he was just a carpenter, but he had red hair and freckles and since his wife left him there had been plenty of girls.

"Here," she said.

She moved around the yellow Formica and chrome-edged table. On the floor, fused into the gold-flecked linoleum, was a charred circle of black. It was a twelve-inch spot, so badly burned that the linoleum had melted, sinking into the subflooring, and probably below.

"How'd it happen?"

"My aunt—"

"She start a campfire?" He had seen the results of stranger behavior.

"Spontaneous human combustion."

He looked at her.

"She burned, from the inside out. The chair was destroyed," she said.

"Your aunt was sitting in a chair and she exploded."

She paused. "It was a kitchen chair, just like that one."

She gestured to his hand where it rested on the back of a yellow-vinyl-and-chrome chair. Roosevelt jerked his hand away, wiped it on the front of his gray coveralls, put it in his pocket.

"Sorry."

She shrugged. "Look at the curtains."

Directly above the liquefied linoleum was a window framed in white curtains. A row of skinny daisies crawled along the bottom. They were Kmart grandmother ugly.

"Nice," Roosevelt said.

"They're hideous," she laughed, "but that's the way I found them. Not burned, not even singed. Nothing. And six inches from the chair."

She looked at the curtains. He looked at her. Her T-shirt was white, white like it had never been dirty. The round neck scooped low. He could see her collarbones, the thumb-sized indentation at the base of her throat.

"Do you have a basement?" he asked.

She turned her head, looked at him slowly without blinking. "Why?"

"I, I, I need to go down there," he said. "Look at these floor-boards."

"Okay."

She tossed her almost-finished ice cream cone into the deep porcelain sink. He held on tightly to his toolbox as she led him to the basement door.

He passed a rack of cups and read one of the inspirational sayings: SCREW THE FUCKING BASTARDS. Quickly he read another on a sugar canister: JUST SAY NO. NO FUCKING WAY.

"How old was she?" he asked.

"Sixty-eight," she said as she opened the basement door.

A cool stench of rancid air escaped. Roosevelt's palms were sweating.

"Shit," she said, "I forgot to empty the freezer."

Roosevelt let out a breath, nodded.

"The electricity was off for a week. Look in that long cupboard there, will you? Get me a plastic bag."

Roosevelt turned to the cupboard at his left.

"Not that one." She sounded exasperated. "The one behind you."

Roosevelt quickly opened the right cupboard. He was anxious to please her, worried that he'd seem slow or stupid. The cupboard was neat, a blue-handled mop and broom set stored in their proper places. On the broom handle was taped another motivational message, RAM IT UP HIS ASS!

Roosevelt found the large-size plastic trash bags and pulled one from the box. He handed it to her. She didn't say thank you.

The basement was badly lit, a single bulb hanging from a wire in the center of the room. In a corner was the chair. The yellow vinyl was gone, burned away. The frame was mangled and dripping black chrome icicles. The chair had melted.

"Jesus Christ," he said without thinking, then looked at her. "Sorry."

"It takes your breath away, doesn't it?"

He nodded. That was it exactly. "And that's how they found it . . . her?"

"Yes," she said. She walked to the old upright freezer and readied the plastic bag. "The chair, the burn on the floor, a pile of ashes." She took a deep breath. "And her legs. Just from the knees down. Did you see the picture? On the eleven o'clock news?"

"I only watch the news when I'm in the hospital."

He wasn't kidding, but she laughed. It was a nice sound, her chortles surprisingly deep and joyful.

"Anyway," she said, "the TV didn't do it justice."

Her white T-shirt twisted against her breasts as she reached in her back pocket and took out a black and white photo and handed it to him. It was just a copy of the police photo, but he could clearly see the ruined chair and beneath it a hill of cremated ash. Two skinny old-lady legs, from the knees down, protruded from the dusty gray mound.

"See her shoes?" She leaned in to look over his shoulder. A strand of her blond hair brushed his cheek. "I had to ID what was left." He felt her breath in his ear. "That's how I knew it was her."

He struggled for something meaningful to say, managed a grunt, a nod. Idiot.

She put the photo back in her pocket. She stepped away from him and opened the freezer. The stink of rotten meat was stunning. He gagged.

Matter-of-factly, she began tossing soft, bloodred packages into the trash bag.

Roosevelt turned his face away to take a breath. "Tell me again what happened to her."

"From what I've read," she said, "this is always how it is with people who spontaneously combust. Their extremities, usually their legs, sometimes an arm, sometimes their head and neck, are left behind, virtually burn free. The rest of the body is vaporized."

His eyes were watering. The packages of meat slapped against each other in the bag like a hand on a wet thigh. He shifted his toolbox. He wanted her to keep talking. He didn't want to look away, look up at the damaged floorboards, not just yet.

"Why does this happen?" he asked, and he meant more than just the old woman who had erupted.

"No one knows for sure."

Slap. Another flat package of rotten meat.

She continued, "I thought there would be visitors. Experts. Scientists who knew about this phenomenon. But no one's called. No one's been by." Slap. Slap. "They even called it 'Spontaneous Human Combustion' on the news. But then they laughed."

Roosevelt would have laughed too. "She was your aunt?"

Slap.

"Actually she was my mother's best friend. No real relation. But I called her Auntie Ned. We were very close." She paused, sighed.

She looked sad and young and Roosevelt wanted to comfort her, dead meat and all. He didn't move. She bent over, reaching to the lower freezer shelf. Roosevelt stared at her ass, heart-shaped in lavender cotton.

"Help me with this, will you?" She stood up and turned to him, handing him the bulging trash bag.

"She ate a lot of meat," he said.

"Sure did. It's something we had in common." She tossed her hair off her shoulder. It fell heavily, giving her a pat on the back. "You vegetarian?" she asked.

"I am now," he said.

She laughed and took the bag from him. She held the top with one hand and spun the sack with the other, twisting its neck. She was strong. He saw the muscles in her forearm, the clench of her hand on the bag. He took a step back from her without knowing why.

"So, there it is," she said and nodded with her head toward the furnace.

"What?"

"The spot where it happened." He looked at her stupidly. "The floorboards."

"Oh, yeah. Right."

He had to blink to come back, to concentrate on the job at hand. He stepped over a Christmas box and slid behind the furnace and looked up. He couldn't really see anything, just a dark circle, a scar from the burning linoleum. He took a pencil from his pocket and stepped up on his toolbox. He poked the beams, the flooring. Everything seemed solid.

"Doesn't seem to have damaged the floor joists or even the sub-flooring."

"I told you it was weird."

"This'll be an easy job."

She shrugged and headed up the purple wooden stairs.

He picked up his toolbox and trotted up behind her.

"Get the light, will you?"

Obediently, he turned and went down again. He pulled the string and took the stairs back up two at a time. He didn't want her to close the door and leave him down there, alone.

He began in the kitchen. He heard her upstairs humming to herself. He moved the table, lifting carefully. He took down the ugly curtains and laid them straight across the olive green sofa in the living room. There was an odor in the couch cushions, sweet and cloying.

He crouched over the hole, measured carefully. He would have to cut away the edges, make them straight, scrape away the remaining mastic, replace the plywood. He couldn't match the linoleum. It was ancient, discolored, unavailable.

"Excuse me?" he called to her from the bottom of the stairs.

"Come on up," she called back.

She was stripping the bed. She looked at him over an armful of faded turquoise sheets. He felt embarrassed, as if he had caught her dressing. The bare mattress, old and covered in blue ticking and buttons, was too obvious a surface between them.

"About the linoleum," he said. "I can't match it."

"Let's replace it. All of it."

He nodded, agreeing with her. "You could go to Carpet Land, one of those places. Watch the sales."

"Can't you do it?"

"I could. I mean, I know how."

"But you're busy. You don't have time."

"No. I have time."

"Great. I want something plain, and white."

"I'm not sure what it'll cost—"

"Whatever."

He tried to be quiet going down the stairs. His work boots were clumsy and he was aware of his hazardous steel toes and his black soles that left scuff marks wherever he went.

"Cup of coffee?" She clattered down after him, her pale sneakers surprisingly loud.

She poured him a cup of black, thick coffee; didn't offer any milk or sugar. She took out a glass for herself, filled it with ice. She poured hot coffee over the cubes. The ice cracked and clattered in the glass.

"I love that," she said.

He moved the table back into the kitchen. And a chair. She sat down. He leaned against the counter.

He wanted to take this woman out on a date, to dinner and the movies. He wanted to bring her back home, kiss her under the yellow porch light, follow her upstairs. But he knew that was not her kind of date. He looked at her and imagined her head against a damp wall in a dark alley, half-dressed groping, the smell of garbage and sex.

He was chewing on his bottom lip. She smiled.

"How long do you think this job will take, Mr. Roosevelt?"

"Roosevelt's my first name. My whole name is Roosevelt James Montgomery. I think my mom thought I'd be a movie star."

"I guess."

"Your name is Clark?"

"That's my last name. My first name is Amy. Amy Clark."

"Pleased to meet you, Ms. Clark."

He put out his hand, anxious to touch her, even just to shake hands hello. Her fingers touched his and shocked him. Painfully. He yanked his hand back, wiped it against his leg.

"Sorry," she said. "Did I shock you?"

He was embarrassed, but didn't try to shake her hand again. "It's fine." He rubbed his fingers, saw her watching him, put them in his pocket.

"Amy is a pretty name," he said.

"My kid sister's name is Gwendolyn." Her face got soft, thinking of her sister. "I was always so jealous of her name."

She raised her brown eyes to him over the glass of coffee and ice. Her lashes were long, blond like her hair, a fringe of sunlight. Her nails were very short and even. Her hands looked capable, capable of anything.

"Have you heard of it?" she asked.

He thought hard, couldn't remember what they had been talking about. "Gwendolyn?" he squeaked.

She laughed. "Spontaneous Human Combustion."

"Oh. Yeah. Sure."

"I think my aunt really did combust," she said. "There's no other explanation."

"There always is," Roosevelt said. "I mean, in stuff that seems spooky or weird. It turns up later—that other explanation. You just don't see it at first. A lighted candle, a spark from the stove, lightning."

"The stove wasn't on. She didn't like candles. We don't have lightning in Los Angeles. At least not very often."

"Was she a smoker?"

"No."

"A drinker? I mean, did she drink alcohol?"

"Occasionally."

"Could she have been drunk? Alcohol-soaked flesh will ignite."

"The curtains didn't burn. The table wasn't even scorched."

"Did she have a microwave?"

"Don't be ridiculous." Amy shook her head. Her thick hair moved and fell right back into place.

"Sorry."

"It's okay. Nobody believes me."

She said it with a smile, but he could see her disappointment settle over her pretty face like the cover on a cake plate.

"Then again, what do I know?" he said.

"Good question, Mr. Montgomery. What do you know?"

He turned his back to her and put his coffee cup in the sink. He didn't need this. It was just a job. He didn't need to feel like this. She was a kook. People didn't explode or implode; there were causes for events. Physics. Explanations. Fires weren't spontaneous, not really. He didn't know anything about her or her aunt and he didn't want to. He was done trying to know anything about women. It didn't get you anywhere, and it loused up the sex.

She left her empty glass on the table and went back upstairs.

He carried her glass to the sink, emptied the ice, rinsed the glass under the water. He moved the table out again—dragging it this time, noisily.

He worked until two o'clock without seeing her. He peeled back one-third of the linoleum. It was brittle, cracked into odd pieces in his hands. The mastic below was too old to scrape. And underneath he could see many more layers of past flooring. He would have to do a lot of chiseling, removing, digging. He was actually a finish worker, he had a talent for cabinetry, but a job was a job.

She came downstairs and stood in the kitchen doorway. He kept working without looking up. Finally, she spoke.

"I'm leaving now."

"Okay."

"Just close the door when you leave. It'll lock."

"Okay."

"Tomorrow could you come a little later? At nine?"

"Okay."

He looked up at her. She had brushed her hair, put on some lipstick or something. Her nipples were hard. He frowned.

"Something else?" he asked.

Amy paused. She pushed her lips together, pulling in her cheeks. Then she let her mouth fall open with a little sucking sound. "I'm moving in," she said.

For one brief, confused moment, he thought she was moving in with him. His tiny one-room apartment flashed in his mind, the futon on the floor, his dirty laundry in the only chair. She walked in and took up the entire room.

"Here. Starting tonight. My sister, Gwendolyn, and I are moving in. Auntie Ned left this house to me."

Roosevelt stood up, crowbar in his hand. He watched her walk away. Her hips rocked from side to side. Her golden hair swung back and forth in opposition. He had never seen lavender look so good.

At the door, she glanced back over her shoulder and caught him watching. She grinned. And left.

Roosevelt knelt back on the floor with a thud. He knew he liked her. His skin was vibrating. His throat was dry, his tongue too big in his mouth. He was nuts, that's what he was, out of his mind. He had a date tonight with Sheryl, the buxom twenty-six-year-old airline ticket agent. He liked the way the buttons on her uniform cried out for his help. But Sheryl's cantaloupe charms flattened when compared with Amy. Maybe tomorrow, Roosevelt thought, maybe it will be better tomorrow.

Gwendolyn bent over her work. In the back room of the Fantasy Bakery of Beverly Hills, surrounded by stainless-steel bowls of colored frosting, she was decorating a three-tiered wedding cake. The bride wanted frosting stairs to spiral around the cake and end at the happy plastic couple on the top. The cake was white, the stairs to begin at the bottom in the darkest red and gradually ascend to the palest pink. It was hard work. Gwendolyn's long dark hair fell across her face. She tossed it back. She was supposed to wear a net, but it made her scalp itch. She usually pulled her hair back into a ponytail, but this morning she'd been late and forgotten her clip.

This morning. Gwendolyn felt her cheeks heat up. Her toes curled and she felt a twitch inside her underpants. She could use more of this morning. Right now. Right here. She closed her eyes and imagined herself spread-eagled on this white-papered counter. She was covered in frosting flowers, roses, daisies, and chains of mint-green leaves crossing her breasts, growing out of her.

She straightened and shook her head; she was turning into some sort of sex freak.

She tucked her heavy shank of hair down the collar of her white bakery coat. She forced herself to study the wedding cake steps. The dark red looked like blood, too much blue. It needed yellow to be the red of poppies, of fire trucks, of hell. She sighed, took her flat spatula, and began scraping off the bottom stairs. It was the third time she had to start over. Her heart just wasn't in it.

Gwendolyn loved to make cakes. As a child it had been her favorite thing, her response to any celebration or disappointment. She made rabbit cakes for Easter, heart-shaped cakes for Valentine's Day, cakes that looked like straw hats for Mother's Day. There were black cakes for bad days and cakes shaped like guns when her big sister, Amy, wanted to kill someone. Her friends talked on the phone, or shopped, or went to the movies. Gwendolyn baked. She didn't even eat her work. Her sole pleasure was in making them. Usually she loved her job. But these stairs were killing her. The bride had explained that they represented her road through life, climbing ever higher until this, her peak of joy, her wedding day. Gwendolyn nodded and smiled supportively and thought of how her sister, Amy, would laugh about it later.

Staircase number three. She started fresh, with a clean steel bowl and new white frosting. She dropped in two squares of the red coloring, a half square of yellow. She put the bowl in its slot on the base and turned on the mixer. The single wire beater chopped through the frosting, then began to spin and blend. Swirls of red through the white, a touch of yellow. A sunrise in a bowl. The colors merged, brightening and blending with each other. The bowl circled, the beater undulated.

Again, Gwendolyn found herself thinking of this morning. The breaking sun turned her window shade golden. Her lips were sore from kissing. She stretched on the white sheets, then drew her knees up, curled her smooth brown body into a circle around her lover. Why had it taken so long to come to this? Why suddenly now? She was twenty-eight, had been sexually active since she was thirteen, and she had never felt anything like this. She couldn't wait to leave work and climb back into bed.

But the floor guy would be there. Roosevelt. Amy liked him. Gwendolyn couldn't imagine why. They were hardly moved in. Boxes. Piles of crunched-up newspaper. And no kitchen floor. The repairs were taking longer than he'd thought, of course. The upstairs hall windows were still coated with the slimy ochre soot from Auntie Ned's demise. They had cleaned the two bedrooms, but nothing else. She'd put her own white sheets, piped in blue, over the rolling mattress. Her clothes were still in the suitcases. She had thought they should wait to do anything about the kitchen floor, put a rug over it. But when Amy got something in her mind, she did it. She said Roosevelt was just what she wanted. How much did that mean? Gwendolyn wondered.

"Gwen! Wake up!" It was Tony, her partner, co-owner of the bakery, business side of the business. And her ex-boyfriend. Serious boyfriend. He smiled, but his eyes were dark. "This cake leaves tonight, remember? Not next year."

She stuck her tongue out at him. She was her sister's opposite, almost as tall, almost as strong, but reversed. Gwendolyn had dark hair, and startling pale blue eyes. The sisters were like white chocolate and milk chocolate. Amy, white, was more pungent and unusual. Gwendolyn, brown, creamier, friendlier. She tanned easily. She was tan now and it was only January, just from walking, being outside. Her white bakery coat accentuated her color, her white teeth.

"Stairway to heaven," said Tony. His hand went around her back, slipped onto her ass. It stayed there, not moving, just resting on the curve of her butt.

Gwendolyn shook her hips, tried to shake him off.

Tony just laughed.

"Come on, Tony." Gwendolyn hated the whine in her voice. She had been saying no for two years, a long time, but he just kept at her.

She had met him at her last job, where he was the boss and she was just one of the cake decorators. He was small, dark, and attractive. She was impressed with his Italian manners and the easy way he discussed cake sizes, flavors, and thousand-dollar price tags with movie stars. She fantasized about theirs being a perfect match. Cake heaven. He was not a good lover, but he was a good talker. He told her everything she wanted to hear. She borrowed money. They opened the Fantasy Bakery of Beverly Hills together. He told her this was it. He told her this was all he ever wanted. On their first Friday she caught him in the back room with a delivery girl. On Saturday night with a sales representative. And on Wednesday morning with a customer. She stopped listening.

Gwendolyn sighed. "I'm working."

"I can't help myself," Tony laughed. "You're lookin' so good. Must be getting it regular."

She didn't want to, but she blushed.

"I knew it!" Tony was both triumphant and jealous. "What's his name?"

14

Gwendolyn shook her head, tried to concentrate on the bleeding red in her bowl. It was too dark again. "Shit," she said.

"Don't tell me who it is," Tony whispered in her ear, and he wasn't laughing or even smiling anymore. "But he better not get in the way of business."

"Don't worry about it."

Tony looked in the bowl. "More white, another square of yellow, it'll be fine. Just right. Just like you."

He ran his finger down her spine so hard it hurt. He grabbed one cheek of her butt and squeezed. She jumped away from him. He laughed and went back in the office and shut the door.

Gwendolyn followed his instructions. She plopped white into the bowl, another yellow bit. She tried to get back that good feeling about her morning, tried to reimagine herself covered in frosting for her lover, but Tony had spoiled it. She could feel the scrape of his fingernail on her back, smell his breath in her nostrils.

And the floor guy, Roosevelt, was coming earlier tomorrow. He'd be there tonight and he'd be there tomorrow. There was something not quite right about him. He was a watcher, his washed-out blue eyes stayed open too long without blinking, his freckled face was too young for someone his age. Amy had started inviting him to stay for dinner, hang around, have a beer. Gwendolyn beat at the frosting with her wire whisk. She sighed. Tony wasn't just a businessman, he really knew about cakes. He was right. The color was perfect. She began building the bride's staircase.

Amy set the picnic table in the backyard for three. She was glad Roosevelt was staying. She liked to watch him eat. It was important to her, what a person ate, the way they did it. He ate well. She had chosen a carpenter wisely.

As a child, Amy ate what no one else wanted. She gnawed on the scavenged lamb chop bones; pulled the rubbery bits of sinew from the chicken legs; crunched on the skin clinging to vertebrae her family left behind. She preferred it.

When she was a teenager, her friends all became vegetarians. She never did. Amy loved meat. In the grocery store she gazed at the clear plastic-wrapped packages of sirloin and boneless chuck. She traced the pattern of marbling, pushed her fingers down to leave indentations that quickly filled with puddles of watery blood. She frequented the butcher's counter. Her nostrils opened to the odors of the bodily fluids of cow, chicken, and pig, metallic and elemental. She loved barbecue and broiling, stews and especially steak tartar.

It was a love that she and Auntie Ned alone had shared. They had sat in Auntie Ned's kitchen, this kitchen, and consumed, devoured, gorged on great slabs of beef, sharpening their teeth on the bones, sucking on the marrow until they wore the grease like lipstick.

"Good," said Auntie Ned.

"Great," said Amy.

"Two peas in a pod," said Auntie Ned. "That's what we are."

"Two pigs in a blanket."

"Two wolves in the henhouse."

They laughed and laughed.

Auntie Ned was always there with a T-bone dinner. One night in high school, Amy was sad and hungry. She passed up the cookies, the ice cream, the leftover cake Gwendolyn had made. She needed meat. She called her Auntie Ned, knowing she would have a steak in the freezer, knowing she would defrost it in the microwave, carry it dripping and limp to the frying pan, cook it just for her.

Amy had made a conquest, realized her power to its fullest potential for the first time. That boy, the one Gwendolyn thought was so cute, had broken up with his girlfriend just because Amy had asked him. Then Amy asked him, no, told him, to take Gwendolyn to the prom. So he broke up with his steady, the girl he'd been dating since he found his first pubic hair, and asked Gwendolyn. He did it for Amy. Amy thought Gwendolyn would be happy. She wanted her to stay home with her, celebrate, but Gwendolyn was furious and went out and left her.

So Auntie Ned turned the meat in the pan and Amy found comfort in the familiar sizzle. She felt reassured watching the steak cook, seeing the flesh shrink from the heat, the color change from pink to maroon to brown. Auntie Ned vowed that eventually Gwendolyn would understand, Gwendolyn would appreciate all that Amy did for her.

"She will," Auntie Ned said, "I promise."

Auntie Ned got out beers and Amy watched the meat. Suddenly, she noticed her skin, her own skin, smoking. The back of her right hand was red, hot, blistering. A splash of fat and a terrible smoldering had begun.

Amy gasped and Auntie Ned was there. She plunged Amy's hand into a bowl of leftover soup and dirty dishwater, pulled it out to look. The skin had not broken. There wasn't even a blister. The redness receded. Bits of celery and carrot, a feeble cluster of gray bubbles clung to the smooth young skin. There was no real damage.

Amy felt better. She knew at any time she might be hurt, permanently disfigured, the flesh seared from her very bones. This boy was nothing, this prom date for Gwendolyn was unimportant. But she saw the realization of her strength. She had to use it to protect those she loved. Auntie Ned. Gwendolyn. She had to work hard, be vigilant, do what she could, for as long as she could. Otherwise, she was just like everybody else, nothing more than a piece of meat.

Chapter Two

U se the downstairs bathroom," Amy said to Roosevelt, "under the stairs." She was in the kitchen, standing barefoot on the untreated plywood unwrapping an enormous piece of meat.

He scrubbed his freckled hands and washed his face in the downstairs quarter bath. The red ruffled shade over the light made his cheeks look flushed, the whites of his pale eyes rosy and feverish. The wallpaper was covered in turquoise Eiffel Towers and crimson French poodles.

The floor was taking longer than he'd thought. The plaster under the baseboards had rotted. There was water damage behind every piece of wood he removed. The house was practically falling apart, although it looked all right on the outside. He could have patched it up, left them with what he called a Hollywood overhaul, saved himself an enormous hassle. But he didn't work that way. And he was not unhappy being there.

He left the water running to mask any possible squeak when he opened the medicine cabinet. He just wanted to see what was inside, that was all. A clue maybe to Amy or her sister or even Auntie Ned. But the cabinet was empty except for one square condom packaged in gold foil. It sat as if on an altar, in the middle of the second shelf, right at his eye level. He had the definite feeling Amy had meant for him to find it. He wanted to think it was a promise, an affirmation. Not a joke. He took the condom and put it in his pocket. In high school the boys had carried their condoms proudly, letting their folded leather wallets wear down in a suggestive ring. He turned off the water and closed the medicine chest door obviously, with a loud click. I have it, he wanted her to know.

But when he came out of the bathroom, Amy was in the backyard at the barbecue grill. Barbecue. He had never eaten so much meat in his life. She made him hamburgers for lunch, brought in red and white grease-stained paper bags of ribs, sent him home with leftover lamb chops. He threw the lamb chops away in the Dumpster behind his building. That night he heard the cats fighting over them. In the morning he had to step over the bones to get to his truck.

The other night he had woken at three A.M. sick to his stomach, and thrown up. His puke was red and chunky brown. He clutched the cool, slippery sides of his not-very-clean toilet and vomited, thinking of meat. He felt sluggish, distracted by all the flesh. Her flesh, the flesh on all the plates in front of him, his own raw red flesh, hands and knees scraped and irritated from working on the splintery floor.

The front door opened and Gwendolyn came in from work. She looked past him at the kitchen floor.

"Coming along, I see," she said.

Smart-ass bitch.

She started upstairs. "Amy? Hey, Amy?"

Go ahead, he thought. He wasn't going to tell her Amy was out in the yard. He took a beer from the refrigerator and went out the back door.

Amy didn't smile at him either. She laughed at him sometimes, but she didn't seem to smile much. That was okay with him. Sometimes at the end of the day as the light softened and the orange walls of the kitchen glowed romantically like the embers in some movie fireplace, she stood in the doorway and watched him work. He liked looking up at her from his knees. Her flat stomach, the upward curve of her breasts. Always in pastels, like a child, like a piece of candy.

He was hoping he would get inside that hard outer shell soon. He was tired of waiting. The kitchen floor was only foreplay. He used the proper tools, struggled to get the moves just right, worried about his performance.

There were layers and layers of flooring. No wonder Auntie Ned hadn't burned through to the joists. He was an archeologist, studying her history of bad taste. She liked meat and she liked color. The kitchen floor had been green and lilac and lemon yellow and a multicolored polka dot. It seemed when one floor got dirty, she simply laid another. He offered pieces of the various floors up to Amy.

"Remember this one?" he would ask.

She always did. She was saving one scrap from each era along the side of the garage. A memorial linoleum garden, Amy said. Gwendolyn would plant flowers later, when he was finished.

He sat down on the back steps to watch Amy. Gwendolyn came out and walked around him.

"Didn't you hear me calling you?" she asked Amy.

He watched Gwendolyn walk barefoot up to the grill and lay her dark head on Amy's baby-blue-sweatered shoulder. Amy turned her face and gave her sister a kiss on the forehead. They were beautiful together, Botticelli paintings in an art book, marble statues come to life from another time, another world. Roosevelt often imagined them naked, the same smooth skin, the same strong hands and feet, each metatarsal visible, straining against the perfect skin. He wanted to like Gwendolyn, but it was obvious she had no use for him. She was always sorry to see him still there when she came home. She had a lover. He knew by the way she shifted her hips in her chair and frowned when Amy teased her. But she wouldn't bring the guy around—not when Roosevelt was there. Maybe he was married. It made Roosevelt smile that she thought he would care.

"Bad day?" Amy asked. "How are the stairs?"

"Finished and delivered." Gwendolyn sighed. "Tony."

Roosevelt saw Amy's face tighten, her eyes go flat and annoyed.

"He's a pig. I told you that a long time ago."

"Don't start, don't."

Gwendolyn wrapped her arms around her sister and kissed her neck. Amy shrugged her off. Gwendolyn looked over to see if

Roosevelt was watching. He was. He couldn't take his eyes off the two of them. Gwendolyn blushed, stepped farther away from Amy.

"Don't tell me you still feel anything for him." Amy stabbed viciously at the charring steak.

"Tony's not so bad." Gwendolyn crossed her arms in front of her chest.

"He's disgusting."

"Who is Tony?" Roosevelt smiled, opened his eyes wide. "Old boyfriend?"

"Yes."

"No. He's your business partner."

"I was in love with him."

"I want to kill him," Amy said. She poked and jabbed at the flesh on the grill. "Kill him for me? Please, Roosevelt? Please?"

Roosevelt gulped back his "yes" before he said it. She could hold him to it.

"Maybe I'll invite him over for dinner." Gwendolyn walked up the three steps to Roosevelt. "It's so nice to have company for dinner."

"Wendy." Amy was angry. Her voice rough.

"I'm going to my room, to read."

"Dinner's ready."

"I'm not hungry." Gwendolyn smiled at Roosevelt and licked her lips. "But he is." She went inside.

Roosevelt stood up. He finished his beer.

Amy looked over at him. It was one of those looks. He had gotten them before. What am I going to do, the woman was asking. What am I going to let you do?

He put his empty bottle down on the steps, crossed the lawn to her side. He hooked one finger in the belt loop of her butter-yellow jeans and pulled her to him. He kissed her. She was tall, taller than the last woman, taller than Sheryl the ticket agent, and it felt good not to bend so much, simply to tilt. Her lips were soft, but substantial. They met his own without giving up too much. He slid his tongue into her mouth. She gave him the right reply. They explored, tasted. She was fresh, with the faintest flavor of iron, of blood. He felt this kiss in his knees, in his hips, in his shoulders. The muscles in the back of his neck tensed, everything in him stretched toward her open mouth. He hadn't even touched her. Only their lips. Only his finger on her belt loop. Her hands remained poised with the barbecue tools, fork and tongs ready to work.

She stepped away before he was ready. He was off balance and he stumbled. As he caught himself, he looked up into her eyes, lit by the setting sun. But she was looking up—away from him.

He turned, knowing what he'd see. Damn her, he thought. Gwendolyn was watching from the upstairs window. Damn her.

He took Amy by the arm, but quickly let her go. She was done with him. She was busy with the steak, her face obscured by her wall of blond hair. He wanted more, but he wasn't going to get it. Not tonight. He felt his hands open and close, his knees actually shake.

She put the steak on a platter.

He didn't want any more meat and he didn't want her to think she was winning, which she was.

"I've gotta go," he said.

"Now?"

"I have to." He thought she'd try to convince him to stay, but it was the second-story window she watched as he left.

She ran out as he started his green truck.

"See you tomorrow." She was breathless, her cheeks pink, her hair glittering around her face.

"I guess," he said. "If something better doesn't come up."

"It won't." She leaned into the truck and kissed him again, quickly, hard, her tongue darting into his mouth and out. Brief as it was, he felt a tug in his pants, a warmth there he hadn't felt by the barbecue grill.

She ran back up the walk and into her Auntie Ned's house without stopping or looking back.

At home in his studio apartment, he lay on the unmade futon and watched the blue television light dance on his ceiling. He usually had the Spanish language station on. He didn't understand what they were saying; it was just background, like music with pictures. On the

Spanish station everything seemed so simple. The men wore mustaches and suits with wide lapels. The women had big hair and big breasts and long skinny legs. They were always angry and yelling at each other and then the men would go out and get in a fight.

In the hospital, after the accident, the television was always on. He had no control. It was always on and it was on in every room. He came to hate its incessant chatter, the drone of newscasters and talk shows, exposés and daytime dramas. All the heads looked the same. All the voices sounded the same, said the same words, "shocking, astonishing, you will be amazed." He was amazed. There was so much to be bewildered by in his own head, he couldn't stand to hear the words.

But when he got home, when they finally let him go home, it was too quiet. He didn't want the declarations, but he wanted the noise. Channel 34 was the perfect solution. He slept with it on, ate with it on, made love with it flickering and humming when he couldn't get a woman to take him to her place.

He turned on his bedside light and picked at a splinter in the top of his ring finger. He could still feel Amy's kiss tingling around his lips, smell her breath, taste her saliva. He felt a squeeze in his stomach, like hunger. Or anger. An empty but frantic urging. An incendiary desire. He wanted to get something, he wanted to have something now, but there was nothing in his tiny apartment that he hadn't had a hundred times, a million times, over and over again.

There was a sewing kit by the bed, not for sewing but for splinters, the carpenter's curse. He took out his favorite needle, dug at his finger until it bled. He sucked the blood and tasted her again. He flung the needle down. It missed the box by the bed and was lost forever in the dirty beige rug.

He stood up, took off his pants and T-shirt, turned off his light, lay back on the futon. The sheet rubbed against his bare arms and legs. His skin felt inside out; he was trembling. He was getting sick. He knew it. He tightened his muscles, searching for the preflu ache, breathed in and out of his nose knowing it would be completely clogged by morning. He pulled his blanket over his bare shoulders, curled on his side, tried to concentrate on the beautiful gesticulating señorita on TV.

Had a woman ever made him feel like this? Even Julie, his ex-wife, even with her it had never been this bad. She'd wanted him as much as he'd wanted her, right from the start. He had felt her up the first time they met under the stairs in the political science building. They had quickly progressed to her dorm room, the ball closet in the gym, the front seat of her little car. That was his favorite. She sat astride and facing him. The windows would steam up. He would watch her concentrate, her eyes closed and her teeth clenched together and kind of chattering. It was a funny little squirrel face and he would forget his own orgasm watching her work so hard.

On their wedding night he tried to get her to do it in the car, but she was disgusted by the idea and then furious with him when he begged.

I should have killed her then, he thought, and immediately felt the familiar nauseous guilt. It was just a line that came unbidden sometimes. He had never meant to kill her. It was a bad joke, a smart-aleck line, a tasteless crack he couldn't help thinking sometimes. The doctor said it was normal and relieved the pressure, but it wasn't normal and it didn't. It made him feel worse.

He had been driving. They had been fighting. It was after the divorce, a year after the separation. He begged her to go out with him. He was driving. They were fighting. He drove the car into the tree. But he'd meant to kill himself. He was hoping to die, put his death in her face, make sure she never forgot him. He didn't think she would be hurt. The tree was not supposed to fall on her. It was a ridiculous joke, a cosmic witticism, just like Wile E. Coyote sawing the branch under the Road Runner. The complete opposite of what was logical had happened. He hit the tree. She died. That was what he couldn't get over. He hit the tree as hard as he could and she died. She had her seat belt on. He didn't. She was innocent. He wasn't. She just didn't love him anymore. It wasn't her fault. He went from loved to unloved to unlovable. But that wasn't her fault.

It was okay now. It was more than two years ago and he had spent enough time in the white rooms and blue light of the hospital to understand that. It was okay to be alive. He enjoyed the work he did every day. When he mitered a perfect corner, when he sanded and polished a slice of beautiful wood, when the measuring came out just right, he was even happy.

"I didn't ask him to kiss me." Amy was standing in front of her, hands on her hips, bottom lip stuck out. It was a pose Gwendolyn had seen all her life.

"You're always asking for it."

Gwendolyn sat down cross-legged in the middle of her bed, her back to her sister. Amy came around and lay on her side in front of her.

"He kissed me."

"You kissed back."

"I did not."

"I can't stand him. He's silent. He's always watching us. His eyes blink from the top and bottom, like a snake, like a lizard."

Amy stretched out on the bed. She arched her back, thrusting her perfect breasts in the air.

Gwendolyn had tried to sculpt those breasts in cake and frosting. She knew them as well as her own, but she could never get them right. She threw a leg over her sister, sat on her stomach, pinned Amy's arms down with her knees.

"He's a Lizard Man. Say it."

"No."

"Say it."

"He's such a boy, a guy, a man." Amy wasn't smiling. "Don't you think so?"

"Yuk."

Gwendolyn climbed off, lay down next to her sister. What did Amy need him for? But she couldn't confront her sister, not any more than she already had.

"Lizard Man." Amy stared at the ceiling and laughed. "That's funny."

"His freckles make his skin look weird. He moves his eyes and then he turns his head—"

"You've been studying him."

"Don't ask him to stay for dinner anymore."

"Roosevelt is special. He is, baby, he is. You'll see."

Gwendolyn sighed. She knew Amy wouldn't let him go. "Don't sleep with him. Don't. No matter what. Just don't."

"Are lizards good lovers?"

"To other lizards."

"What kind of penis does a Lizard Man have?"

"Slimy."

Amy chuckled, gave a deep breathy snort. Gwendolyn rolled over on her side. They faced each other. Amy brought her hand up to Gwendolyn's face, stroked her cheek, ran her fingers over her eyelids, down the bridge of her nose.

"I need him," Amy said. "It's not what you think. Think of him as an experiment."

"But—" Gwendolyn began.

Amy put a finger on her sister's lips. Gwendolyn opened her mouth, took Amy's finger gently between her teeth. Amy was salty; Gwendolyn could taste the garlic from the steak. They looked into each other's eyes for a long moment. Gwendolyn had always found Amy's dark eyes unfathomable, their black blankness disconcerting. There was never more to see in them than what Amy let out.

"Hungry?" Amy asked.

Gwendolyn grew angry again. Her own blue eyes didn't lie; she thought what she wanted was obvious. She bit her sister's finger, hard.

"Ow!"

"I'm not hungry." Gwendolyn sat up on the side of the bed. "I'm going to the movies tonight."

"With who?"

"Jane and Suzanne and you're not invited."

"Why not?"

"I need a night off."

"From what?"

"You." Gwendolyn looked at her older sister. "Why don't you call Lizard Man? I'm sure he'd be thrilled to slither right back here."

Amy got up. She left the room without a word.

Gwendolyn felt her nose get full and tears start in the corners of her eyes. She missed her own little apartment. She missed evening plans, the promise of a date after work, dinner or a movie, even a night curled up on her couch with a book. She hadn't read a book or seen a movie since she'd moved in with Amy. She wasn't really going out with Jane and Suzanne. She hadn't spoken to either of her friends in a long time. But she was going out.

She took off her bakery clothes, her white chef's pants and white V-neck T-shirt, and stood in her underpants in front of her closet. She pulled out a black dress that Tony had given her. It was tight, bare, perfect.

She heard a crash, the sound of glass breaking, and Amy's unhappy cry.

Gwendolyn ran downstairs.

Amy crouched on the back steps. There was blood, a lot of it, around her foot and on the step. Roosevelt's beer bottle lay broken on its side.

"I stepped on his stupid beer bottle."

"Goddamn him."

Gwendolyn took Amy's foot into her lap, first pulling the black dress up and out of the way, leaving her long tan legs bare. The cut was on the side of Amy's foot. It wasn't big, but it was jagged. Gwendolyn looked at her sister's face. It hurt.

"What a mess," Gwendolyn said.

"Wendy?" Amy whispered. "I'm sorry."

"You didn't do it on purpose."

"Don't go out tonight. Please?"

"No. Okay, no. I won't."

Gwendolyn helped her sister hobble inside.

Chapter Three

Across the country in Pittsburgh, PA, Dr. Gustave Minor, Professor of Pyrophenomena at the Pittsburgh Center for the Study of the Paranormal, received an e-mail from a colleague in Los Angeles. Dr. Minor's fat but fluttering hands flapped and flew while he read the message. Was he too late? When he got there would there be anything left to see? Why hadn't he heard about this earlier?

He hopped off the special stool in front of his computer, skittered around his specifically designed office in agitated confusion. It was the office of a child, a very smart child. Diminutive chairs, four-foot-high bookshelves. But Dr. Minor was forty-three. He was also a dwarf; not a midget, but a dwarf. His head was distorted, but normal size; his torso was almost ordinary. His arms were shortened and his hands were corpulent and tiny, the hands of an overstuffed rag doll. His legs were too short and bowed under the weight of the rest of him. He lived with a lot of pain.

The pain was not important right now. He was excited. There was a lot to do. He had to find someone to teach his classes. He had to call Los Angeles, find out if anyone was still living in the house where it had happened. Who had cleaned it up? Had the damage been repaired? He hoped not. He was an expert. Spontaneous

Human Combustion was his area of expertise. He picked up the phone, dialed his wife. His wife. His beautiful, normal, ex-fashion-model wife. She made him feel good. Their new baby boy was only six weeks old, but she would understand. She would have to. She'd even call the airlines and book him a ticket. ASAP.

Amy took a deep breath and opened the closet door. Auntie Ned's clothes, shockingly bright, a cacophony of polyester, hung neatly on cloth-covered hangers. Amy had saved this job for last. This was real. These were her clothes; Auntie Ned had worn them, her naked body had touched them.

Amy opened a large garbage bag. Since Auntie Ned's death, she had gone through boxes of garbage bags. If Auntie Ned were still alive she would have put her clothes in a suitcase, or at least a cardboard box if she was moving. Now it was just a large army-green plastic garbage bag. Extra strength.

There was a mystery about Auntie Ned's death that Amy needed to understand. It was unsettling, a loose end that made Amy uncomfortable, incomplete, as if there was something important she had forgotten. A healthy, sixty-eight-year-old woman burned to death in a kitchen chair. Amy had gone to the library, done her research. Spontaneous Human Combustion was a fact. She looked at pictures, read case studies. Charles Dickens had even written about it in *Bleak House*. The human body could ignite, an internal cremation. It was inexplicable, but it was not supernatural. It couldn't be so completely out of control. There must be human choices, rational explanations, some kind of science involved. But why Auntie Ned? Why her?

No one else, not even Gwendolyn, seemed to care.

"She was pretty old," Gwendolyn said. "She didn't go out much."

The implication was so what, who cares if she died, even if she did burn up sitting in a kitchen chair. She was old. She was odd.

"No husband?" the policeman had asked her again and again. "No children? She was completely alone?"

Me, she has me, Amy had wanted to shout. She wouldn't let

Auntie Ned just go. Her life had been lonely and sad, but her death was remarkable. Amy saw it as some final gift to her, although she couldn't explain why or how. She just knew Auntie Ned had not gone for nothing.

Amy missed her. Auntie Ned. Ned, short for Naomi. Amy had shortened the name herself when she was two years old and couldn't say "Naomi." Naomi had been a permanent fixture in their house during Amy's childhood. There had been a lot of women, interesting, beautiful women, poets and artists and actresses, who spent hours at their house. Amy remembered flamboyant jewelry and bright red lipstick, black turtlenecks and shockingly short hair.

She remembered her father's face when he appeared in the kitchen doorway, home from work in his wilted gray suit, looking startled and embarrassed by all the women clustered around his kitchen table. They would get up, make room for him, but he would never stay. He fled to the garage or the basement or the den. "Scared him away again," someone was bound to say, and the others would laugh.

They drank coffee and scotch in the winter, gin and iced tea in the summer. Amy, and two years later baby Gwendolyn, would lie on the kitchen floor coloring or playing with dolls and the world would be warm and soft and only women, laughing women who loved them.

Then Auntie Ned left town with Melody Winters, a big-busted singer from Chicago, and one by one the other women stopped coming by and Amy's mother, Helen, was depressed. Amy's father tried to cheer her up, but he failed and then one day he left too. The world again was filled entirely with women, but it was just Amy and Gwendolyn and their mom and it wasn't really enough. Helen never perked up again; the corners of her mouth pointed perpetually down. She wouldn't speak to Auntie Ned when she came back to town without Melody and bought this little house, lived so nearby. When the girls were out of high school, Helen moved to Hawaii. She wouldn't even come to Auntie Ned's funeral. Amy hadn't seen her mother in over a year.

Amy could hear Roosevelt working downstairs. The steady thump of his hammer, the squeak of the crowbar prying up the mistakes and very occasionally his voice, just to swear or exclaim, were comforting to her. She liked having him in the house. She liked being home all day while he was there, while Gwendolyn was out at work. She liked the shopping, the cooking, cleaning up the mess that Auntie Ned's body had deposited on the walls and windows. And Roosevelt was part of it. The man around the house. Amy never thought she'd need one, even want one on a permanent basis, but now she could see the appeal.

She had decided not to go back to work. Auntie Ned had left her plenty of money, and Gwendolyn too. The house was a gift, mortgage paid for, free and clear. Amy needed to grieve for her aunt, to contemplate, and to put things in order. And after that, there would be plenty of time.

She avoided Roosevelt this morning. He let himself in, later than usual. Gwendolyn had already left for work and Amy was upstairs in Auntie Ned's room. She knew it was him, heard the clank of his toolbox, the two syllable *ca-lump* of his work boots on the bare floor. She hadn't even called "hello," but closed the bedroom door so he knew she was there. She heard him pause at the bottom of the stairs, then continue into the kitchen.

She wouldn't let him kiss her again, not today. It was too soon. She knew he wanted to. She had heard his desire in that pause when he came in the door, the heavy step afterward to the kitchen. She bent over from the waist and shook her hair, then stood up knowing her blond hair was tousled and pretty and her cheeks pink. Time for a cup of coffee.

But he wasn't in the kitchen.

She was surprised at the sharpness of her disappointment. He was supposed to be here. She wanted to see him. Then she heard the familiar clunk of his hammer and turned to see the basement door open. She was surprised to feel so relieved.

"Hey," she called down to him, "you want a cup of coffee?"

There was a bang—he hit his head on something—and a pause. Then, "O-kay." His voice broke and squeaked.

"I'll bring it down."

Amy hummed to herself as she made the coffee. She didn't hurry and when it was done she poured two cups and bit her lips gently to bring the blood to them, just for color.

The basement stairs felt cold on her bare feet, the coffee cups hot in her hands. Roosevelt's face was ghostly white and hopeful in the gloom. He tried to smile at her, but couldn't. She felt her resolve weakening. He wasn't lizardlike at all. His eyes were soft and wanting; his lips too large to be reptilian. He was so obviously warm-blooded with his curly red hair and freckles; he was an Irish setter or a spaniel. His desire to please was pure in his face.

He took the cup from her, but didn't take a drink.

She looked at him sideways, from under her long blond lashes. "I'm sorry you didn't stay last night."

"No, you're not."

His words were unexpected. His disagreeing with her gave her a jolt.

"You have dirt on your face," she said and reached to brush off his cheek.

"Don't," he said, grabbing her hand before it touched him, surprising her again.

She frowned and blushed.

"It's not dirt," he said. "It's oil. You'll get it all over you."

"Oh." She shook her head. "I thought . . ." She stopped. He knew what she thought. Her blush deepened. She was unaccustomed to being embarrassed.

He didn't let go of her hand. He wasn't hurting her, but he wasn't letting her go. He took a step toward her. She took a step back. They were each holding a full cup of coffee in their other hand. She felt trapped.

And then she saw his eyes flicker to her mouth, and down to her breasts. She took a deep breath. She pulled her hand from his and touched the front of his gray coveralls.

"Do these come in other colors?" she asked.

"Blue," he said. "Green. Tan."

He took another step toward her. She stayed where she was and lifted her face toward him and the single sullen light. He kissed her and today she closed her eyes. She let him think she was surrendering to his lips, his tongue. It was better than last night. It was less tentative. She pulled her mouth away and saw his lips stay open, waiting. She leaned into him again, opening wider, running her tongue around the inside of his mouth. She slid her hand up his chest and felt him shudder. She reached into his hair. It was wispy, softer than it looked.

He put one arm around her, then the other. He screamed.

"What?"

"My hand!"

His coffee had spilled, burning the back of his hand. He put the coffee cup down and waved his injured hand in the air. He hopped backward and stumbled into the mangled chair, final resting place of Auntie Ned. He fell onto what was left of the vinyl seat and leaped up as if burned there too.

"Jesus Christ!"

Amy began to laugh. "I'm sorry," she said. "I'm sorry. Stop. Let me see."

He calmed down and held out his hand to her. It was red, would probably blister.

"It's not funny," he said. He sounded like a five-year-old. She wanted to laugh again.

"Here," she said and kissed his hand. "And here." She kissed his cheek. "And here." His lips.

He backed up against the worktable and she ran her hands up his coveralls to his shoulders. He put both arms around her and kissed her properly, with the entire length of their bodies touching, toe to lip.

Poor thing, Amy thought. She could feel how lonely he was, how much he wanted. She could feel it in her blood. It was what she wanted to feel.

She pushed herself away.

"You have work to do," she said.

He looked confused, childlike again. "You started it."

"And I'm ending it," she said. She picked up her coffee cup, started up the stairs.

"Wait a minute," he said.

She stopped. She watched his eyes narrow, the muscles in the back of his jaw tense and release and flex again.

"Is there someone else?" he asked.

"No." She could feel his relief. She bowed her head, stared at her bare feet on the peeling purple paint of Auntie Ned's wooden stairs.

"Then what?"

"It's . . . let's just say it's my problem," Amy said. Then she shook her head. "Just forget it. I don't want to talk about it."

"What?" He leaned toward her. His face went soft; his features seemed to lose definition in the gloom. He was so nice. She could touch his concern, put her hands around his kindness.

"I know about problems," he said. "I really do."

"Let me think about it." She smiled at him, sadly, but not too sadly. She left a bit of hope on her face. "I'm not sure yet."

"Okay." He paused. "Okay."

She was going to have to watch him, she thought when she was back upstairs, watch him carefully. She cranked the twist-tie around the garbage bag of clothing. He had surprised her and she didn't like that. Still, she was glad to know he could, that he had it in him. She felt her attraction to him expanding. What she had to do would be good for many reasons.

"Stop it!" Gwendolyn's voice was high. She hoped it wasn't desperate.

Tony laughed and pushed his weight against her. His hands pinned hers above her head and against the wall. She felt the soles of her sneakers sliding out from under her on the waxed linoleum floor. Only his hips grinding into hers kept her from falling down.

"Cut it out!" She wiggled under him.

He nuzzled her hair, her neck, not kissing her, but sniffing like an animal. She felt his growling breath on her collarbone, the wet exhale from his large nostrils. She wanted to bring one knee up sharp between his legs, but she couldn't get a firm push off the floor.

"Don't, Tony," she said, embarrassed by the tears in her voice. "Get off."

"Come on, baby."

He dipped his head, put his mouth over her breast covered by her white T-shirt. He bit down, too hard, then laughed. He pulled one of her hands down to his penis, rubbed it back and forth, back and forth. He squashed her hand between them.

"You know how much I want you." He groaned and released her a little, pulled back, hoping she would get a better grip on him.

"No. No. No."

"I miss you. I love you. I do, I do, I do."

The front bell rang the opening notes of "Here Comes the Bride," signaling that a customer had entered the shop. Tony groaned a different groan and pushed himself off her. She slipped and almost fell to the floor. He didn't try to help.

He ran his hands through his hair. "You get that, Gwen, will you?" He gestured to his penis making a pyramid in his pants. "I . . . uh . . . I'm kinda indisposed."

Gwendolyn pulled her white coat over the wet marks on her T-shirt left by his slobbering mouth. She walked through the swinging door to the shop area without saying anything.

A Beverly Hills mom was looking through the design book. Her handsome husband stood back by the door, talking on his cell phone. Her two fair-haired children danced between her and their dad, asking for sweets, demanding to see the book, wanting, wanting, wanting. The well-oiled mother looked up at Gwendolyn as she came in.

"I need a—"

Gwendolyn began to cry.

The husband looked up from his black plastic conversation. The children stopped their clamoring and stared at her. Gwendolyn saw the mother put a protective arm around each child, the long painted fingernails unconsciously caressing the straight shiny hair.

"I'm sorry," Gwendolyn managed.

"Bad news?" the husband asked.

She could tell he was a take-charge kind of guy. He made the dinner reservations, bought the new car, threw the ball in the backyard with his son, yelled "come on" when he missed it.

"I'm sorry," Gwendolyn said again. She was sorry for everything.

Gwendolyn walked past the khaki-panted husband, past the trimmed and manicured mom, past the cake that looked like a basket of flowers, past the circus tent with cookie animals, past the chocolate '67 Corvette complete with hubcaps, past all her work, through the shop, and out the door. She could feel them staring at her, even the children aware that something odd was going on.

Outside she pulled off her white bakery coat and dropped it on the sidewalk. She left it there for them to stare at. She walked around the back of the building to her small red car, took her keys out of her pocket, and opened the door. She got in and drove away.

Roosevelt knew something was up when he heard Gwendolyn come home in the middle of the day. He was still working in the basement, but he could hear her car pull up outside. He heard the front door open and slam shut. He heard the footsteps above him: Amy, loud even with bare feet, coming down the stairs and meeting Gwendolyn in the living room. They were hugging, he could tell. Then Gwendolyn walked over and sat down on the ugly couch and Amy began to pace. He didn't need to hear their voices to know that Amy was angry. That Gwendolyn was crying. That Amy was too angry to stop and comfort her sister.

He figured Gwendolyn had gotten fired. She was such an abrasive bitch, it didn't surprise him. He didn't really care about what she did—he thought she just worked in a fancy bakery—but it seemed she'd been having troubles with her boss. Amy was really angry, he could tell. But Amy was blind where Gwendolyn was concerned. She thought everything her little sister did was perfect and remarkable.

He heard Amy walk over and sit with Gwendolyn. Then he heard Gwendolyn laugh. And Amy too. Then silence. He waited, hammer in his hand, and listened. He heard the old couch springs moan and the scrape of the small wooden legs as they shifted against the floor. Gwendolyn must be lying down, her head in Amy's lap. Amy would stroke her dark hair, tickle her ear, be a good big sister.

Roosevelt didn't want to go back to hammering and disturb them. He felt like a Peeping Tom, an Eavesdropping Eddie, a sneak. But he couldn't stay in the dark basement forever. He ran his lips over the blister that had come up on the back of his left hand. He had thought of nothing all day except Amy, her kisses and her problems. And his hand. He needed some ointment, a bandage. His wound was throbbing. He would probably get an infection. She wouldn't begrudge him a trip up the stairs for antiseptic.

He was more quiet than usual coming up the stairs. The door to the kitchen was open and he felt like he should tiptoe. There was no sound from the other room.

He stopped in the arched doorway leading from dining room to living room. He couldn't see them. Had they gone and he didn't hear? How could he have missed the back door opening, or the front door, or a car leaving?

His boots squeaked on the floor as he looked around. Amy's blond head, disheveled, sleepy-looking, popped up over the back of the couch. She looked caught, startled to find him there. Then Gwendolyn, her eyes red from crying, sat up. She glared at him.

He faltered, stammered, "You all right?"

He could tell from Amy's face she had forgotten him. Forgotten him completely. Like yesterday's breakfast he'd been digested, and expelled. His hand was pulsing now with pain. He felt queasy. He knew he was coming down with something.

"I need a Band-Aid, something." He waved his hand at her.

"Have you been in the kitchen this whole time?"

"The basement." He saw relief on both their faces. "What's going on?"

Amy ignored his question. "What did you do to your hand?"

"The coffee, the coffee burned me." It hurt more that she didn't remember.

"Oh. Right. Right. Upstairs. I think there's stuff in the upstairs bathroom."

"Okay." He started for the stairs. The two sisters sat on opposite ends of the couch. He wanted Amy to come with him, to take care of his hand.

"Hot coffee splashed on his hand," Amy explained to Gwendolyn.

Gwendolyn didn't care, he could see that.

"I'll help you," Amy said. "Come on."

She ran up the stairs in front of him. He trotted up behind. He couldn't help a triumphant glance back at Gwendolyn. She was staring at him, hating him, her cheeks tracked by tears, her nose shiny and wet with snot. Roosevelt felt suddenly sorry for her. She probably hates all men right now, he thought. They've all let her down. He smiled at her. She stuck her tongue out at him.

"Are you coming?" Amy called.

In the bathroom, he tried to kiss her. She bent over his blistered skin, her face hidden behind her curtain of blond hair. He ran his good hand up her bare arm, fingered the edge of her toilet-paper-pink sleeve. He pulled her hair back and put his lips on her cheek. She brushed him off. He tried again. She squeezed his sore hand, pressed down on the blister.

"Jesus Christ!"

"Don't bug me."

"That really hurt."

"I think you should go home, rest this hand."

"I can't believe you did that."

"Take the rest of the day off."

"I didn't fire your sister."

"She wasn't fired. She owns the bakery—with him, with that dog."

"Jesus, that hurt."

"Tony tried to rape her, okay?"

He shook his head, disbelieving. "I thought they used to, you know, go out."

"No is still no."

Amy went back downstairs, closing the bathroom door behind her, leaving him alone to put the cap on the antiseptic and put it away.

Roosevelt walked outside to his truck. Gwendolyn had gone to her room. Amy was in the kitchen when he left. She hadn't said another word to him. He blew on his hand. The blister hadn't popped, but the throbbing had increased. His head was starting to hurt. He was definitely getting sick.

Across the street, the neighbor kids, two Latino teenage boys, were watching him. They had shaved heads and tattoos on the backs of their bare necks. Their baggy pants hung low enough to see the red stripe on the waistband of their underwear. They were homeboys, gang members, and they watched him sullenly. They were always outside. Always watching.

"What happened over there?" the older brother called out.

Roosevelt was startled. He looked over at them, confused. How did they know something had happened?

"Yeah. What happened?" said the other one, the younger, skinnier brother.

"I heard the old lady exploded."

Roosevelt let out a sigh of relief. He nodded, shrugged, noncommittal.

"Was it a mess?" They each took a step forward, leaning toward Roosevelt to hear the gruesome details.

"I don't know," Roosevelt answered honestly. "They cleaned it up before I got here."

"So what are you doing?" They were so obviously disappointed.

"I'm fixing the hole in the floor."

"From her? From her blowing up?"

Roosevelt nodded, yes. The boys smiled.

"Shit."

"Fuck, man, I'd've liked to have seen that."

The younger one punched his brother's arm, danced around him, laughing, shaking his head.

"I mean," said the older brother, "she was a nice old lady and all, but shit . . . blowing up."

"I think she just dropped a match or something. She just burned up," Roosevelt said and glanced toward the house. He hoped Amy wasn't listening.

"I dropped a match plenty of times and I didn't burn up."

"You could smell this weird-ass sweet smell all up and down the street."

"It's odd," Roosevelt said, "I agree."

"Yeah. It's fuckin' paranormal."

"And now those sisters are living there? They're nuts."

The dancing brother giggled high and wild. Roosevelt laughed.

"Be careful, man." The older brother lowered his voice and spoke quietly to Roosevelt. "You watch those *chiquitas*, those weird girls in there."

"Careful you don't explode!" the baby brother crowed, not caring who heard him.

Roosevelt laughed again, but not really. "Thanks," he said and got into his truck.

Chapter Four

He drove past the street leading to Dodger Stadium and turned right on Sunset Boulevard, back toward his neighborhood, Hollywood. He could be in Mexico or El Salvador; the signs in the store windows were all in Spanish. The billboards too, advertising cigarettes and beer, admonishing men to wear condoms; he recognized the pictures but not the words. He stopped at a red light and the music blared from a strip mall minimarket, fast and loud with trumpets and a panicked beat.

He should have stayed in the basement. If he had started hammering they would have heard him and thought he was just down there working. Not listening. Not caring.

He didn't want to go home. He wasn't prepared to go home in the middle of the day. His bed was unmade. His dingy curtains still closed. He should be working, but Amy so definitely wanted him to leave. She hadn't said don't come back, and the work wasn't even close to finished, but he didn't know if he should go tomorrow. He would call in the morning. He would telephone her, see how things were going.

Two o'clock on a weekday afternoon. He had already eaten his lunch. He didn't drink this early in the day; daytime bars were too depressing. He was usually working. When he wasn't working he made sure to fill up his day with errands, the grocery store, a movie at the three-dollar theater around the corner.

He continued slowly, moving with the traffic. The cars were well used, pickup trucks, El Caminos, battered jalopies. Two men in most of them, too many people in the others. There were some words he was beginning to know. *Cerrado*. Closed. *Abierto*. Open. *Carnicería*. Meat store, or something. He wished his mother was here to see this. She would have loved it, the foreignness, the world so much different from her own. "Oh, look at that." He could hear her midwestern voice flatten and lengthen each word. "Well. I never."

But his mom was gone. She had never even come to Los Angeles, except that one time for the wedding, and he had been too busy getting married to show her around much. He missed her. They had been close. He had never known his father, dead before he was born; growing up, it was just him and his mother, the two of them. They had had a good time, a confidential life; she had been his date for the senior prom after his girlfriend broke up with him.

Still, he was glad she died when she did. She never knew that Julie stopped loving him. Never knew that she moved out, taking everything with her, even her smell. His mom never knew how angry he was, how frightened, how much he wanted to die. She never knew he tried, tried to die and join her in the whatever that came next. Instead he found himself alive and left behind. Completely and all alone. If you believed in heaven, which he didn't, Julie was with his mother. He could imagine they got along pretty well, and if they were watching him, they weren't surprised, but similarly resigned in their disappointment.

He made an abrupt right turn onto the Hollywood freeway. He knew where to go. He hadn't been there in a long time. He used to go a lot, before the work was more regular. Two exits up, around behind Ralph's Grocery Store, squatted the Hollywood dog pound. He guessed it was really called the ASPCA. He loved dogs, but couldn't have one of his own. They weren't allowed in the apartment and he wasn't home enough anyway.

The shelter had the comforting smell of dog pee and disinfectant. The attendant at the counter, full head of thick black hair, brown city uniform, looked up but didn't smile or acknowledge Roosevelt in any way. He stared past him, out the double glass doors. Roosevelt turned and looked. A short, plump woman was dragging in an old dog, a mutt, big-boned and bad-hipped. The dog didn't want to go. He knew that pungent smell meant the vet's office or worse. He sat down on the blacktop parking lot and spread his front feet. The lady cajoled, begged. From inside Roosevelt could hear her voice, high and desperate. He and the guy at the counter watched her stamp her white and turquoise sneaker. She yanked on the dog's leash, threw her weight into it, pulling as hard as she could. The dog's collar choked up around his ears, but still he didn't move. Now she was angry. She began to yell and tug and stomp both feet. The dog was immovable. Finally, she ran her hands through her hair. Roosevelt could feel her going out of control. Her turquoise sweatpants trembled. Her fists clenched. She took the leather leash and walked back to the dog and began to beat him with the strap, hard, mercilessly, yelling at him the whole time. The dog took it for as long as he could and then he lunged and snapped at her. The woman screamed, dropped the leash, and retreated. The dog, admirably, sat its ground.

"That's my cue," said the attendant. He took a pole with a nooselike collar on one end from its hook on the wall and went out the front door.

Roosevelt watched the man approach slowly, head down, talking softly to the dog. The dog eyed him sadly. Roosevelt could see him drooping, feel the fight leaving him. The attendant crouched and the big old dog gave a pathetic thump-thump of his tail on the hard asphalt.

Why was that his cue? Roosevelt wanted to know. Why not before, when the woman couldn't get her dog to move, or when the woman began to yell, or when the woman began to beat him? Now he was a bad dog; he would be labeled "dangerous, unadoptable" and put down in seven days.

The attendant slipped the noose over the dog's neck and squeezed a trigger to tighten it. The pole kept the dog at a broomstick's length. The attendant gave a gentle tug to the pole. The dog stood, the pain in his old hips obvious, and limped along with the man, tranquil, even willing. Only when the woman began to follow did he stop, turn his head, and look at her. She dropped back, followed more slowly. Roosevelt knew the dog had won. A warm, dry cage for a few days, regular meals, and then a quick, painless death were a victory that Roosevelt could understand.

His hand hurt as he walked through the rest of the cages. Amy, he thought with every throb. He thought of her kiss, her taste. He thought about the way she had looked at him in the morning, before the coffee had burned him, not when she was angry and he was leaving. He had been happy this morning. It was odd about happiness. He had learned in the hospital that there really was no rhyme nor reason to it. Sometimes you felt happy; sometimes it was just the cessation of pain; sometimes it was all wrapped up with the pain. The pain almost made it better.

Amy left her sister sleeping and tiptoed downstairs. She loved napping in the afternoon. She loved waking just before dark, when the light was leaving and the house gray, the corners indistinct. The neighborhood was still and expectant, waiting for wives and children and fathers to come home from work and soccer practice and music lessons and get dinner started and turn on the television and argue about homework. It was the last quiet pause before the evening began. It was her favorite time of day.

She looked at Roosevelt's phone number, written in his masculine scrawl on Auntie Ned's multicolored pad by the phone. It was that weird name of his. It stuck in a person's mind. She remembered it so clearly from the newspaper articles two years before. Roosevelt James Montgomery. During the trial they ran his picture on the news. The cute young man who killed his wife. The man who went catatonic at the trial and ended up in the mental institution. When she saw his name under "Carpenters" in the Yellow Pages she remembered and she knew he was the one.

She felt a brief twitch of guilt. She had been mean to him, but he had startled her. She hated him to be unexpected. She wanted him predictable, like Tony. Tony, the sugarcoated pig. Amy hated

Tony with every crimson corpuscle of blood in her veins, but she could sympathize with him. Gwendolyn was hard to resist. Amy loved to watch her sister work, her long hands stroke and caress the cake, lovingly create every flower, every nuance. Wendy's cheeks flushed when she concentrated; even her earlobes turned pink.

It wouldn't be hard for Roosevelt to see her charms when Amy was ready. And eventually Gwendolyn would come around, see him as Amy did, her perfect solution. He was what she wanted, after all, work boots, denim, dirty fingers, male. He would be there for Gwendolyn, take her places, fix things around the house, be her answer to everyone's embarrassing questions. You live with your sister? Don't you want to find a nice boy and get married? He was the shovel to remove Amy's only stumbling block to their perfect future.

Amy stood on the new plywood subfloor in her aunt's kitchen and felt herself between, at the edge of something new, still leaning on what had been. Her sister lay upstairs in the white and blue bed. Roosevelt was down here, only a phone call away.

The ugly daisy-decorated curtains moved gently in the warm Los Angeles winter wind and caressed the back of the kitchen chair.

"Amy."

A woman said her name, but there was no one here, no one with her. It was just the curtains, whispering against the chrome edge, murmuring to her, "This is where she sat. This is where it happened. This is all she was."

Amy watched the curtains moving and the light fading on the yellow Formica tabletop. When it was dark, she would move. One way or the other, she would move.

Across the country in Pittsburgh, Dr. Minor was boarding a plane for Los Angeles. It was the last flight of the day, all-night traveling with a long fluorescent-lit layover at five A.M. in St. Louis. Cheap and uncomfortable. But for someone his size all traveling was unpleasant. Nowhere to put his feet, his head hitting awkwardly below the padded headrest, forcing his neck to bend forward. He was surprised at how much he missed the baby, his son, already. He and his wife had named him David; he could grow up and fight Goliath if necessary. David was normal-sized, six weeks and smiling, lifting his little head and looking around.

Dr. Minor had not been able to get much information about the case of Naomi Fitz over the phone or on the Internet. His colleague had said someone was living in the house now, but he didn't know who. The number had been changed. Dr. Minor realized he would have to make the trip blind, show up on the proverbial doorstep. He hoped he wasn't too late, that it would be worth it. The flight attendant helped him with his suitcase, tossing it into the overhead compartment with an ease he could only dream about. He thanked her navy-blue pleated skirt, the two points of her vest hanging over her waistband. She seemed remarkably tall.

When Roosevelt returned home from the pound, he knew he needed something ordinary. Or as ordinary as his life ever was. He paced his dirty apartment, stepping around the unmade futon, looking down at the stains from his own personal gropings. He dialed Sheryl, the ticket agent. Their first—and only—date hadn't been a disaster. One nice kiss, the promise of more.

Sheryl was pleased to hear from him. "Hey, you," she said. He could hear the airline counter business behind her, phones ringing, the plastic clicking of computers, people leaving, vacations, holidays. "Where've you been, stranger?"

Her voice was round, like her figure. There was something so American about Sheryl. Her large breasts were like the front fenders on a 1950s Plymouth, as comforting as Jell-O molds, as familiar as a La-Z-Boy recliner in front of the TV. Nothing she said would surprise him.

"I've been working."

"Not too hard, I hope." She giggled.

He sighed. "What are you doing tonight?"

"Tonight?"

He heard the hesitation. She was considering. She wanted to see him, but she didn't want to seem too eager or too easy.

"I was having dinner with friends," she said. He smiled, noticing she had already put it in the past tense. "Wanna come along?" It was obligatory, not sincere.

"No."

"I . . . I could rearrange," she surrendered, and he knew the night would end as he wanted it to, without subterfuge, in her fluffy bed with the flowered duvet cover and ruffled shams.

"Great. That'd be great," he said and meant it.

She was a relief to him. He showered carefully. When Amy, her lips, her hands, the thick shaft of her sunny hair, spilled into his mind, he used the technique the hospital had taught him to move her, put her in a back drawer. "Cancel, cancel," he said to himself, mentally folding her away. "Cancel, cancel." He had to say it often as he dressed, ran his fingers through his curly hair, cut his toenails, laced his boots. "Cancel, cancel."

Amy picked up the phone and dialed Roosevelt's number.

He answered on the second ring. "Hello?"

"It's me, Amy."

There was a pause. She let him hear her breath; the warm sigh in his ear.

"How's Gwendolyn?" he asked.

What a nice guy. That's what she counted on. He was such a nice guy.

"She's sleeping," Amy answered.

"What's she going to do?"

Right question. She liked that. "I don't know."

"It'll be fine."

It was her turn to pause. He sounded different on the phone, more sure of himself, more male somehow.

"Is someone there?" she asked. There couldn't be, could there?

"No," he said. "Well . . . no."

She wasn't convinced. Did he have friends? Guy friends whom he talked to about her?

"What are you doing tonight?" Amy asked him.

"Why?"

That wasn't what she wanted to hear. "I thought . . . Well, I'm sorry about today. How's your hand?"

"I took a long shower. Put some cream on it. It's better."

"That's good."

"Yeah," he said. "Listen, Amy. I'm sorry too—about today, I mean. I wasn't very . . . sensitive."

The words were nice, but he was guarded, distant. "We could get together later," she said, "for a drink."

"I can't tonight. Another time would be great."

How normal of him. How disappointingly normal. "Sure."

And then he said quietly, "Amy." And again, "Amy."

"What?" She heard him take a deep breath.

"Will I see you tomorrow?" he asked.

"Aren't you coming to work?"

"Yeah. Of course. I just didn't know if . . . you'd be there."

"I'll see you tomorrow."

When Gwendolyn came downstairs, Amy was crabby. She wasn't in the mood to cook. She sat at the kitchen table with a glass of old red wine and an older *Sunset* magazine open to the barbecue tips.

Gwendolyn took a sip of the wine and shuddered. "How can you drink that?"

"Tastes okay to me."

Amy felt hot all over, a burning rawness in her throat that the vinegary wine didn't help. She had been wrong to take Roosevelt for granted.

The phone rang and she leapt for it.

"Hello?"

"Is Gwendolyn there?"

It was Tony. Amy's irritation grew, in her stomach, behind her eyes. "Maybe."

"Come on, Amy. Let me talk to her."

"She doesn't want to talk to you."

"Is it Tony?" Amy didn't like the hopeful sound in Gwendolyn's voice. "Is it? Tell me." Gwendolyn was insistent.

Amy looked at her sister and knew. Gwendolyn wanted to go

back to work. She liked Tony. She was too nice to fight with him, to kill him like he deserved. Gwendolyn was too nice to everybody. Amy handed the phone to her. She walked out of the room. She didn't want to hear Gwendolyn listen to Tony's apology. She didn't want to know that Gwendolyn was going back tomorrow as if nothing had happened. It had been a terrible day. She went upstairs, slowly, wishing for her Auntie Ned. She felt sweat pooling under her arms, collecting on her upper lip and temples, bubbling on the bridge of her nose. She would take a cool shower, change her clothes and go out to have a beer and an oversized, very rare, hamburger.

Roosevelt contemplated another shower. He was hot. He had been unprepared for her phone call. When he heard her voice it had been a shock, the voice of a dead woman calling him from some place he had forgotten. He didn't want to remember. He had worked so hard to put her away. He was anxious now to see Sheryl. He would pick her up at work. He wouldn't wait. He was the man. Sheryl's short, top-heavy body and little skinny legs were a beacon, a light circling, flashing through a warm fog. It was clear with her. He anticipated getting exactly what he wanted.

Gwendolyn went upstairs to talk to Amy. She heard the shower running. She knew Amy was furious with her. She felt queasy. She would explain and Amy would understand. It was her bakery too. She and Tony could work it out. They had to. Gwendolyn loved the bakery. Amy would understand that.

Gwendolyn burped up the bad wine. She swallowed, stroked her nervous stomach. She knocked on the bathroom door. She went in. The bathroom was warm and cloudy. The air was moist and comforting with the familiar smell of Amy's citrus soap.

"Amy?" Gwendolyn spoke above the shower and waited.

She leaned against the wallpaper, a faded interpretation of the ocean. There were tarnished gold and silver fish on the wallpaper and matching fish peeling off the transparent shower curtain.

Gwendolyn could see Amy's strong body, head back under the water, long hair sleek against her neck.

"Amy."

Amy pushed back the shower curtain and looked at her sister. "It's okay," she said.

"You mean it?" Gwendolyn waited for Amy's anger.

"Sure." Amy's voice was tired, but not unhappy. "If you love it there, you should stay."

"Really? Come on."

"You come on."

Amy reached a wet, slippery arm out to her sister, grabbed her T-shirt, and pulled her close. The warm shower spray felt good on Gwendolyn's face. The lemon scent tickled her nose. Amy's smile was small, but genuine. Gwendolyn exhaled relief, her stomach calmed.

"You smell like the bakery," Amy said.

"I need a shower."

"You do."

Amy leaned toward her sister, wrapped her wet arm around her neck, and kissed her. Gwendolyn melted into that mouth, dissolved into those soft lips. Amy's tongue was loose and undemanding. It was like kissing herself, the best kiss imaginable.

"You're getting wet," Amy said.

"I am," Gwendolyn replied.

"Take this off." Amy tugged at her T-shirt.

Gwendolyn pulled it off over her head, snapped open the front closure on her bra and wriggled her shoulders back to let it fall. Amy struggled with the button on the white pants.

"I'll do it," Gwendolyn said.

She slid her pants and underpants together down over her hips and legs, stepped out of them and into the shower, into Amy's waiting arms, into the only place she wanted to be. Amy's mouth was blazing hot, hotter than the shower water. Gwendolyn cupped her sister's breasts with both hands. The nipples burned her palms, a conflagration of excitement. Steam rose from them both. She took her sister's earlobe between her teeth, breathed into her moist ear. She kissed her neck, smooth and white as the shower stall. The water fell on her nose and closed eyelids, the side of her face, in her own ear.

She kissed and licked and caressed her way down the orchard-scented body. On her knees in the shower she felt the waterfall covering them both, a warm wet rhythm. It drummed on the top of her head, massaged her shoulders, pulsated down her back before plunging off her curves. Her tongue probed and searched, tasting soap and shampoo. Her fingers helped gently at first, then more insistently as Amy gave up to her. Gwendolyn felt grateful supplication. She opened her eyes, looked up without stopping what she was doing. Through the wet blur she watched Amy's hands try to grasp the slick white tile, her head arch back, and her mouth fall open, drowning in the water.

Chapter Five

Roosevelt groped awkwardly at Sheryl's official airline ticket-agent uniform. He caught his thumb on the metal edge of a button, surprisingly sharp and too big for the buttonhole.

"Shit," he said.

"Slow down," Sheryl complained.

He could tell she wasn't exactly flattered by his ardor, his rush to get on with it. He had tapped his foot incessantly through dinner, drummed on the table with his good hand through coffee and dessert, been less than impressed with the slowness with which she could eat a hot fudge sundae. Her tongue and the whipped cream were not the turn-on she had hoped for.

Finally he was in her bedroom. Now she was being shy, coy, sweet, disgusting. He needed to move forward if this was going to be any sort of meaningful experience for him. She put her head on his shoulder, pushed one hand with the fire-engine-red fingernails into the back pocket of his blue jeans. He looked around. Her bedroom was not the pastel garden he had imagined, but overly modern, Swedish, pared down to essentials. He had expected ruffles and flounces, an abundance of stuffing, not the platform bed, the navy blue, the treadmill in the corner. It didn't matter. If they could just lie down.

He lifted her hand and kissed it. She sighed. He turned his head and kissed her hair, her forehead. She tilted her face up to him and he did his duty. He pulled her to the bed, led her with his mouth, his hands around her waist. They sat, still kissing, and he put a hand on her shoulder and actually pushed her to a prone position.

Once she got with the program, she was competent, qualified, efficient, ever the ticket girl helping him get where he wanted to go. She undid those recalcitrant buttons. She removed her pesky skirt and panty hose quickly, before he could complain. She navigated his pants for him. He buried his face between her twin mountains and hoped he had reached paradise.

"Cancel, cancel," he said.

"What?"

He hadn't realized he'd spoken out loud. "Nothing." He could not think of Amy now. "Cancel, cancel," he said again.

Sheryl giggled. "What does that mean?" She giggled again. She giggled too much.

"I'm just trying to forget everything but you."

"Oh. You're so sweet." She kissed the top of his head like a mother.

Roosevelt closed his eyes and moved on, followed the map and the directions. She was warm, naked, willing. She smelled good. He thought he was there, he was about to reach his destination, when she laced her fingers through his hands and squeezed and her nails scratched his burn. It was not the pain, it was Amy. She came to him and wouldn't leave, her bare feet tan and clean on the peeling steps, her strong straight thighs coming down the stairs to him, the column of her white neck framed by soft cotton and blond hair. He couldn't cancel her out now. He felt his erection wilt, a flat tire only a few feet from the finish line. He lay on Sheryl and groaned into her ear.

"What happened?" she asked.

"I dunno," he said. His head was hurting. His nose felt suddenly stuffy. The cold, a terrible flu was coming.

"Did you . . . did you, you know, did you?"

"Sure," he tried to lie.

"You did? When?"

"Listen, my hand really hurts."

"Oh."

He sat up, started pulling on his underwear, his pants.

"Maybe you should see a doctor," she said.

"That's a good idea," he said, buttoning the cuffs of his shirt. "I think I'll go right now."

"At eleven-thirty? Where? The emergency room?"

"The emergency room. Great idea. Thanks."

"Want me to go with you?"

"No." He was sorry he sounded so emphatic. "I mean, you have to work tomorrow. I'll probably have to sit there all night. But thank you."

"Okay," she said. Her voice was small. There was a quiver that meant tears were just around the next corner. He hoped he would be gone before she got there.

"I'll call you," he said.

"Okay," she said again. "Okay." Then, "Thanks for dinner."

"No problem." He couldn't even bring himself to kiss her good-bye. He fled.

What an asshole he was. He got in his truck and rolled down the windows to get rid of the smell of her perfume. He felt terrible; he felt out of control. In bed with a naked woman who was not unappealing, had in fact been very appealing only a month ago, and he had failed. Amy, Amy, Amy. His hands were shaking. He was freezing. He was definitely getting sick. He couldn't wait to get home and turn on the TV. Amy.

And suddenly he was calm. It was Amy. She needed him. He couldn't be with Sheryl. Not when Amy needed him.

So he headed crosstown to Amy's house. He wanted to, had to, just drive by and look at her dark windows, make sure that her house was quiet. It was a long way to go, but not a bad trip this time of night.

He left Sheryl's neighborhood of Westwood and college kids, sports bars and clothing stores, and turned right onto Sunset. He would take Sunset back across. It was the only way he knew to go. He used to have a *Thomas Guide*, the big, thick, and essential map of

Los Angeles, but someone had stolen it out of his truck when it was parked in front of Amy's house. He'd left the window open a crack and someone had used a stick or a wire to catch it off the seat and pull it out. The thief had left torn sections of pages 534 and 622 behind; maps of Pomona, West Covina, places he would never go.

He drove through Beverly Hills. It was quiet. The only other cars on the road were Westec Security and policemen. They followed him with their eyes. His old truck. His panel van was the perfect place for rapes and murders and hiding small expensive children. He drove the speed limit, didn't change lanes, kept his windows down, and tried to look casual.

Then it was Hollywood, guitar shops and music clubs. There were people on the street. He stopped at a red light. A teenage tourist was lying on the sidewalk where that young movie star had overdosed and died. She lay there with her tongue lolling out, playing dead, while her friends took a picture. She scrambled to her feet and someone else took her place. He could hear them laughing. They were loud and silly, high-pitched; children who had grown up whining. It seemed everyone could hear them. The dead movie star could hear them in heaven.

The music district disintegrated into all-night fast food and boarded-up businesses. The fluorescent lights from a white and red tiled hamburger place illuminated the night and bleached the faces of runaways and drag queens, prostitutes and other escapees. He had sat there himself when he was first out of the hospital. He had felt at home, damaged as he was, used to the watery coffee and the lights that were too bright and always on. Did he recognize anyone? He couldn't tell. The people were the same, but the faces different.

He felt the familiar chill of uncomfortable fear down the back of his neck and in the soles of his feet. When he had first lived away from home, in his first apartment, just on the other side of his midwestern hometown, near the junior college, he was so scared of the dark. He lay awake listening, and worrying, afraid to be in the blackness, but also afraid to turn on the light and expose himself. He curled in the small twin bed of the furnished room and wondered where he might be safe. Only his mother's house, only at home, but when he thought of her there alone, he panicked. He invented excuses to stay with her, time after time, until finally he gave up his apartment entirely.

His mother finally told him to move. She wanted him to finish college in California where his father went to school. She had been saving up his whole life. She wrote away for the application, helped him fill it out. He went and graduated and killed his wife.

Now he passed into the scarier sections of Sunset Boulevard. Closer and closer to Amy. Silver Lake. Echo Park. The vampire hangouts. The leather clubs. The twenty-four-hour adult bookstore. There were skinny junkies in the doorways, *cholos* hanging out on the corners. They watched him go by, their eyes as malevolent and distrustful as those of the Beverly Hills police force. Cadavers in black walked out of the Devil's Hole, an occult curiosity shop. Their white faces glowed. Their clothes absorbed the night. They disappeared when they turned their backs to him.

He was frightened. As he used to be frightened for his mother, he could feel his heart pounding for Amy and Gwendolyn, isolated; their little house an island in the dark. He pressed on the gas pedal, speeding up, hurrying to them. They did not know he was coming. He thought of them sleeping, like his mother always had, deeply, waking refreshed and content. Not aware of the tragedies around them, the dangers, the chances for disaster.

Their street was quiet. Most of the houses were dark, a porch light on here and there, like any other neighborhood. It worried him. He knew what lurked in normalcy. He thought of what had already happened in that house, their house. A woman had burst into flames. For no apparent reason. The combination of heat, electricity of some kind, all that meat in the freezer. Heat, electricity, and meat. He had to gulp for breath. Amy's blond hair sizzled in his mind; he saw it tighten and contract, crinkle up into the tight curls of pubic hair. He saw flames licking her feet, lapping up her calves, her knees, her thighs, to the curve of her ass.

He didn't realize he was driving so fast until he pulled up in front of her house and his brakes squealed as he stopped. He sat, panting and sweating, looking at the dark house. Not a light was on, not a single spark of life. The yellow clapboard looked gray in the dimness, the row of flowers along the walk planted for ghosts. The quiet was unnerving, not peaceful. It appeared to him as a house of death, past and present. His hand began to throb. He looked down at it. He could see his blood pulse and undulate under his blistered skin. The threat of fire was too close and too strong. He couldn't leave her alone, not tonight. He locked the truck doors and slunk down with his back against the driver-side door, his eyes on the house. He was shivering. He couldn't breathe through his nose. He grabbed an old painting tarp from the back and wrapped it around his shoulders and over his legs. The smell of paint and varnish and turpentine reminded him of daylight and safety. He wouldn't let her sleep alone.

Chapter Six

Gwendolyn stood outside the truck watching Roosevelt sleep. He looked cold, uncomfortable, and very young. His freckles stood out on his white face. A curl of his hair was stuck in his ear. It was street-cleaning day and he was parked on the wrong side of the street. He was bound to get a rude awakening and a hefty ticket. She picked up the newspaper and went back into the house.

"Your boyfriend's outside," she said to Amy. "Roosevelt. He's sleeping in his truck. Looks like he was there all night."

Amy smiled. "You're kidding."

"Nope. Wrapped in an old sheet with paint all over it and sleeping like a baby."

"Oh, brother. Isn't he perfect?"

"He's your kind of man, that's for sure."

"Shut up," Amy said and kissed her sister on the lips. It was a good kiss, a lasting one. Gwendolyn felt warm butter in her veins.

"I think we should give Roosevelt a present," Gwendolyn said.

"Why?"

"For putting up with you."

Amy laughed. "Like what?"

"I'll get it for him," Gwendolyn said and smiled at her sister again. "I know just what to give him."

"You're feeling very generous."

"I can afford it. Poor lonely Lizard Boy."

"He is not a lizard."

"Yes, he is. He is. He is." Gwendolyn said it just to annoy her sister. "Let's go wake him up."

"What for?"

"He's going to get a ticket. It's street-cleaning day."

"Aren't you considerate all of a sudden."

"I want to watch his face when he wakes up and sees you, the little woman, handing him a hot, steaming cup of coffee."

"You're a bitch."

"You taught me everything I know."

They walked out to the truck, bumping each other, Gwendolyn half trying to spill the coffee that Amy carried. They laughed as their smooth hips collided. Their hair tangled together, the dark and the light. Their hands intertwined. Gwendolyn was in no rush to go to the bakery. She wanted this morning and last night to go on for as long as it could.

"How can he sleep like that?" Amy asked.

Roosevelt's head was bent between the door handle and the arm rest. His knees were curled around the emergency brake that stuck up between the two front seats.

"His lips look a little blue." Amy spoke again.

"Think he's cold? Or dead?"

"He's not dead," Amy said. "I can see the pulse in his throat."

Amy went quiet and Gwendolyn looked over at her sister. She saw the look, recognized it, the mother look, the I'll-take-care-of-you look, the poor-thing-let-me-make-it-better look. Gwendolyn didn't have a single maternal bone in her body, but Amy had lots of them. That's so odd, Gwendolyn thought. I'm the nicer one.

She said, "Lizards have pulses in their necks."

"Shut up." Amy snapped out of it and pushed her sister.

The coffee spilled on the walk between them, splashing Gwendolyn's bare foot.

"Watch it." Laughing, not caring.

"You watch it."

They looked back at Roosevelt and were both startled to see his eyes open and looking at them. He hadn't moved, lay frozen in his awkward position. Only his eyes had changed, the watery blue irises a tiny rim around the large, black pupils.

Gwendolyn and her sister stared back. Then Amy lifted the cup of coffee, half empty now and dripping. Roosevelt smiled at her, Gwendolyn thought, like she was a gift from heaven. Not for him, Gwendolyn thought, not for him.

He sat up. Gwendolyn was annoyed at how cute he looked, even charming with his hair flat on one side and the curls in every direction on the other. His little-boy grin, his genuine happiness at seeing them, both of them, was dismaying.

He leaned forward and unlocked the passenger door.

Amy opened it. The car released a warm, sleepy, childlike smell.

"What the hell are you doing?" Amy asked with a big smile.

"I was worried about you," he answered. Gwendolyn could tell it was the truth. "I get spooked sometimes," he said. "I just do."

"Spooked," Amy repeated. "About me?"

"Yeah. It was a strange night."

"Come in. I'll make breakfast."

And breakfast was great, Gwendolyn realized. Amy made eggs and lots of bacon, barely cooked the way she liked it, the fat loose and dripping. Gwendolyn made a quick batch of no-rise biscuits that Roosevelt said were the best he'd ever eaten. They ate and ate. Roosevelt reached out at one moment and touched Amy's hair. The sun had come through the open kitchen window and Amy's blond strands sparked in the sun; when she moved her head she gave off alternating currents of light. Gwendolyn wanted to touch it too, but she felt shy suddenly, a woman and a sister.

It had never seemed an odd thing, her relationship with Amy. They were constantly intertwined as children, in the backseat of the car, on the same side of the table, in the bathtub fighting over bubbles and toys. They knew each other; touched tongues to see what it would feel like; plucked the hairs from each other's breasts; examined their skin with a magnifying glass. Gwendolyn's skin, two years younger, was smoother, smaller pores, freckle free. Amy examined the inside of her own fair arm. Then she tilted the magnifying glass, oversized, black-handled, to catch the sun. Gwendolyn watched, shook her head, her voice high and pleading for Amy to cut it out. Amy waited until it cooked, until her skin blossomed crimson and blistered. Gwendolyn remembered Amy's wet eyes, the blood on her lip as she turned to her and smiled. The burn was not a wound, but a badge.

One junior high school night when Gwendolyn was thirteen and Amy was fifteen, the full moon made a window-shaped shadow across Amy's yellow bedspread, stretched out on the floor next to her bed. In the cool, voyeuristic moonlight, Gwendolyn looked down at their two naked bodies curled together and could not tell where her body ended and her sister's began.

Amy had lost her virginity and thought Gwendolyn should be prepared to lose hers. To not be frightened. To not care so much about it. Amy planned it, but Gwendolyn was caught unaware. Surprised by the way her body responded, the warmth, the perfect natural bliss.

And when Amy started college, there had been an easy move apart. There were boys in both their lives. Better boys, ones with knowledge, at least competence, and occasional brilliance. At one point Gwendolyn thought she'd never do that thing with her sister again. These men were too satisfying in their ordinary way.

Tony came along to confirm it. Gwendolyn told Amy she expected to marry him, to say yes just as soon as he asked. They opened the bakery, Amy didn't come to opening day. Gwendolyn didn't know why Amy hated him so much. When he broke her heart, Amy could have said I told you so, but she didn't. Instead, Amy tried to cheer her up, took her to dinner, movies, bought her chocolate, the special things sisters do for each other. Perfect things only sisters share.

Two years went by. They saw each other, looked without touching. Then one night, the week before Auntie Ned died, Amy had shown up at her apartment. She was crying. Gwendolyn never saw Amy cry.

"I miss you," Amy said.

"We had lunch together yesterday."

"I miss all of you, more of you, I don't know."

Amy was seeing Nick. A guy, nothing more or less, an actor, a typical LA guy with a low black car and a prosperity crystal hanging on a genuine Native American leather thong around his mirror. He was okay. He liked Amy a lot. They'd met at the Chinese herbalist's tea garden.

"How's Nick?" she asked.

"Useless," Amy said. "I . . . I met someone else."

"Well. Good, then. Who?"

"A . . . woman."

Gwendolyn was crushed, furious; the hurt and anger fell like a red curtain behind her eyes, down her throat, a shower of hot coals falling into her bowels. "What?" She thought she might be screaming.

It was unspoken between them, but it was also true. They only loved each other. Men could come, and come inside them, but there were other places reserved for just each other.

"No," Gwendolyn said. "No."

"It's nothing."

"No."

"Wendy. Baby. Please."

"No. Go away. Go away." She meant it when she said it. Amy left and Gwendolyn didn't call her, didn't see her, but thought about her and that woman every day for seven days. Seven days exactly until Auntie Ned caught on fire and died. Thank God Auntie Ned had died.

After the funeral they came home to Auntie Ned's house and Auntie Ned's bed and Auntie Ned's messages for living and took her advice. Forget the rest of the world. They lived, they lived in each other, and Gwendolyn felt like she was dead every moment without Amy. It happened suddenly. Just like that, a snap of the fingers. She never wanted anyone else, ever again. And Amy said the same thing, even more vehemently, passionately, desperately.

"I have to go to work," Gwendolyn said.

Roosevelt nodded sympathetically, innocently, the annoying innocence with which he seemed to do everything.

"What are you doing today?" she asked Amy, wanting Amy to tell her to stay home.

"Thought I'd pull the wallpaper down in the upstairs bathroom."

"The upstairs bathroom?"

"It's so ugly."

It was insulting that Amy would think to change the bathroom, their bathroom, today. "Aren't you ever going back to work?"

"No." Amy looked at her. "You know that."

Gwendolyn hated that look, hated it when Amy tried to make her feel stupid.

"What do you do?" Roosevelt asked.

Amy ignored him.

"You never told me your plans," Gwendolyn said. Amy never told her anything.

"Okay. What did you do?" Roosevelt grinned. Gwendolyn saw he was trying to defuse Amy, get between their fight. She was surprised he was that astute, sensitive, warm-blooded.

"I worked on the phone," Amy said.

"A salesperson?"

"Sort of. I sold the future. I was a phone psychic." Amy paused to let it sink in. "I told fortunes over the telephone," she continued. "Pay was good. My time was flexible. I could work from home."

Gwendolyn could see that Roosevelt was a little shocked. She thought her sister's job was funny, but it was sleazy too. The company advertised in the back of the free papers, after all, mixed in with 1-900-EAT-PUSY and all-night party lines. All the sex talk. And a lot of Amy's job was about sex. It was just another form of 900 number, cloaked in pseudo-mysticism.

"Tell me your problems. I can solve them." Amy's face was dark, closed, completely serious. "What is your name?" she said to Roosevelt.

"You know my name."

"Play along. What is your name?"

"Roosevelt James—"

"Just your first name."

"Roosevelt."

"Hmmm, Roosevelt." Amy closed her eyes, took some deep breaths, and pretended to drift into the other world, the spirit world. "I can see this is a time of great change for you."

"Oh, yeah." Roosevelt was grinning, trying to enjoy this. "Tell me about the tall blond stranger. Her name begins with an *A*, right?"

"Quiet. Concentrate." Amy wouldn't smile. She spoke slowly. "This is a difficult time in some ways. You are on a precipice. Things are about to change. It's good, but it is also frightening. You're not sure you're up to it."

Roosevelt's grin looked suddenly wired, his lips too red, too wide, dangerous tracks across his face, bent and twisted.

Amy opened her eyes. She didn't look at him, but stared into the beyond. "There is something in your past you want to forget. Something you want to leave behind."

"Amy," Gwendolyn said.

"You want this thing to leave you alone. It bothers you. It makes you sad. Haunts you in your dreams. I see a white room, a man in white. A doctor? Could it be a doctor?"

Roosevelt's face dissolved, went blank, stalled in the light of the oncoming train.

"A doctor, yes, some kind of doctor." Amy, Madame Amy nodded knowingly.

"Amy," Gwendolyn said again. Amy was saying too much. But she looked at Roosevelt. He was trapped, caught, run over and flattened.

"You don't like this doctor, you are afraid of this doctor, but he is trying to help you. He is. And he does. He has helped you. Now he's gone. The doctor is gone. That's good, Roosevelt, it's good. It is time for you to help yourself. And help others. Yes, it is time. You can save others. Like you have always wanted, but before it has always gone wrong, hasn't it? This time it won't. This time everything will be right. The time for redemption. Redemption."

Amy stopped. She closed her eyes. A moment passed. Then she shook her head, tossed her pretty hair, like she was coming back to this world. She smiled at Roosevelt, shy, blushing, asking his approval.

"How was I?" she asked.

"How do you do that?" The color was coming slowly back to his face. His eyes glittered with admiration.

It had been the right thing to do, Gwendolyn realized. He did believe. Her sister the psychic always knew.

Amy laughed. "They train us. You listen for audio clues in the other person, the way they say 'uh-huh,' or even breathe. I could hear your hands moving. And some things are universal. Most people are afraid of doctors."

Roosevelt looked relieved, if not convinced. But Gwendolyn knew there was more to it than that. Amy had a talent. Gwendolyn wasn't convinced it involved telling the future for desperate strangers, but some kind of intimate power was there. Amy knew the first and, more importantly, the last thing people wanted to hear.

"I better go," Gwendolyn said and looked at Amy.

"I wish you'd stay home with us," Amy said.

It was what Gwendolyn wanted to hear. She stood, smiled. "I have to go."

"I'll miss you," Amy said.

Gwendolyn believed her.

Roosevelt was relieved to be out of the basement and back to the kitchen. He liked it better working upstairs in the light than down in the dim clutter. The melted chair was always there in the corner of his eye. The hum of the upright freezer—the meat locker—was insistent, pervasive.

He knew they thought he was crazy, but he felt good. He really had protected them last night. He didn't know how, but he knew it. When he woke up in his truck and saw their brown and yellow heads haloed by the early morning sun, he knew he had done a good job. They were safe. Thanks to him.

A time for redemption, Amy had said. He couldn't believe she was really a psychic, but he thought she was right. He felt good about his future. He felt like the future had actually begun.

He stripped the last piece of baseboard off the wall, gratified to see that there was nothing surprising behind it. He had ordered the new floor. Amy would like it. It was white as she requested, but with gentle flecks of yellow and peach. Her colors, he thought, and her sister's.

He liked Gwendolyn better today. He saw another side of her making those biscuits, hanging out at breakfast. She even gave him a smile when she left. He felt appreciated. His nose was clear, his head wasn't hurting. Whatever ailment he'd been coming down with seemed to have passed over. This time.

Amy appeared in the doorway of the kitchen. "Let's go to the beach," she said.

"Huh?" He hated to say "huh"; his mother had taught him it sounded ignorant. "Excuse me?"

"Let's go to the beach. Walk in the sand. Eat a basket of shrimp for lunch."

"I . . . I'm behind."

"I don't care."

"I'm not even close to finished."

"I don't want you to finish," Amy said.

She walked over to him, stood next to where he was working in the corner. He looked up at her from his knees. She leaned against the wall, but didn't move her head to look down at him, simply lowered her eyes, filtered her gaze through her eyelashes. Her face looked calm, almost as if she were sleeping.

"I like having you here," she continued.

"I like being here."

He leaned his red curls against her thigh. She brushed her fingers along the top of his head, tapping lightly.

"It's raining," she said in a child's singsong. "It's pouring. The old man is snoring."

He didn't know what that meant. "Where do you want to go?" he asked.

"I'll drive."

Abruptly she walked away. Losing her support, he almost fell over. He got to his feet. He was still wearing the clothes of last night, the ones he had slept in, that he had removed for Sheryl, but they smelled like bacon now, not a ticket agent's motionless perfume.

"It's up to you," Auntie Ned said. She wrote it on a slip of paper and taped it to Amy's lavender sweater.

Amy tilted her nine-year-old perfect face up to her favorite aunt. Her only aunt, Auntie Ned thought, but her favorite nonetheless.

"Say it," Auntie Ned said. " 'It's up to me.' "

"It's up to me." Amy smiled, went back to singing that nursery rhyme about the rain and the old man who bumped his head.

Auntie Ned was taking her to the beach, leaving Gwendolyn behind. She wanted Amy to herself. There had been an unhappy moment at the house. Gwendolyn crying. Amy feeling guilty. Helen not speaking.

Auntie Ned apologized to Gwendolyn. "I'll take you next time." She turned to Helen. "Both of you."

Helen took Gwendolyn's arm, pulled her inside, closed the door behind them hard.

Auntie Ned saw Gwendolyn's little face at the window, her palms pressed to the glass, as they backed out of the driveway.

"Wendy," Amy called.

Auntie Ned could hear the longing in her voice.

"Don't give up," Auntie Ned said, "Don't let her get away. Don't give up. Like I did."

Amy drove Auntie Ned's canary-yellow Dodge Dart. There was one of her aunt's inspirational messages, written in her slanting, grammar-school hand on a yellow Post-it, taped to the dashboard: GET OFF MY FUCKING ROAD.

"Was she always like this?" Roosevelt asked, gesturing to the slip of paper in peeling Scotch tape.

"She was tough," Amy said.

"But it doesn't say get out of my way, but get off my road. Like it was hers."

Amy looked over at Roosevelt. He looked good this morning. She had watched him slurp his bacon, dunk Gwendolyn's biscuits in the runny egg yolks. Good eater.

"It *is* her road," she said. "Or it was when she drove on it."

"What are you talking about?"

"Now it's my road." Amy laughed at Roosevelt's confusion. "Haven't you ever thought of it that way?"

"I never feel like it's mine," Roosevelt said.

"You think you borrow everything," Amy said, "is that it? Nothing's really yours. It's only loaned to you."

"Well—"

"But if you borrow it," Amy went on, "then you have to feel obligated to someone, or at least grateful. To who? The guys who made the road? The city council? Some long-dead urban planner who thought this road should go in this direction? It's demeaning."

He scrunched down in his seat to think about this.

Amy opened her window. It would be cloudy at the beach, she could tell by the haze in the distance. It would be gray and windy and the sand would look dirty and there would be the smell of old garbage and seagull crap. Just the way she liked it, she thought, and laughed.

She looked over at Roosevelt and was very glad he didn't ask her what was funny. She hated that. She hated people to ask her what she was thinking, what made her frown, even how she was feeling. It was none of their business.

"Don't you have a girlfriend?" she asked.

She startled him into the truth. "No. Well . . . why?"

"Then why couldn't you see me last night?"

"I had a date."

"Didn't go very well, did it?"

"It was fine."

"You slept in your truck at my house. Couldn't kick her out of bed at your place?"

"No, no. She . . . she wasn't at my place. No, never, no."

"Okay, okay." Amy looked at him, made her face soft and wistful. "It's not my business to ask, anyway."

"Sure it is," he said. "You have every right to ask me whatever you want."

Amy put her hand on his thigh. She felt his muscles tighten, saw a minuscule flex in his groin. She was very familiar with a nice hotel near Topanga Canyon that wouldn't mind a daytime rental. She loved the impersonal response allowed in a hotel room, any hotel room.

He put his hand on hers. Their two hands were almost the same size.

"Your burn looks much better," she said.

"I haven't even thought about it," he replied. "Truly. Doesn't seem to hurt today at all."

"Good," she said. "Or am I sorry that you don't have a little constant reminder of me?"

"I don't need a burn on my hand," he said, "to think of you."

She had to admit she liked it when he talked that way. Too many men she met were timid, reticent, and frightened by her. Roosevelt was an idiot, but he had a certain sexual smoothness, possibly even the strength she required. Yes, oh yes, definitely. He was perfect.

Chapter Seven

Dr. Minor barely made a dent in the king-size bed in the low-budget Vagabond Motor Hotel in Glendale, CA. His tiny body was a bump under the bland, floral bedspread, a day's worth of laundry, a wet bath towel discarded. He was exhausted, but not sleeping. Too tired, too excited, too many diet sodas on the plane. In the St. Louis airport he had rushed to the men's room. He surprised a father and his toddler son at the urinal. The sleepy little boy looked over at Dr. Minor and burst into tears. His nightmare come to life. Dr. Minor smiled. The boy screamed. The father let go of his penis and smacked his son, hard, on the back of the head.

"Shut up," he said. "That's not polite." He smiled and apologized to Dr. Minor. The boy moved away, to the other side of his strong and protective father.

Dr. Minor knew he wasn't bad looking, for a dwarf. He was a surprise, that was all. Something unexpected, especially at five in the morning in the unpleasant light of a public men's room in a strange city where everyone would rather be asleep. He flopped uneasily on the hard motel mattress and saw the boy's frightened face, the father's big wet hand, the top of his own misshapen head in the mirror.

People laughed at his size. And when they heard what he did for a living, they laughed harder. Enrollment was down in his classes. The thrill was gone, not enough new evidence. Dr. Minor prayed for someone famous to combust. An actor would be best, but a rock star, even a politician would be all right. And if he could examine the evidence! If he could document it, prove it beyond anyone's unreasonable and ridiculous doubt, his future would be insured.

He felt his overworked heart beating desperately in his odd chest. He was aware of each frantic beat and grateful for it. His doctor had told him he should be dead by now. He didn't take a breath for granted, willed his compressed lungs to keep pumping as long as immortality took.

When Gwendolyn was little, she loved to go to Disneyland in the summer, at the most popular time, the most crowded. Amy wouldn't go to Disneyland. There was no way for her to be special, to stand out. There were too many pretty blond children in lines and groups. Amy tried temper tantrums and sneaking cigarettes in the bathroom and finally refused to go. Gwendolyn was happy to disappear, to blend into the multitude.

Going to work was like that too. She liked going across town in the morning with all the other cars on the freeway, a commuter mug on her dashboard, the morning show on the radio. She liked the routine, the idea that this was what everybody did. And the cakes she made were part of it too, parties and weddings, baby showers and bon voyage. She knew they didn't last, they were only sugary moments, but her cakes were always surrounded by people who wanted them.

Tony was being extra nice. He wore the corduroy shirt she had given him for Christmas and a pair of faded blue jeans. He looked handsome. She had loved him. Maybe his advances were all her own fault; maybe she sent mixed messages.

She was working on a hot-air-balloon cake, one of her trademarks, complete with a woven basket in different straw colors, sandbags, a bottle of champagne in an ice bucket festooned with ribbons and bows, all made entirely of icing. She would attach a real helium balloon and matching ribbons later. She had baked it yesterday before she walked out. Last night she had thought about it, regretted that she wouldn't get to finish it.

Tony hovered over her, admiring, complimenting, until she shooed him away. In a moment he was back carrying a slip of pale pink stationery.

"Here," he said. "This came for you."

She took the note from him and read it. It was praise from the bride of the bloodred stairway, how lovely the cake was, how everybody commented, how she absolutely hated to cut into it.

"Thanks." She meant it.

"Gwen . . . I'm really sorry."

"I know."

"I've been having trouble with my girlfriend."

Gwendolyn knew his girlfriend, knew his trouble, knew that trouble was what he liked. "Pass me that toothpick."

"I promise to be a good boy. Keep my hands to myself. You can take some time off."

"Tony."

"What?"

Gwendolyn wasn't sure what she wanted to say. Men always looked so young when they apologized. They turned into boys caught at the cookie jar, beside the broken window, standing over the dead squirrel. "I didn't mean it." "I'm sorry." "I didn't know it would happen." But the glass was still broken and the squirrel still dead, the cookies all gone. That's what boys didn't seem to understand.

"Let me work," she said.

"Suit yourself." He turned away, pouting, rejected.

Gwendolyn knew he was begging to talk, to explain himself. She didn't want to give him the satisfaction, but she couldn't work knowing how much he wanted.

"Is there any coffee?" she called after him.

"I'll make some. I'll make it." He smiled at her, grateful, happy.

She put her tools down and followed him into the back. He hummed as he filled the coffeepot, replaced the filter, carelessly measured the black espresso blend. She watched him. She liked watching him do a domestic task. She couldn't remember her father in the kitchen. She couldn't remember her father; not his face or his voice. He was only a cool smell of mint and tobacco, a scratchy feeling, the breeze from a brief ride in the air over his balding head. She had grown up with women, her mother and her sister, and Auntie Ned who drifted in and out of their lives.

"So?" she asked.

"Hmmm?" He was busy frothing milk, making her a treat.

"Your girlfriend doesn't understand you."

"It's true."

"It's a cliché."

"I think she's seeing someone else."

"You sleep with a hundred women."

"I'm a passionate man."

He handed her a cup, her favorite, round like the sky, a sunny blue and yellow Italian morning.

"Do you make her coffee?" Gwendolyn asked.

"Are you kidding?"

Gwendolyn lifted her eyebrows at him over the cup.

Tony shrugged. "She makes the coffee."

"Bet it's not as good as this."

Tony grinned. "You like my coffee. You always liked my coffee."

"Yeah," Gwendolyn said, "but that's all I like."

"Time off," he said. "That's what you need. Go away for a few days."

"How am I supposed to do that?"

"I want you to go," Tony said. "You'll spend every night thinking of me. I know it, because I'll be thinking of you."

"Up yours."

Tony laughed. "Back to work," he said.

Enough discussion, Gwendolyn realized, before either of them said too much.

He was not a bad guy. He really wasn't. She didn't know how to explain it to Amy. Amy hated him so much. Gwendolyn didn't hate Tony; it was just that sometimes he made her feel like trash. He reminded her of the neighbor's dog when she was a kid. Mom had given her and Amy a puppy, a little white girl dog. They named her Buttercup. The big boy dog from next door, King, a flop-eared sweet-faced mutt, dug under the fence, jumped over the fence, slid around the fence to hump Buttercup day and night. It wasn't flattering. It was just exhausting.

Dr. Minor's colleague, Jeffrey Woodrow, met him in the lobby of the Vagabond Motor Hotel at ten o'clock.

"I know where the house is," Jeffrey said as they got into his battered station wagon, "but I couldn't, I mean, I don't know who lives there."

"That's fine, Jeff," said Dr. Minor. "I'll take over now."

Jeff was apologetic, nervous, thrilled to be squiring the renowned Dr. Minor to the scene of a possible combustion. Dr. Minor was gratified to be so admired. The bad taste of traveling was melting away.

But when they got to the house and rang the doorbell, no one answered. Dr. Minor tried to look in the window. There was nothing to see but the back of the drawn curtains.

"Are you sure someone has moved in?" he asked.

"Oh yes," Jeff answered. "Two girls, women. I talked to the old lady neighbor, but she didn't know their names. Over there, in that house." He gestured next door to a high and ratty bamboo fence.

Behind it Dr. Minor could see the top of a ramshackle stucco box, paint peeling, roof tiles missing.

"What a weirdo she was. A real freak," Jeff said, then looked at Dr. Minor, mortified. "Sorry."

Amy's hand rested on Roosevelt's thigh. He liked it there. His attention centered on it. He hardly noticed where they were going.

"Tell me about her," Amy said.

"Who?" Roosevelt had to think a moment to remember her name. "You mean . . . Sheryl?"

"Is that who you had the date with last night?"

"Yes." He stroked the back of her hand, firm and possessive on his thigh. It was a large hand, but smooth, flawless, feminine. He traced around the top of each of her fingers. Her nails were so short he felt only soft skin, no edges, no sharpness. He thought of Sheryl's professionally red talons and shuddered.

Amy laughed. "That good, huh?"

"She was nice enough," he said. He looked at Amy, took his hand off hers, reached and pulled her hair back. He touched her cheek. He figured why the hell not. "But she wasn't you," he said.

Amy looked at him. He saw he had surprised her again. He knew she thought he was an idiot. He knew, but he didn't want her to know he knew. He knew she wanted something from him. He also knew that she was hurt in some terrible way; she held back in their kisses and when he touched her. The reserve came from deep within her, a childhood pain, he had decided, a longing for something that he knew he could supply. He would go slow, let her confide in him, trust him. Years of his own therapy had let him in on some of the tricks of the trade, some of the ways of providing help, some of the special understandings.

They took the number 10 freeway all the way to the end where it dumped out by the ocean under the Santa Monica pier like so much sewage. Roosevelt thought of Santa Monica as a fallen paradise, once beautiful, but now a beach in high contrast; the dirty sand and the unhappy ocean under sunsets made glorious by smog; the Westside professionals stepping over and around and through the territories of the homeless. He saw volleyball players jumping over bearded veterans who had never left the war; skaters circling winos; blonds in BMWs avoiding the gray-green turtle-men with garbage bags on their backs. Everything was the most and the least and the best and the worst and basically he hated it.

Of course, to be honest, he hated all beaches. He lived in southern California, but he hated the beach. There was too much water in the ocean, too much sameness, waves and sand and sand and waves. He'd grown up in the Midwest occasionally watching *Hawaii Five-O*. Men in tropical shirts, women who did business in bikinis; it all looked hot and bland and ridiculous to him. He had come here for something else. He'd had a faint idea he would work in movies. Not as an actor, of course, but designing houses for the reactions of television couples, or building the mountains of another planet. As a child he had been imaginative, artistic. After he moved here, he had worked one month in a scenic shop, part-time during college. But it had all seemed so temporary, so fake, so spectral. He couldn't keep up his enthusiasm.

At least now, when he fixed a woman's broken doorjamb, never mind that her husband broke down the door trying to kill her, never mind the bloodstains he pulled away with the splintered wood, at least he was doing something that really existed.

He had talked about leaving town a lot at the hospital. He thought he should make a new start somewhere else.

"You can't run away from your problems," chanted a member of his group every time he brought up the subject. It was a liturgy, a statement and response like the prayers at his mother's Episcopalian church. "God be with you." "And also with you." "A new start." "Same old problems."

And he didn't leave. He knew why too. For as long as he stayed he had leaving as a possibility. The minute he left, there was nothing else he could do.

He sighed as Amy pulled in to the beach parking lot, no charge for parking today, a mobile home and a shiny black pickup truck their only companions. He had hoped the beach would be closed.

"What's the matter?"

"Nothing," Roosevelt answered. "You must be a real beach girl. Growing up here. I can see you at fifteen, sixteen, blond and really tan. I bet you wore a lime-green bikini."

"How did you know?" He was glad to make her laugh.

"I have an eye for trouble. You were trouble, weren't you?"

"I had Gwendolyn to slow me down."

Amy tossed her slip-on sneakers in the back. Her feet were made to be bare. Roosevelt looked down at his boots. He wondered if, in this great outdoors, she would be able to smell his feet when he took his socks off.

"Afraid your feet will stink?" she asked.

She was a remarkable girl. "Actually, I have been wearing these boots a long time."

"If they do, I promise I'll pretend not to notice."

"Okay," he said and sat down on the curb to take them off. "But I think I'll leave them outside the car."

"Meet you at the water," Amy said and skipped off across the sand.

Roosevelt could never run like that in sand. She seemed like a nymph, a sand sprite, a commercial for the good life. She stripped off her sweater as she ran, leaving on only a white sleeveless undershirt. He was fascinated by the stretch in her lean thighs, covered by robin's-egg-blue cotton, her straight back, the firm brown skin on the back of her arms.

He stared at his own yellow-white toes wiggling on the sandy sidewalk. He took off his plaid shirt and shivered in his T-shirt. He hid his clothing behind the tire of the car and took off after her, running clumsily, awkwardly, feet digging too deeply into the sand, always on the verge of falling.

He reached her out of breath and stumbling. A wave spilled on the beach and caught his toes. He screamed, an embarrassing squealing girl of a scream, and jumped away. Amy stood motionless and let the water cover her feet, her ankles, the bottoms of her pants.

"Jesus, that's cold," Roosevelt said and realized how stupidly obvious that was. "I mean, it really surprised me." Another astute observation.

Amy didn't reply. He took a step back toward the water to be next to her. He forced himself to stand in the aftermath of the receding wave. The wet sand was glacial. He wanted to shiver, but he compelled his body to be still. He was going to catch pneumonia this way, he knew it. It was supposed to be warm here in southern California, but he had never been colder anywhere in his life. His first apartment, a nice one, had no heat. At restaurants they sat you outside in sixty-degree weather. The movie theaters kept their air-conditioning on year round. He missed the boiling hot summers of Missouri, no cool evenings sneaking up on you at a barbecue. And when it was wintertime, you wore a coat, a hat, gloves. You put on the heat and stayed indoors. You did not go swimming.

Another wave came in. He gritted his teeth, tried not to cry out. Amy leaned her head on his shoulder.

"I knew you liked the beach as much as I do," she said.

"Nothing like it," he said.

"I couldn't live anywhere else," she said. "I mean, I don't get down here enough. But I have to know it's here."

He was too cold to talk. He reached one bare arm around her waist. He could feel the heat of her body through her little shirt. He put both arms around her.

"Hey," she said and snuggled into his neck. "Ever made love in the sand?"

"No." It was a terrible thought.

"I can tell you're thinking about it."

His balls were shriveled to the size of raisins. The image of less clothing was not appealing, even though he had been dreaming about her naked body forever.

"You're tougher than I am. It's too cold for me," she said. "But it's tempting."

She turned her face up to him and he kissed her. Her lips felt heated, a radiator carrying steam up from below.

"Let's go," she said.

"Great." But first another kiss. Even as cold as he was, even with his pale feet frosty to the point of pain, he needed to kiss that mouth again. Right away. It was the one warm spot in all of Los Angeles.

She kissed back, circled his mouth with her smoldering tongue. She pressed her chest against his. She wasn't wearing a bra and her breasts were obvious against him. Her hands found an untucked opening in his T-shirt and she slid her fingers under and against his defenseless skin. He gasped. Fingers of ice, so cold they burned him.

"You're so warm," she breathed into his mouth.

She slid her hands around from his back to his chest and over his nipples, frozen hard in the cold. He groaned.

"Let's go," she said again and stepped away from him.

He followed her doggedly across the sand, neither of them running. They had a purpose, a mission, a warm car ahead.

He looked around. Amy had parked far enough from both the pickup and the Winnebago. They could be alone on the black vinyl backseat. It was daylight, but it was overcast. A single jogger in the distance. And if a single jogger got surprised, that was his problem, not theirs.

Amy got to the car first. She got in and started it right up and

Roosevelt knew she wasn't going to make love to him in a parked car by a dirty beach in the middle of the day. But he didn't think she'd make love to him in her aunt's house either. He could suggest his place, but he knew she'd have to be pretty desperate to drive into Hollywood, step over the dog shit and broken bottles to the twisted front gate of his building. It had cooled a woman's enthusiasm in the past. He didn't want to risk it.

He retrieved his boots and his shirt and slid into the passenger seat. Before he had the door closed she was backing up, pulling out of the parking lot.

"Where are we going?"

"I have a fantasy," she said.

He nodded. He knew she did. He had already imagined it. A meat locker, a steel grate in the floor for hosing down the blood. She would push him up against the hanging carcass of a cow; her hair would intertwine with the veins and sinew. He had seen it in her eyes as she stared at him over dinner, over rare hamburgers, ribs, and chops. She pictured him naked and drawn on, mapped out pound by pound, rump roast, dark meat, breast and thigh. She would put him on platters covered with gravy and vegetables, cooked carrots, boiled potatoes.

They turned right on Topanga Canyon Boulevard. Patrick's Road House was on the corner. Roosevelt and his wife had gone there on an early date. He remembered Irish stew, green beer, and soda bread. Must have been St. Patrick's day.

Amy turned right again immediately behind the bar. There was a small hotel. The Fleur de Lys or something—the sign was too small to read quickly. He had never noticed a hotel here before. It was odd, a redbrick building with fancy wrought-iron curlicues, stone gargoyles, black shutters. Something out of a New Orleans nightmare. Were there hooks in the walls and the ceilings, he wondered, places for the chains and the whips? He wouldn't be entirely surprised.

They drove around back and parked in front of a red door marked OFFICE.

"Here?" he asked.

"I've always wanted to come here," Amy said. "On the top floor I bet you can see the ocean."

"This is your fantasy?"

"Not much of one, I guess. You were expecting whips and chains?"

He laughed. She licked her lips and he could taste it.

"I'm paying for this," she said. "That's part of it. I put out the money. We can tell them we're tourists from Ohio."

"Missouri," he said. "I'm from Missouri."

"I know."

She got out of the car. He followed. They didn't look like tourists. They didn't have any suitcases. This was an obvious nooner. But he didn't mind a bit.

The receptionist didn't mind either. He barely looked up from the golf tournament on the small television. The perfect green lawn on the screen was bright in the room, turned the man's hands grassy as he reached for the book. He had gray hair and wore a short-sleeved purple polo shirt and a belt with whales on it. A golfer himself, no doubt.

Roosevelt smiled at Amy. She shifted from foot to foot, blushed when the guy asked how long they'd be staying.

"Just one night," she said. "We're here from Ohio. I mean, Missouri."

Now the guy looked up. "May I have your credit card?"

"Do you take traveler's checks?"

"With two forms of ID."

"Better save my cash." She lied badly. "For all that sightseeing. Here."

She handed him her credit card.

She reached her hand down behind the counter where the man couldn't see and brushed her fingers over Roosevelt's crotch. Roosevelt snickered and the man looked up at him.

"Top floor, please," said Amy.

"Here you go."

There was a view of the ocean from their room. Roosevelt could appreciate the beach from this distance, in the comfortable, modulated temperature of a motel room. It was hard to tell where the gray sea ended and the gray sky began.

"Hey," Amy said.

He turned from the window. She sat on the king-size bed, her legs squeezed tightly together. Her arms crossed in front of her chest. He never imagined she would be shy, or awkward. It was up to him. He had made love to women in motel rooms before. He had even paid them sometimes. Those were the strangest temporary rooms, the ones where women worked. They were oddly personalized, a picture of their kid stuck in the bathroom mirror, a pair of panty hose hung up to dry, the drawer in the bedside table filled with condoms and jewelry, lubricants, Band-Aids, and tampons.

He stood in front of her, cupped her face and lifted it to him. They kissed. But he could feel her holding back. Not like at the beach, not like it had been.

He sat down next to her, put his arm around her.

Suddenly aggressive, she turned to him and pushed him back on the bed. She straddled him, leaned down, and kissed him, hard. She slid her mouth off his and kissed his neck, stuck her tongue in his ear.

"I have to ask you—" she whispered.

"Anything," he answered. She had put her sweater back on in the car and now he pulled at it, trying to remove it. He thought of her small undershirt and her distinct breasts.

"Wait," she said and kissed him again, easier this time. She rolled off him and they lay face-to-face on the bed kissing, continuing to kiss. She traced his mouth with one finger. Her lips were warm, her tongue hot and wet, her finger salty and cool. He didn't think he could stand it much longer.

"I . . ." she began.

"What, what?" He didn't want to rush her, but he was close to begging now.

"I want you to experience something with me."

"Me too." It was a stupid thing to say, but he couldn't help it. She laughed.

"Something not ordinary."

"Okay."

"Something special."

"Great." He'd do anything now, he knew it.

"I think it's the only way."

"Tell me," he said.

She pulled away from him and sat up. "It won't be easy for you."

Roosevelt sat up, confused.

"I can't have an orgasm," Amy said. She looked down in her lap, suddenly young, scared, worried.

"You can't? Or you won't?"

"I don't. I never have."

"Never?"

"Not . . . well, once. I have once, by myself. I mean, I know it works, it's physically possible, but . . ."

He knew someone had hurt her. He imagined some filthy uncle, some lying teacher, some scum of the universe standing over her.

"I've been working on it," she said, "and I want you to help me. I think you can help me."

"I can," he said. His breath came faster. "I can," he said again. He had waited for this.

"You're not like anybody else."

She smiled at him, timidly. He smiled back and grew taller, broader, more handsome. He knew she was scared to reveal so much to him. He could help her, he could go slow, he was not inexperienced. His penis thumped a little.

"Close your eyes," he said.

She obeyed and he kissed both eyelids, then her nose. Her lips parted and he kissed her mouth. They were good kissers, they fit just right together. He touched her neck and her shoulder and finally her breast, round and cotton-sweater-covered. She didn't pull away. He felt he had reached a goal. Second base. He had been running from first for a long time.

Amy pulled her sweater and her undershirt off over her head. She stood up and peeled down her springtime pants. She stepped out of her panties. He wasn't surprised they were white, cotton, tiny.

She stood naked before him.

"Here's the deal," she said.

It sounded like she meant business. "Okay." He tried to keep his eyes on her face.

"Until I do"—she paused and looked at him—"you can't."

"Can't what?"

"Orgasm. You can't have an orgasm."

"Inside you?"

"No. At all. Not until I do." She put her strong hands on her naked hips. "I mean it. It's important. The minute you do, it's over between us."

It was ridiculous what she was asking. What was the point? But he looked at her face and knew she was serious.

"Can you do it?" she asked.

It was hard to say no to the perfect bare body standing in front of him. Her pubic hair was blond. Her belly flat. Her breasts beautiful, palm-sized orbs. He was a sucker for that middle part of a woman, the curve of her hip, the slight outline of a rib, the ripe swell of her tit.

"Say it again," he said. "Tell me the deal again."

"No orgasm, until I say so."

"Can I go in the bathroom, you know, just to relieve some tension?"

"No. And not at home either."

She would know if he cheated. He knew she would.

"How long will this take?" he asked.

"I don't know."

"Are you talking about today?"

"It'll take longer than that."

"You mean we're going to do this more than once?"

"I think we'll have to do it a lot. Often."

"But no . . . no . . ."

"No."

Here was a woman he couldn't get out of his mind, a woman he wanted so much, offering him repeated sex. A lot, she said, and often. But without the diploma at the end.

"What if I wear a rubber?"

"That has nothing to do with it."

"And you think this will help you?"

"I know it will. You will."

She came closer to him. His face was just the right height. He could smell her lemony soap and something darker, muskier. He tried to focus on her eyes, but she looked at him and then looked away, tilted her head back to stare at the ceiling. She was pure body now in front of him.

"I'm sorry," she said. He could hear a moist gurgle in her throat.

"It won't be easy," he said. "But I'll do my best."

"Thank you," she said. "Thank you."

He reached for her. She stepped back, out of range.

"Men and women are different," Amy began. Her voice was abruptly efficient, a schoolteacher in front of her class. "A woman is slow to be aroused, but slower to finish. A woman's sexual energy is like a wave. Once it's started, it keeps cresting. It can roll on for a long time. A man is the opposite. He is quick, singular, and finished."

"But give me fifteen minutes, less with you, and I'm ready again." Roosevelt smiled at Amy. But she wasn't laughing.

"This is important," Amy said. "It's important to me. To us. A woman's power is called Sakti. It means cosmic, kinetic. A man is Siva, inert, base, grounded in the here and now."

"Makes us guys sound great."

"I know a method." She ignored his comment. "A method that helps us to combine our forces. Have you heard of tantra? Tantric sex?"

"I've never been real into this eastern stuff."

"Don't think of it as eastern. Think of it as an ancient truth. There's a path I want us to take. It's called the Tantric Way. Tantra means 'woven together.' It's about the union of male and female. About worshiping a nonorgasmic sexual union and recognizing the presence of the divine in both of us. It makes a lot of sense. I've done a lot of reading."

Roosevelt had to keep himself from laughing. "You don't need to read about it."

"I do," she said.

He sighed.

She crossed her arms in front of her breasts, thrust a hip to one side. "It's about making it a conscious act."

"I'm usually conscious."

"Don't make fun of me." Her hair trembled on her shoulders. "I need to know you're present, cognizant, that you're thinking of me. We have to practice."

"Practice," he said unhappily. "Sex is supposed to be—I mean—" He looked at her pale body in front of him. It glowed. He could smell the ocean. His dick tugged at his pants, beseeching him to just say yes. He shrugged. "It's just not very spontaneous."

"There's no such thing as spontaneity. Every single thing we do is premeditated."

He realized that for her that was probably true. She was a thinker, an analyzer, a worrier.

"No laughing," she said. "Can you do that? I need you to do that. Don't laugh at me."

"I promise," he said, and he did promise, he really did.

"There are steps we have to follow. They're called the Nine Rewards."

"Nine."

"Nine specific things I want you to do, us to do together."

"Sex things."

"Obviously."

He frowned. Nothing was obvious with this woman. "Before I get to . . . ?"

"Right. And at the Ninth Reward, it'll be amazing."

"And you'll . . . you'll have an orgasm?"

"I believe I will." She looked at him. "For the first time ever."

He was anxious now, anxious to begin. "Can we do all nine things at once? You know, one after the other?"

"No. We do each one until we get it right. It might take some time."

"Jesus."

"Fine." Amy stood up. "Then don't bother."

She turned her naked back to him. There was a freckle low on her back where a tail would be. He was hungry to kiss her there, let his tongue linger over that spot, the ducklinglike hairs tickling his lips.

"Okay," he said. "Okay. What's number one?"

She turned and smiled at him, her relief and joy filling her face. She was beautiful, luminescent. He had to close his eyes.

"Get undressed," she said.

He had never taken his clothes off so quickly.

"Lie down on the bed," she said.

He did.

"I lie on my side next to you," she said and did so. "You turn toward me."

He rolled over to face her and ran his hand down her arm.

"Don't touch me," she said. "Not yet."

He looked at her, stared into her dark eyes, listened to the ocean, faint but constant, and the traffic noise, louder, but comforting. He thought of every man out there, every poor sucker on his way to work, to a meeting, to pick up the kids from school, and how they would envy him. He was the only one in here. The light in the room was mottled, watery. They were safe, two fish inside a dark green aquarium. Okay, he thought, this is okay. He saw her desire in her eyes. She wanted this to work as badly as he did. He was content.

Amy lay on her side facing him. Stupid man. How could he lie there, staring at her, and not see? His pale eyes looked at her without blinking. A fish, she thought, he was a fish hooked to her line, her orgasmic, tantric line. Gwendolyn would be his release. She looked at him. He would do what she expected. He would service them both. What was that old joke, about keeping a man in the basement? She wanted Gwendolyn to know, to appreciate what her big sister went through for her. She would tell her one day. They would laugh about it. Gwendolyn would be impressed and grateful.

Roosevelt sighed. She could feel his desire, she could see it in his freckled face. She didn't want this to go on too long. She only needed to get him addicted, get him doing whatever she told him. Maybe she should have told him there were only Six Rewards. Maybe they could skip over a couple of them. Time off for good behavior. She dug her thumbnail into her fingertip. The pain felt good. Stupid man.

Then she saw his penis hardening. Just by looking at her. That was a good feeling. She licked her lips, as if unconsciously, knowing that her tongue would hasten his arousal. She was right. His eyes left hers, stared at her mouth. He was unaware his own mouth had opened, his tongue protruded slightly. She closed her eyes, and thought of Gwendolyn. Gwendolyn's mouth. Her mouth on Gwendolyn's breasts, their firmness, their taste, a dryness she felt in the back of her throat. Her nipples were tingling. It was working.

Roosevelt knew he was hard. Amazing. They were just looking at each other and he thought he could probably have an orgasm. This is really safe sex, he thought, and laughed.

Amy frowned and he winced.

"Sorry," he said.

"Shh."

He felt his penis wilt a little. Then he noticed her nipples standing up and felt himself stiffen again. This was wild. He had never been so connected and yet so distant from his own body before. He wasn't worrying about entertaining her, or if his breath was bad or if he was too heavy on top of her, or going too fast, or not fast enough, or if they should roll over and try another position. They were both just lying here, turning each other on. This was good.

But he also knew he couldn't do this forever.

Amy felt him shift, just slightly. He was thinking again, pulling away from her. She needed to move on. She put her head back and moaned just a little. She opened her legs.

She knew what Roosevelt was looking at.

She heard his breath louder, quicker.

Good, she thought. "I want you," she said.

Instantly he complied, moving toward her, pressing his body against hers. His penis immediately found its way. She thought of Gwendolyn, then didn't, pushed Gwendolyn away and thought of a visit to the doctor instead.

"Nine strokes," she said.

He groaned. "Nine?"

"Nine and then quit. Slowly. Pause between each."

One.

Two.

Three.

Four.

Five.

"Slow down," she said.

Six . . .

Seven . . .

Eight . . .

He took a deep breath. She could tell he wasn't ready for nine, for the end.

Nine . . .

He rolled over on his back. Then she did. They both stared at the ceiling. The light fixture glittered above her, winking at her, laughing at her. She felt herself on edge. Her finger hurt where her nail had pressed. But she had to pretend. She sighed as if happily, got up her on her knees, and kissed him, noticing, but not mentioning, the frustration, the pain, in his face.

"Thank you," she said and left to go to the bathroom.

Roosevelt felt as if he had run the marathon with his pants on fire. He was sweating, sick to his stomach. His erection bounced in front of him. It didn't want to go away.

"Come in the shower," she called from the bathroom.

He lay where he was, naked, spread-eagled on the bed.

"Come on," she said. "This water is unbelievable."

He was afraid to get in the shower with her. Would she let him touch her, slide soap across her flesh, rub hotel shampoo sweet and flowery in her hair? He got to his feet. His knees were trembling, but he felt strong. He never thought such a thing was possible. Nine strokes and stop. The shower would be okay. He really was an extraordinary guy.

Chapter Eight

There was a lizard, a real one, caged in a Plexiglas box on the center of the kitchen table. It was green like its artificial fern perch, but the brochure said it could change colors depending on its background. Amy could see its toes, bulbous, splayed, gripping for dear life on the slippery plastic.

"Can't it have real plants?" she asked.

"Sure," Gwendolyn said. Amy could hear the excitement in her voice. "He can make it a whole jungle habitat. You know, a terrarium."

Roosevelt looked stunned. Amy frowned.

"I'm not responsible," she said to him.

"Of course you're not." Gwendolyn shook her dark hair, smiled with her sky-blue eyes. "I wanted to get him a present."

She has lost her mind, Amy thought. A present, a lizard, so green and fragile.

"What does it eat?" Roosevelt asked.

Gwendolyn grinned and handed him a white Chinese food box. Something scrabbled and scratched inside.

Roosevelt started to open it.

"Don't!" Gwendolyn stopped him. "They'll get out."

Roosevelt held the box gingerly, away from his body.

"They're crickets," Gwendolyn said with relish. She almost licked her lips as she spoke. "Baby crickets. She's just a little lizard, after all."

"I thought lizards were vegetarians."

"Definitely carnivorous. Eats them alive. The guy showed me. You should see how fast she is. Have you ever tried to catch a cricket?"

"I like my food dead," Roosevelt said. "And on a plate."

Amy shook her head. She could smell Roosevelt on her fingers, in her hair. The shower had caught her off guard. She had thought he would succumb in the shower. Then he would beg her to give her a second chance, promise to try harder, concentrate. She would be magnanimous, offer it to him, wounded but understanding.

But Roosevelt had surprised her. He focused on her at every moment; he never gave up although she knew he was close several times. It was disconcerting. She didn't like surprises. They had practiced the First Reward again afterward, because she wanted to. She needed to remind him who was in charge.

Then they came home, found Gwendolyn and this lizard. Another variable she had not been expecting. She watched Gwendolyn and Roosevelt as they talked, heads bent together, his red curls, her shiny brown hair, almost touching.

"So I just give it a cricket?" he was asking.

"First you put on a vitamin drop. Squeeze it right on the cricket. Then drop it in her cage."

"It's a she?"

"Why not?"

Amy slipped her hand under his shirt, touched his back, felt his skin ripple away from her. Like a horse, she thought, horse and rider.

"What will you name her?" she asked.

"Amy," he said. "The meat eater."

Amy saw Gwendolyn look from Roosevelt to her and back again. Amy knew Gwendolyn was seeing Roosevelt's untucked shirt, his hair still damp from the shower and frustrated sweat. Amy saw the possibility of their busy afternoon breaking on her sister's lovely face.

She leaned over and gave Gwendolyn a kiss, a quick one, on the lips. Amy heard Gwendolyn breathe in, sniffing. Amy smiled. There was nothing to smell.

"You're sweet," Amy said to her. "It was a sweet thing to do." She turned to Roosevelt. "Now you won't be lonely at night."

"Maybe I should leave it here."

"Take it," Gwendolyn said, her voice suddenly quiet. "It needs to go home with you."

"Thanks, Gwendolyn," Roosevelt said. "My first pet. Ever."

Amy would have sworn he'd had a dog as a child, a Spot that followed him everywhere, chewed on his G.I. Joes, tagged along for games of kickball and kite flying. A real midwestern kid's dog.

"My mom was allergic to dogs," Roosevelt continued, "and I never really wanted anything else. But," he stumbled, "I mean, this is great."

Amy hurried him out the door soon after. She didn't linger, no long good-bye. She could see his lips pucker for that farewell kiss, but she wouldn't give it to him. She closed the door behind him—and his lizard—with relief.

Gwendolyn was waiting for her. "So?"

"So what?"

"What happened this afternoon?"

Amy shrugged. She was too tired to argue.

"Where were you?"

"We went to the beach."

"It's January."

"I felt like swimming."

"Naked?"

"He was a sport about it."

"What is it with him? What are you doing?"

"You gave him the lizard, not me."

"Were you swimming naked with him?"

Amy wanted to scream. The whole thing was for Gwendolyn.

Everything. Everything she ever did was for Gwendolyn. Instead she sighed, tried to smile. One day Gwendolyn would understand; one day she'd see how much Amy did for her.

"How was your day?" Amy asked.

"It was fine. I did a balloon cake. I got a nice note from a bride."

"You know what I'm asking."

"He made me coffee."

"And?"

"He apologized."

"Until next time."

"He's just a guy with an overactive dick. Don't make a federal case out of it."

"You sound like an idiot."

"I mean it."

"Idiot."

There was a pause. Gwendolyn crossed her arms. She looked twelve years old. Amy wanted to hold her, caress her, shake her silly.

"Did you see it?" Gwendolyn asked.

"See what?"

Gwendolyn wrinkled her nose at her sister. "You know. Is it slimy?"

"Why did you give him that lizard?"

"Did you see the way they blinked at each other?"

"He's a puppy dog."

"They're a perfect match."

"He'll never take care of it. He'll kill it."

"Good. Then he'll feel guilty."

Gwendolyn had a valid point. Guilt was good. She could use guilt.

"Are you hungry?" Amy asked her.

"Starved."

"Bet you'd like a cricket."

"You eat applesauce with worms."

"You eat peanut butter with bird poop."

"Jell-O and snot globs."

"Spaghetti and hair balls."

"Beans and doggy wieners."

There was nothing like a sister, Amy knew. Her sister. Only her. "Actually," she said, and put her arms around her precious baby, "there's only one thing I'm hungry for."

Roosevelt drove home with the lizard on the seat next to him. He tried some different names for it, Elizabeth Lizard, Lizzie Lizard, Lila, Lily, Lola. Larry. It hadn't moved from its perch. So far it had only blinked at him a couple of times back on the kitchen table. He couldn't help it, he had blinked back.

He came to a stoplight and put his hand out to steady the clear plastic cage as he stepped on the brake. His penis felt raw, chafed, wounded. It complained between his legs, but it wasn't after completion, only rest.

It had been so different from not coming with Sheryl. There he had pounded away with only one thought, one goal on his mind. Do it, do it, do it, and get it over with.

But with Amy. Nine incredible strokes, slowly in and slowly out, he tried desperately to make it last, for it never to be over.

And then, the shower. He held Amy's perfect wet breast in his mouth; he drank the water from her belly button. She touched him, let him touch her. She told him they shouldn't, but neither of them wanted to listen to her. He had been on the brink of orgasm twenty times in their small wet world. And each time, just when he felt himself about to go, she had stopped. She had pulled away from him. She had looked into his face and he had known and seen and shrunk away from her disapproval. She had been close a couple of times herself. He was sure of it. He had worked hard, fingers, lips, tongue, the court jester juggling desperately to stay alive, but nothing quite pushed her off the edge.

Afterward, she held out her wrinkled fingers and said she wanted nine more, the First Reward again. He never thought he could do it. But in that nine, the Reward repeated, slower, more agonizing, he gave up his own desire. Instead he thought about everything: his mother; the sky; driving on the freeway; Amy's eyes; his third grade teacher; Amy's toenails; the place he had eaten once in Oklahoma; the theme music of National Public Radio. His whole life passed before his eyes to the count of nine. He had almost screamed his dead wife's name, not because he wanted her, but because she was there.

In the car heading home, she had said that they should stick to the plan. No more showers together, unpredictable encounters. She looked like she might cry. He promised he would wait for Reward Number Two.

His answering machine was blinking when he entered his apartment. He hoped it was her. Come back, come back.

He pushed the button, heard the single beep.

"This is Stan Waters. I'm trying to reach Roosevelt Montgomery. Got a job for you, buddy. Apartment complex down in Newport Beach. All new cabinets in every unit. Please call."

It was work, then. Good work. Big work. Money. He had been wishing for something like this to come through. He had to finish Amy's house first. He might have to finish quickly. And he didn't think that was what Amy had in mind.

He dialed Stan's number.

"Hello? Stan? This is Roosevelt Montgomery. I got your message."

"It's big, Roosevelt. Lot of work."

He had done one other job for Stan a couple of months earlier, a kitchen repair, small job, just to get acquainted. Stan was a nice contractor. He had big dry hands with calluses to be proud of, thick, yellow, and cracked.

"Sounds good. When does it start?"

"Right away."

Roosevelt nodded. He had expected that, but didn't want to hear it. "I'm finishing a job now," he told Stan.

"How long?"

"Not long," Roosevelt said, and knew it was true if he worked and didn't take any more afternoons off.

"What kind of job?" Stan asked.

"Replacing a floor. There was a fire. Private home."

"Shit, man, that's not your kind of work. I got a guy—a floor guy—he can do it."

"I've already been paid."

"Not a problem. You pay this guy something, whatever, not much. He needs the work." Stan laughed. "Otherwise I deport him."

"But—"

"I need you," Stan said. "I need a real cabinet man. This is no fuckin' in-and-out job. It's real. Asian client. Big money. You do these Del Amo Apartments, you are in. I'm talkin' loyalty. I'm talkin' security. You and me, we're not goin' anywhere. That's what it's all about. Shit, Roosevelt, you were my first call."

Roosevelt stopped listening. Stan confused him. The lizard was doing something. The long thin jaws were like tweezers, opening slowly, then pinching closed. Open and shut, open and shut. Roosevelt hoped it wasn't hungry.

"What do you think?" Stan asked and waited.

"Sure," Roosevelt said. What was he talking about?

"Great."

Roosevelt could tell Stan was happy and that made him glad.

"Here's this guy's name, Manuel Juarez," Stan continued. "He's a good guy. You don't have to watch him. He'll do an honest job. You won't be sorry."

"No," Roosevelt said.

"Tell you what." Stan sounded downright ecstatic now. Roosevelt could hear the magnanimous pride in his voice. He was giving everybody just what they wanted. "I'm gonna see Mannie tomorrow, I'll tell him to call you. He'll be pleased as punch. Then you come down to the office and I'll show you the plans. Client's going Kitchencraft, quality all the way. We're not talkin some Swedish shit from someplace, you gotta glue it together. I'm talkin' longevity. I'm talkin' stability."

"Great, Stan. Sure, great."

"Say two o'clock?"

"You bet."

Roosevelt didn't even know the address of Stan's office. He'd have to call him tomorrow and say he was sorry; say he got more work from this private house and he felt obligated. Remodeling the kitchen or something, something Stan would understand. When he thought about Mannie, Manuel or whatever his name was, on his knees in Amy's kitchen, he felt physically sick. He was supposed to pick up the new floor the day after tomorrow. He didn't want another man to bring it in from the truck, unwrap the brown paper, and receive Amy's grateful smile. He didn't want Gwendolyn to come home and compare this new worker to him, how much faster it was going, how easy it was for him. And it would go faster. And it would be easier for a man who was thinking with his whole mind.

There would be other big jobs. Stan would understand. Roosevelt and Amy would get married, once he had solved her dilemma, proved to her what a sensitive, caring man he could be and shown her the mysteries of meaningful lovemaking. Redemption. Wasn't that what Amy had said when she told his future? Did she know it was her he would save?

He would invite Stan to the wedding. Stan would take one look at Amy and know that Roosevelt had done the right thing. Whatever Roosevelt had done in his life, whenever, it had to be all right to come out like this, him and Amy. There would be gold letters printed on the white napkins, Amy and Roosevelt Forever.

The lizard moved. It turned its head and stepped higher along the fake branch. Its mouth continued opening and shutting. Roosevelt suddenly realized he was starving. Breakfast had been a long time ago and there had been a lot of fervid activity in between. He decided to feed Lizzy or Larry or Lola Lizard first and then himself.

He contemplated the carryout box of crickets. It was a puzzle, a true Chinese puzzle box. How to open it and free only one cricket. How to hold the cricket while he put on the vitamin drop. How to remove the lizard's mesh cage lid and drop the cricket inside. Carefully, he pulled apart the top flaps on the white box. Did he imagine it, or did the scratching increase, amplify into a frantic churning? The collective death awareness of crickets. He had read that ants could always tell when they were going to die; probably crickets could too. He peeked inside, brought his eyes level to the box top. The crickets were tiny. Babies, prepubescent, translucent like dusty half-sucked butterscotch candies. They were the size of his fingernail. He poked two fingers in, shuddered when they hopped maniacally against him. He pinched a cricket, using his fingers like chopsticks. Too hard, the cricket snapped, crunched. He dropped it, scalded by cricket blood.

He washed his hands. The hot water ran between his fingers. Amy. Amy. Amy. His hands on her wet shoulders in the shower. His lips on her steaming breast. He turned to the crickets with new resolve. He opened the box. They were little crickets, a jump to freedom impossible for them. He tried not to look at the one he'd murdered oozing in the bottom of the box. The other crickets hopped over it, around it. He thought maybe its leg moved. A post-mortem reflex, that was all. He got a spoon from the drawer and scooped a cricket into it. The bottle of vitamins reminded him of something. Binaca, that was it. Junior high school breath freshener.

He untwisted the top with one hand, flicked it off with his thumb. He was feeling capable. Maybe he could take the job with Stan, maybe he could do both, Stan during the day, Amy at night. The cricket hopped off the spoon. Maybe the secret was to do the drop first, then scoop the cricket directly into the cage.

He chose a cricket who was bigger than the rest and slower. He squeezed a drop on its back. The cricket shuddered, but didn't hop away. Roosevelt stuck the spoon behind it and scooped quickly. He closed his other hand over the spoon, careful not to press down at all. At all. He pushed off the lizard's cage lid with his elbow and dropped the cricket in.

Stunned, the cricket froze. The lizard moved its eyes to watch, and then turned its skinny head. It took a step down the branch. The cricket woke up, hopped once against the Plexiglas. The lizard was there and in a split second had the cricket in its mouth. The cricket's back legs flexed and straightened, looking for dirt, grass, the backs of its companions, anything, any other life it knew. Liz or Lucy or Lila was motionless with the cricket thrusting in her mouth. She took another gulp. Only the cricket's tiny hairlike feet were still visible, but the skin under the lizard's jaw was moving, the same kicking motion, pulsing, pushing, now from inside. Roosevelt couldn't watch anymore. How long would it take for a cricket to die?

He was tired and hungry and suddenly sad. His apartment was dirty and lonely. The Donner party came unbidden into his mind. When they ate each other, who did the carving? Which body part did they start with? How did they make themselves eat? He knew it wasn't a good sign for him to be thinking about the Donner party. He turned on his television and sank onto his crumpled futon. He watched the blue light flicker on the lizard's Plexiglas box. The crickets were quiet. He was glad. He didn't want to know they were there.

Chapter Nine

Gwendolyn sniffled, on the verge of crying. Instead she sneezed, the tears squeezed from her eyes. She slid out of bed, leaving her sister sleeping in the crisp white sheets with the navy-blue piping. She pulled on her L. L. Bean flannel bathrobe. It was Black Watch plaid and brand-new. Auntie Ned's house was cold even when the days were warm and sunny. Amy had taken to wearing their aunt's old robe, hot pink and daisy-covered, chenille fraying at the cuffs. Gwendolyn had grown up in Amy's hand-me-downs. Now she wanted new things.

She tiptoed downstairs. Amy slept hard, but Gwendolyn wasn't taking any chances. She wanted to be alone, to indulge her sorrow, cater to the grief she knew her sister would never understand. She turned on only the small light over the stove. She put the water on for a cup of tea. She didn't like tea very much, but it was what she drank in the middle of the night. It was what most people drank at night. She liked the ritual of making it. She liked sitting at the table with the cup between her hands, the steam rising in the single kitchen light.

She had never been a good sleeper. She wandered room to room or lay on her back and tried to make sense of the ceiling. As a child she loved the house at night. Mother sleeping. Sister sleeping. And herself alone, the youngest, the smallest, but the guardian, the only one aware. In the fairy tales it was always the youngest who listened to the old man's advice, who didn't touch the treasure, who walked straight down the path and didn't look back. She saved her unfortunate sibling, pushed the wicked witch into the stove and cooked her.

She was hungry. She and Amy had gone out for dinner. They ate enormous hamburgers, rare and dripping, and onion rings. Waiting for the check, Amy moved to the same side of the booth as Gwendolyn, her pastel thighs sliding across the red vinyl. Gwendolyn laughed, then blushed and scrunched closer to the wall. Amy pushed up against her. She took Gwendolyn's hand and licked the grease off her fingers, one by one, slowly with her tongue hot and wet, not caring what other people thought, enjoying the young waiter's covert stares. Gwendolyn didn't stop her, but she was aware of an older married couple watching them. She kept her head down, her face hidden. She couldn't surrender to Amy's warm mouth. And at home in bed, it had been the same. She couldn't, wouldn't quite give it up. She kept wondering about when she and Amy were in their sixties. Where would they go out to dinner? Who would be their friends? What would they do at night? The burger lay in her stomach, pulsing, the busy work of her digestive juices indisputable.

But now, three hours later, she was hungry again. She put a slice of bread in the old, upright toaster. Her nice new toaster oven was in a box in the garage. A lot of her things were in the garage, stacked up, waiting. Amy said they were waiting until Roosevelt finished the floor, but Gwendolyn knew they were waiting for more than that.

She felt the tears start again. The toaster blurred. She turned to look for the tissue box and gasped. A smoke-colored apparition moved in the corner of the dark kitchen, floated out and back. It took only an instant for Gwendolyn to realize it was just the curtains, the ugly kitchen curtains, moving in the breeze.

"Dammit," Gwendolyn said, fear replaced by anger.

She shut the window, hard, remembering too late that Amy was sleeping just above.

"Wendy?" Amy's voice was distant, from the land of sleep.

"I'm okay," Gwendolyn called back in her softest voice.

"Wendy?"

Gwendolyn sighed and walked to the bottom of the stairs.

"I'm fine," she said. "Just having a cup of tea."

"What's burning?"

"Nothing." She breathed in. "Dammit!"

She ran to the kitchen. The toaster was smoking. She pulled up the lever, but the toast would not eject. She could see it in there, the glowing red wires of the heating element, the black charred stripes like wounds on the light wheat slice of bread.

She yanked the toaster's cord from the outlet. She fanned the smoke with her hand. She didn't want the smoke alarm to go off, not now, not ever.

She took out a butter knife and pried the inflamed bread from the toaster's slit. It was ruined. She couldn't eat it. Didn't want it anyway.

"Can't sleep?" Amy shouldn't have been a surprise, but she startled her anyway, standing in the kitchen doorway in just a T-shirt, arms pressing on either side of the doorjamb.

"No," Gwendolyn said.

"What are you doing? Sounds like construction."

"I only closed the window!"

"What are you upset about? You're the one who woke me up."

"I want my toaster oven," Gwendolyn said.

"Have you been crying?"

"I want my things in the kitchen."

"Crying for your toaster oven?"

"This toaster is a piece of shit."

"Your things. Your little things."

"I have a really good toaster oven."

"I'm sure you do."

"It can even bake a potato."

"So go out in the garage and get it."

"I will."

"No, you won't. You'd rather complain about it."

"I am not complaining."

"You want me to get it?"

"No."

"I'll go right now."

"I'm not hungry anymore."

"We don't have any potatoes anyway."

"I don't want a potato! I wanted a piece of toast. I wanted to be alone!"

"Fine. I'm going back to bed."

"Good," Gwendolyn said and meant it.

"Try not to break anything else."

"I didn't break anything!"

"Good night."

"I just put the bread in!"

Amy walked out. Gwendolyn hated it when she did that. Gwendolyn followed her.

"I didn't do anything!"

Amy didn't respond.

"The toaster is old. It sucks!"

Amy shook her head. She looked just like their mother when she did that, exasperated with Gwendolyn's ridiculous inadequacies.

"It's a fucking piece of shit toaster!" Gwendolyn screamed from the foot of the stairs.

Amy went back into the bedroom and shut the door.

So what, Gwendolyn thought, so what. She wasn't going to give Amy the satisfaction of following her up the stairs, standing over the bed, arguing until she won. She knew she was right and Amy was a bitch. She would sit up all night. She wasn't going back to that bed. No. No matter what. Amy would just have to come down here and apologize.

Three hours later, Gwendolyn shivered on the smelly sofa. She was trying to watch an old movie on Auntie Ned's ancient television. Her nice new TV was in the garage. That was another thing she was getting out tomorrow. She would go right now, but it was cold, it was four A.M., it felt too good to be so miserable. Her life was a mess. Her business partner was a pervert; she hated this ugly little house; she was in love with her goddamn sister. An average life was as far away as the moon.

Someone had left the faucet dripping. The light was gloomy, the sun hiding, depressed and on the run. The faucet made a constant trickle just beyond the bed. Amy woke, feeling annoyed, disoriented. Wendy, turn that off. What are you doing? It took her a moment to remember, to stretch in Gwendolyn's tailored sheets and realize her sister hadn't come back to bed. And it was raining. The drip was outside. A hole in a gutter. More repairs.

Amy showered. She left the door open. She sang as loud as she could. She dropped the plastic shampoo bottle, twice, on the tile floor. She got dressed and banged the closet door, threw boots across the room, dropped a book. Wake up, wake up, her whole body called to her sister, tell me you're sorry.

She clattered down the stairs, saw Gwendolyn unhappily sleeping on the couch. Amy lingered on her way to the kitchen, walked slowly past. Wake up, she willed, wake up now. But Gwendolyn slept on. Amy clenched her fists, wanted to stamp her feet. Her scent couldn't wake her, her will, the screaming in her mind. Gwendolyn didn't stir.

Amy grimaced. Roosevelt would be there soon and there wouldn't be any time for kind words and reconciliation. She wiped up the toast crumbs and pushed the remnants of the burnt slice of bread down the drain. It turned soggy and disintegrated in the water, fell apart and washed away.

She picked up the old toaster. She would throw it away. It would be gone and their fight would be forgotten. She went out and let the screen door slam.

The backyard's patches of dirt had turned to mud. The raindrops drummed and thumped in the open barbecue grill. Gwendolyn had left a sweatshirt on the back of one of the lawn chairs. Weather was never expected.

Amy walked down the driveway to the collection of trash cans. Her hair was wet from her shower; the rain on her head was barely noticeable.

Their neighbor had mice. Not in the duplex to the left of the house, but the single-family home on the right. An elderly Filipino woman lived there, had lived there in stucco and ornamental bricks for forty-seven years. Amy didn't know her name. On moving day she had shuffled over and told Amy to call her Mama Girl, but Amy couldn't, not to her face, although she did in her mind. Mama Girl. Ridiculous. Mama Girl never wore clothes, only nightgowns, muu-muus, cheap, flowered, riotous polyester.

Auntie Ned had not been Mama Girl's friend. Mama Girl had invited her next door only once, to help her celebrate her eightieth birthday. Amy had dropped by just as Auntie Ned returned home with a paper plate of unrecognizable fried food.

"I only ate the cake," Auntie Ned told Amy as they tried to define the animal body parts sunk in orange slime. "At least it came right out of a box from the grocery store."

Mama Girl had a boyfriend, a younger man in his sixties. He arrived each morning at quarter to nine in a beige sedan with a HANDICAPPED card around the mirror. There didn't seem to be anything wrong with his arms or legs. He was balding, dressed every day in the same baggy khaki pants and cardigan zip-front sweater, no matter what the temperature.

One day Amy had seen them dancing in the backyard. She was washing the windows in the back bedroom and she could see over the tattered bamboo fence. Mama Girl wore a Hawaiian print shift in well-used floral pink and purple. The boyfriend suddenly grabbed her around the waist, kissed her neck. He let her go and took off his sweater, as if doing a striptease just for her. She giggled, laughed, hid her face behind her knotty hands. He shook and contorted in front of her in just his undershirt. His biceps were wiry; the muscles shrunken, dried, collapsed on themselves like a piece of jerky. Amy didn't know if she saw an old tattoo or a bruise. Mama Girl squealed and swung her eighty-year-old hips. Her feet were bare and the toe-nails polished orange, so bright Amy could see it from the window. Fluorescent. Day-Glo. There was no music playing, but they danced and danced as if there were. Amy watched them for a long time.

Now Mama Girl had mice. She had complained to Amy a week ago and again a couple of days ago.

"Since your aunt, your aunt, your aunt, had her trouble," Mama Girl said as if Auntie Ned was only laid up for a while, "the mice have all run over to my house. They have run, run, run to my house."

Her boyfriend stood behind her. He looked up, into the trees, over at the roof across the street, not at Amy.

"I don't think my aunt ever had any mice," Amy said honestly. "I haven't found any droppings or traps or anything."

"We all have them," Mama Girl said, "all, all, all the houses on this street. We need a hungry cat."

"That's a good idea," Amy said.

"But I don't like cats." Mama Girl shook her head. "They keep their noses, their noses in the air. They look down on us all. On all of us."

Amy wanted to offer some condolence. They were neighbors, after all. "I'm sorry," she told Mama Girl. "Maybe you should get some mousetraps."

She had been nice, but later she found the tortured carcasses of trapped mice in her trash cans. Bent in unnatural positions, empty bellies swollen, their tiny teeth reaching for the moldy cheese, backs broken by their desire. Amy's trash cans smelled, the over-sweet, candied smell of decaying flesh. There were maggots crawling in the bottom, squirming white against the black heavy-duty rubber. Now, as she walked toward the row of containers, she thought she could see the cans actually swell and breathe in the gray morning drizzle. Her hand hesitated, quivered, disgusted on its own, as she opened the lid.

New dead mice inside. She didn't want to throw the broken toaster in there, down on top of them all. She didn't want to hear the squish, the crunch of mouse bones and organs under a toaster anvil.

This was beginning to piss her off. They were her goddamn trash cans. She didn't have mice. She wasn't responsible for the mice in the neighborhood. She felt her anger in her hands, a feverish trembling. She wanted to scream, but wouldn't, wouldn't wake Gwendolyn that way, wouldn't give the neighbor boys something to watch. She grunted instead and threw the toaster over the fence. Crash! It fell on Mama Girl's cement walk. Amy chuckled. She hoped it had broken into a million hard-to-clean-up pieces.

She waited, expecting Mama Girl to come and see what the noise was. She waited, ready to fight, but heard nothing. She was sweating. Her hands were shaking.

And suddenly she was furious with Gwendolyn. She didn't want to be, but she was. It was Gwendolyn's fault. Gwendolyn's silly midnight cravings for toasters and picket fences, Gwendolyn not coming back to bed, Gwendolyn not waking up, not apologizing this morning. Gwendolyn had destroyed her day. Gwendolyn would go and talk to Mama Girl. Gwendolyn would be sweet. Mama Girl would love Gwendolyn. Perfect Gwendolyn.

Amy stomped down the driveway to the garage. All of this was for Gwendolyn. Everything she did was for Gwendolyn. It had always been that way.

"Take care of your sister," her mother was always saying. "She's younger. She's not as strong as you."

Gwendolyn, the baby, crawling toward the basement stairs. "Catch her!" Mother cried.

Gwendolyn getting her hair pulled at school. "Watch out for her on the playground."

And Auntie Ned. "You are everything to her. You are all she has in the world. It's you, Amy. And her. And no one else."

"What about Mom?" Amy asked that afternoon on the beach. "We have Mommy. Wendy has Mommy."

"You can't depend on Helen," Auntie Ned said. And little Amy looked at her tight face and believed her.

"Keep Gwendolyn safe. Keep her close to you. No one else will ever be your sister. Or her sister. No one. You are the only two sisters in the world. In the universe."

"Do you have a sister?"

"I lost her." Auntie Ned dug up two handfuls of sand, threw them into the wind. The fine grains blew back into their faces, like the minuscule feet of tiny creatures running across Amy's cheeks, up her nose, in her eyes, through her hair.

"I lost her, I lost her," Auntie Ned lamented and spit the sand from her mouth. She pulled Amy to her and wiped her eyes with the tail of her shirt. "But you won't."

It was all about Gwendolyn, but Amy didn't mind. It was what she wanted. Since the day Gwendolyn came home from the hospital and Auntie Ned had shown her the blood pulsing under the soft spot on her baby sister's tiny skull, she had wanted to protect her. She craved it. To keep her safe, beautiful, well fed. This, this life in Auntie Ned's house, the future she foresaw for them—Gwendolyn would be so happy. She would never be unhappy again. Never.

The garage's side door hung crooked. It scraped against the concrete floor as she pushed it open. The doorknob wouldn't turn. There was plenty of work for Roosevelt. She would keep him very busy, as long as it took.

Amy put her hand on Auntie Ned's dusty bicycle. It was old-fashioned, squat, pink and white frayed plastic basket between the handlebars, both wide tires completely flat. Next to it was Gwendolyn's bike, the one she had ridden to work before they moved to Auntie Ned's house, so far away. It was twice as high and half as thick as Auntie Ned's. Shiny, silver, the seat a slim black droplet. It looked fast, professional, foreign. Amy didn't ride bicycles. She didn't swim. She didn't play tennis. She didn't do things that left too much up to chance, weather, conditions. Bicycling was something Gwendolyn did away from her, to get away from her.

Amy crouched. She unscrewed the caps on both air valves. She pressed down on the tires. There was a satisfying hiss of escape.

"Hey."

Amy jumped.

Roosevelt stood just inside the doorway.

"Don't sneak up on me," she said.

"I didn't mean to. I thought you heard me. What's the matter?"

He was the last person she wanted to see. Or the first, she thought, surprised. He was male, coveralled in gray cotton. He was larger than she and solid. He was there for her.

"What are you doing?" he asked.

"Looking for Gwendolyn's toaster. Her toaster oven."

"She doesn't know where it is?"

"It's a peace offering. We had a fight."

"I'll find it," he said. "Let me help you."

He didn't ask about the bicycle, why she was on her knees in front of it. He trusted her. He wanted to help her. And she knew it was good for him to feel capable. She saw his back straighten, his eyes open wider and lose that hopeful, worried look. He thought he could help her find the toaster. He thought he could help her have an orgasm. Then he really would help her make her sister's life complete.

"You sit here," he said and guided her by the shoulders to another box. "Sit here while I look."

She sat and watched him. He took the predictable, but serviceable, Swiss Army knife from his pocket and carefully sliced through tape and opened flaps. He looked inside and then meticulously folded the flaps back together, under and over so they would stay closed.

It was in the last box, the one labeled LINENS. The new white toaster oven was tucked under old sheets and tablecloths from their childhood.

"What do you know?" Roosevelt said and laughed. "Should have looked here first."

What a relief it would be to fall into Roosevelt, let him feed her and wrap her up snug somewhere. But she couldn't let herself think that way. It was a trap, the one men laid for women, I'll fill you up, I'll take care of you. Amy wondered if Roosevelt would be willing to die to make her happy, or would he die when she was done with him. Die or just go catatonic again as he had after he killed his wife.

"Thank you," she said quietly.

He looked at her. She held her arms out to him. Gratefully, he put the toaster down and came to her. She wrapped him in her arms, lifted her face.

He brought his mouth to hers, but stopped just short of kissing. She frowned. She looked into his faded eyes, willing him to kiss her.

"I can't get enough of looking at you," he said.

Shut up. She bit her lip to keep from shouting. Shut up. Don't tell me those things. She leaned forward and kissed him. He let himself be kissed and then, finally, kissed back. She could feel him fall. She could feel him forget.

Chapter Ten

Gwendolyn watched from the upstairs bathroom window. She saw Amy go in the garage. She saw Roosevelt hesitate outside, just stand there in the rain, and then go in after her. She knew what Amy was doing in there. She knew Amy felt bad about last night, and retrieving her toaster oven was the perfect peace offering. She knew Amy wouldn't apologize, not verbally, but she would be sorry and she would offer the toaster to Gwendolyn with her strong, tenacious hands.

Gwendolyn stood at the window. She felt cold, distant, shivery from being up most of the night. Her bones felt loose, her muscles slack. The tan on her face was a hard shell. Underneath she was pale, flabby, a scallop living its last moment before the sushi knife.

She wanted to make up with her sister. She wanted to sleep in her own bed for just twenty minutes. She did not want Roosevelt around.

She watched from the window, not intending to count, but counting just the same, out loud, "Seventy-four. Seventy-five." How long would it take for Roosevelt to come out of there? She leaned her face against the rain-spotted glass, cool on her cheek. Her fingers played with the peeling wallpaper. She pulled off a glittery fish

113

without meaning to, not really. She looked at it and tucked it into the pocket of her robe. "Ninety-two, ninety-three." It hadn't been long. Was he helping Amy find the toaster? Gwendolyn smiled. He'd have to open every box. It was with the tablecloths, tucked in tight. The box wouldn't even rattle when shook. Served Amy right. And him too. "One hundred and seventeen. One hundred and eighteen." But it kept him in there longer. The search kept them both in there, together and away from her.

She wasn't feeling any better than she had in the middle of the night. She was out of sorts, uncomfortable inside herself. Something had changed between her and Amy just since they began living together, since being in Auntie Ned's house. Gwendolyn didn't like being jealous of her sister's dalliances. It wasn't a familiar feeling. She had never cared before about Amy's boyfriends or the men she casually slept with or the guys whose fortunes she told who couldn't wait to meet her. They had nothing to do with her. And she knew Amy wasn't straight with those guys. She knew Amy never told them the truth. She knew Amy looked at men as experiments, as experiences, as necessary notches on an already full bedpost.

There was that guy—Richard? Rob?—a year ago. Amy had met him at a bar. He was successful, handsome, happily married to a very pregnant wife. Amy took him to that hotel at the beach that she liked. Afterward, she told him she was not impressed. He wanted her to be. He followed her everywhere, sniffing after her butt like an abandoned dog, head hanging down, his tongue always licking at her heels. She turned around finally and gave him more than he wanted, more than he had ever even imagined. It went on for weeks, hot; Amy was stoked. Then one day Amy showed Gwendolyn the article in the Los Angeles paper. Homicide. Suicide. He had killed his wife and then himself. Left the new baby behind. Gwendolyn had been shocked. Amy cried, but then she began to laugh. Gwendolyn was horrified. Amy told her she had to laugh; it was too awful otherwise. Amy hooted with laughter. Her nose snorted, trumpeted even. Gwendolyn surprised herself by giggling, then chuckling, then laughing hysterically with Amy. Her sister was irresistible.

"Why you?" Gwendolyn had asked. "Why you?"

But maybe the question should have been, "Why him?" Guys like him didn't seek out Amy. She found them. She fed on them like lambs to a wolf, fresh meat on the hoof.

"Two hundred and thirty-three, two hundred and thirty-four." Gwendolyn was afraid they would never come out of the garage. They would like it in there too much. There was something different about Lizard Boy. Amy had something new in mind. Gwendolyn could see it, the way she stared at him, watched him eat. She thought of them together, inside that garage, old blankets, a tarp thrown down. Gwendolyn felt her stomach contract, her bones shrink inside her skin. She had to be enough.

Amy came out of the garage carrying the toaster. It made Gwendolyn happy that she had the toaster, not Roosevelt. Amy didn't look back, didn't stop and wait for him as he fumbled with the garage door. She ducked her lovely head against the rain and hurried inside. Gwendolyn saw the way Roosevelt frowned after her, his tongue out the side of his mouth, a film of sweaty desire on his face. It was impossible that Amy could find his reptilian peculiarities attractive. Amy. Amy.

Quickly she brushed her teeth and ran the comb through her long hair. She tied her bathrobe a little looser, crossing it lower on her chest, exposing more skin. She took off her socks. Amy liked her feet.

She walked down the stairs just as Amy reached the bottom. Roosevelt had stayed in the kitchen or somewhere. Gwendolyn didn't care where he was, but she felt grateful that he wasn't there, watching.

Amy offered the toaster up to her, the ritual sacrifice that Gwendolyn had expected.

"You found it," Gwendolyn said.

"Linens. Of course. Why didn't I look there first?"

Gwendolyn took the toaster from her sister, wiggled her bare toes. "I'm sleepy."

"Roosevelt's here."

Gwendolyn sighed, then smiled. "I'll make you a piece of toast."

"Actually, I've been thinking about a baked potato."

Gwendolyn laughed. She felt better. It would be all right. Roosevelt would do his job and go away. She handed the toaster back to Amy.

"I have to take a shower," she said. "I feel like shit."

"You look good."

"You too."

"Not much longer," Amy said, reading her mind. "He's almost done."

Chapter Eleven

Roosevelt was alone in the house. The rain pattered outside. Gwendolyn had gone to work. Amy was at the grocery store. The doorbell rang. It startled him, made him drop the nails out of his mouth. He put his hammer down, then changed his mind and picked it up again. He carried the hammer with him to answer the door.

There was a midget on the porch. He came up to just below Roosevelt's heart. The man said his name was Dr. Gustave Minor, Professor of Pyrophenomena at the Pittsburgh Center for the Study of the Paranormal. He showed Roosevelt his card. He said he had come all the way from Pittsburgh to inquire about the death of Naomi Fitz.

"She died almost a month ago," Roosevelt said. "Did you walk here?"

He felt protective. He was cautious around doctors, even small ones; they talked a big story, but they weren't all nice men.

"I heard about it so late," the doctor said. "So late. I tried to contact you. I came as soon as I could."

Minor was not young. He was plump like a lot of dwarves or midgets or whatever. He reminded Roosevelt of a fat bird—a penguin or an overstuffed parrot—with a beak for a nose and a little feathery beard. Minor's eyes darted nervously around the room; his pudgy hands wouldn't stay still. He wore a miniature gray suit and a child-sized trench coat, but he looked more like a psycho than a scientist.

"Do you live here?" the doctor asked.

"I . . . I'm the carpenter," Roosevelt said. He had almost said yes.

"I'm an expert on SHC, Spontaneous Human Combustion. Implosion, the conflagration of a human body. Maybe you've read my book, *The Fire Within*?"

"I don't believe in it," Roosevelt said, aware that his chin was up in the air, that he was looking down as far as he could.

"You don't?" Dr. Minor seemed truly surprised.

"No," Roosevelt said and meant it. He hadn't known until this moment how much he didn't believe. "Absolutely not."

"Did you see it?" Dr. Minor's fluffy hair glittered from the drizzle; the shoulders of his trench coat were turning dark, a spreading stain.

"I saw the picture." Roosevelt shrugged.

"Ah, a picture. The real thing—it makes a huge impression. Remarkable. Nothing like it." He rubbed his hands together in that joyful, doctorlike way. The worse things got, the more excited doctors became.

Roosevelt shifted the hammer in his hand. He wasn't sure what to do now. He looked out, over the little man's shoulder. A red rental car was badly parked out front. The sky was getting darker, heavier, the rain continuing.

"Your car?" he asked.

"I drive with some special equipment." The doctor sounded defensive. "Who does live here? With whom should I be speaking?"

"She's at the store." Roosevelt sighed. "You can wait inside if you want."

"Thank you." He followed Roosevelt inside, shuddered like a bird in a birdbath. "Rain. In southern California. Now that's a real miracle."

Amy whistled a little tune in the grocery store. She lingered with the butcher, admiring his big hands, the blood under his fingernails.

She tossed a very sexy smile to a man fighting with his wife. She made him blush, throw up his hands, walk away from the nag, nag, nag. He wanted to meet her over in the frozen food, she could tell, but she went the other way.

Amy enjoyed having a secret. It was like Christmas or Gwendolyn's birthday; the anticipation of Gwendolyn's pleasure almost better than the actual moment of gift giving. And Gwendolyn would be thrilled, Amy knew it. The time for giving was almost upon her. Maybe she should get a bow for Roosevelt's head. Or his penis.

This morning, upstairs, she had had a long good moment with Gwendolyn. Before Gwendolyn left for work they'd had time to make up. She heard Roosevelt downstairs hammering, prying things up, while she and Gwendolyn apologized, made each other feel better.

Amy was going to give Gwendolyn everything she wanted.

Gwendolyn was a southern California driver. She was used to dry roads and sunglasses against the glare. The rain made her nervous. She peered through her spotted windshield, kept her hands at the driver's-education-required "ten and two o'clock" positions on the wheel.

She knew Amy loved driving in the rain. Amy went faster, not slower. Amy swerved to go through puddles and splash the rare pedestrian. Gwendolyn hunched forward. She didn't turn on her radio. She watched the cars on either side and in front of her vigilantly, her eyes glancing left and right and forward again.

She stopped at a red light, watching in her rearview mirror to make sure the car behind her also stopped. She was in Koreatown. The store signs were in Korean. They blurred and swayed and seemed to animate through her wet windows. She loved the Asian writing, like paintings, each character a little picture in black lines. She thought she would take an Oriental calligraphy class. She didn't want to speak the language, but she'd like to learn to write it down.

In the spring, she thought, just another month away, when the rain was over, when the floor was finished and her real life had begun.

She heard a squeal of brakes and a horn. She gasped. Then a muffled, thudding crunch of metal against metal. She saw the spin, a brown blur coming toward her and skidding to a stop just in time. Two cars had collided in the intersection in front of her. A small brown car going straight. A pickup truck turning left. Gwendolyn stared. The small brown car had somehow ended up right beside her. She could see the driver, an older Asian man, through her window and his. If their windows had been open, she could have reached out and touched his face. His nose was bleeding, his mouth hung open, his black eyes turned to Gwendolyn as if questioning her, What happened to me?

Dr. Minor followed Roosevelt into the kitchen. The doctor's bowed legs and tiny feet made a smacking sound on the floor. His shoes were round, the soles flat; the shoes of a doll.

"Is this where it happened?" Dr. Minor's eyes and his head moved left and right, independent of each other. His shoulders jumped up and down.

Birdlike, Roosevelt thought again. For a moment he imagined the doctor's oddly protruding chest covered with soft gray feathers instead of hair.

"This is where it happened."

"And you are repairing the damage?"

"Right."

"Where exactly was she? Ms. Fitz, I mean?"

"There. At the table."

"What did you see? I mean, what was there to fix? Did she burn up the entire kitchen floor?"

"Just a little spot. Twelve inches, maybe. Amy—Amy Clark, her niece—thought it was a good time to do the whole thing."

"Is Amy Clark living here now?"

"Yes. With her sister." It's none of your goddamn business, Roosevelt thought. You doctors are so goddamn nosy.

Gwendolyn screamed. The driver of the pickup truck, too big, red-faced, his hate steaming from his damp head and shoulders in the rain, opened the Asian man's passenger door and pulled the little man from his car. He hit him.

"No!" Gwendolyn cried. "No!"

It seemed impossible. The small man was already bleeding; his nose already broken. Don't hurt him again. She tried to get out of her car, but her door was blocked by the small brown car. She banged against it again and again, not thinking, not remembering her car had three other doors. What is in my way? She struggled. What is it? Move, move, move.

She felt trapped, watching the bigger man pummel the smaller. The truck driver held the little man's bald head in the crook of one arm and hit his face with the other hand, again and again. He let go and the too slender and bleeding Buddha dropped to the wet street. Gwendolyn couldn't see him over the hood of her car.

Dr. Minor was writing things down. That was another familiar doctor-type activity to Roosevelt, but it didn't make Minor more trustworthy. Roosevelt felt the same reticence he had experienced in the hospital, the buzz behind his eyes that meant he wanted to fade out.

"What else can you tell me?" Dr. Minor asked.

Roosevelt hated that question. "Nothing."

"She was right next to the windows?"

"Yes."

Roosevelt wasn't going to tell him that the curtains hadn't burned, or the table.

"Are these the same curtains?" Dr. Minor asked.

Roosevelt realized the doctor was eye-level with the ugly flowered border on the curtains.

"Yes," he said.

"This the table?"

"Yes."

"Was she sitting in a chair?"

Roosevelt didn't want him going down in the basement. He didn't appreciate his enthusiasm. "I told you. I didn't see it. You better wait for her, for Ms. Clark."

"Of course, of course."

Roosevelt went back to the corner where he was working. He looked at his watch. He had to go meet Stan in two hours. He watched Dr. Minor peripherally, without letting on. Dr. Minor was writing things down, looking around the kitchen, shifting happily from one baby foot to the other, back and forth as if he might suddenly take flight. Roosevelt thought how weird it was to be an expert in something that didn't really exist. Like being a priest, he thought; no one could prove what you said wasn't true.

If he had to call Stan and tell him he'd be late, then he would. The idea of Amy alone with Minor was not a comfortable one. Minor had that doctor smell of antibacterial soap, mint, and coffee. Stan would wait. Stan was going to be happy. Roosevelt had decided to do both jobs; he had decided this morning after feeding his lizard another cricket.

The rain fell without stopping. Cars went around them, continued on their way. Gwendolyn wanted to hide her eyes, but couldn't. She watched. The truck driver was kicking him now. She turned off her windshield wipers, but she could still see the big man's upper body, just from the waist up, over the hood of her car. It swayed back and forth with the movement of his leg. He could have been exercising, doing ballet, riding a giant rocking horse.

Dr. Minor looked over at Roosevelt. Roosevelt pretended to be very busy in his corner.

"So," Minor began. "So . . ."

Doctors were always dying to talk. Roosevelt said nothing.

"You saw the picture." Minor had to speak. "You know, the arson investigator ruled it a kitchen fire."

Roosevelt remained silent.

Dr. Minor was undeterred. "Obviously it wasn't a kitchen fire. Nothing in the kitchen burned."

"Except her." Roosevelt couldn't resist. "And she was in the kitchen."

"Exactly!" Minor gave a little cock-a-doodle-doo of exaltation.

"Exactly! She burned, but nothing else. It's classic. It seems to be a classic case."

"I don't know how long she'll be," Roosevelt said. "Ms. Clark, I mean. Maybe you shouldn't wait. She can call you. Set up an appointment."

"It's fine. I'm perfectly happy." He was jovial, this doctor. "I'm only here for her."

"No trip to Disneyland with the wife and kids?"

"My son is too young for Disneyland," Minor said. "He's home with my wife. You look surprised. Neither have achondroplasia. That means they're average size. Both of them."

The doctor wasn't smiling. Roosevelt blushed.

"Why don't you sit down," he said. "You're making me nervous."

"Sorry. Sorry. I'm excited, that's all." Minor pulled out a kitchen chair, then looked at Roosevelt. "Here? Or would you prefer I sat in the living room?"

"Anywhere," Roosevelt said. "Just perch yourself."

Roosevelt was surprised at the tone of his own voice. He was usually nice to strangers, talkative if they wanted, and he never seemed to mind people's disabilities, wheelchairs, crutches, facial deformities. It was doctors. No, it was this doctor. He was an intruder, a possible usurper. Roosevelt remembered that first day he had come to work and Amy's zeal when she told him what had happened to her aunt. She was passionate, and his cool disbelief had annoyed her. This weirdo's fervent fanaticism would only inflame her, stir her up into a new fever about the whole thing.

He closed his eyes, just for a moment, and saw Amy's warm white skin and the dim hotel light on the angle of her pelvic bone. The way she tasted and smelled were inside him now. He could bring them out to be treasured, savored, turned this way and that.

He opened his eyes and put his thoughts away. He didn't want to use them up, didn't want to diminish his memories by dwelling on them.

Gwendolyn tried to get out of her car, but she couldn't. Her door was blocked. By what? She couldn't think. She never realized that the act of beating, of striking, of kicking someone to death could be so quiet. Not a grunt or a groan, just the gentle drumming of the rain on the roof of her car, cozy, soothing.

Amy saw the red rental car as she pulled up to the house and into the driveway. She hadn't been gone long. She didn't want any visitors.

She got out empty-handed, left the keys in the ignition as always. She would send Roosevelt out to the car for the two bags of groceries.

"Missy? Missy?"

Amy turned. It was Mama Girl, standing on a ladder, looking over the fence. Amy burped, a sour taste at the back of her throat.

"Everything, everything okay at your house?" Mama Girl called to her.

"Yes." Amy took a step toward her back door. Mama Girl spoke louder.

"Well, you know, it's the strangest, strangest thing."

Amy waited.

Mama Girl continued, "This morning. It rained."

"It's still raining. Drizzling. Wintertime."

"It rained toasters," Mama Girl said and giggled. "Toasters, toasters falling from the sky."

Amy sighed. She wasn't in the mood. "Isn't that strange? It rained dead mice in my trash can."

"Oh no," Mama Girl said. "No, no, it didn't. I put them there. I don't want them, can't have them, in my trash cans. Not my mice."

"They're not mine either." Amy let out a breath, walked away quickly. Mama Girl was too fragile, her bones too thin and brittle.

"You have a nice day," Mama Girl called. "Be careful a toaster doesn't fall on your head."

The anger fell, a dark crimson curtain in front of Amy's eyes. She couldn't see. She stumbled over a rock in the driveway. Sabotage. Mama Girl was out to get her. Mama Girl hadn't understood Auntie Ned. She didn't understand Amy. Amy couldn't make her understand; her gray matter was too porous, addled; it prevented her from understanding Amy's good common sense. Amy rubbed her eyes. Turned back.

"Leave me alone," she said, her hands fisted, her toes curling inside her shoes.

Through the fence, she could see the boyfriend standing down in the yard. He was beneath Mama Girl, holding the ladder, getting an eyeful under that old-lady nightie, all her dried-up and wrinkled parts. Bile rose in Amy's throat.

"Leave us alone. Leave our trash cans alone. Stay away."

Gwendolyn could suddenly think clearly. Very clearly. She undid her seat belt. She climbed over her gearshift and out the passenger side. A car swerved, horn blaring as it went around her, not stopping, not caring.

"Help him!" Gwendolyn shouted. "Help him! Somebody!"

Amy walked into her kitchen through the back door and stopped. A child in a grown-up disguise sat at her kitchen table. She didn't like children. When they called the psychic hot line she'd hung up on them. Their fortunes were messy, their futures always unexpected.

"Ms. Clark?" The doctor jumped off the chair so quickly he knocked it over. "Sorry!" He picked it up. "Sorry. I'm Dr. Gustave Minor. I'm here," he paused, "about your aunt."

"My aunt." Momentarily she was lost, not a place she liked to be. She looked at Roosevelt. He looked himself, solid, in her kitchen. He was comforting. He rolled his eyes, shrugged.

"I wrote the book," Dr. Minor said, "about Spontaneous Human Combustion, *The Fire Within*. I'm here, all the way from Pittsburgh."

He grinned at her. Amy realized he was just a gnome, a small adult, and he had come for her. He had come to prove her right. She smiled at him and took his hand.

Gwendolyn was screaming.

"Stop it! Stop him. Somebody!"

The big man didn't stop. Gwendolyn tried to run to him, to grab him, bite him, but slipped in the slick, wet oil reflecting a rainbow on the street. She slid down onto one knee, on her way to prayer.

Amy wanted to pat the little doctor on the head, but she didn't.

"I read your book," she said. "And you came all this way."

"You read my book?"

She could see he was taken aback by her youth, her beauty. She tossed her hair back over her shoulder. "Dr. Minor. I'm glad you're here."

"You may call me Gus." He took her hand with both of his. "This is such a thrill for me."

"Ow!" Roosevelt yelled from his corner. He grinned apologetically as they looked over at him. "Hit my thumb."

He was a movie character, the bumbling boyfriend you hated to love. Only she didn't love him. "Are you okay?" she asked.

"Got nine other fingers."

She turned back to Gus. "Did Roosevelt show you where it happened?"

"Yes. Oh yes. I'm sorry he's repaired the floor already."

"I kept the piece of linoleum."

She could see the doctor's chest swell, his cheeks inflate. He looked like he would pop.

"You did?" he said. "May I see it? Please?"

"Sure."

Amy actually had read this guy's book. She had seen his picture on the back flap. There was no way of knowing that he was a dwarf.

"In the basement," she said. "I'm making a little collection of things."

"Want me to bring the chair up?" Roosevelt asked. "I mean, it's so dark down there."

"I'm not afraid of the dark."

"I know that, I only meant—" It was fun to see Roosevelt stumble.

"Would you get the groceries?" she asked him.

"Right now?" Roosevelt said, deflated.

"Thanks," she said. "You're my hero."

There were sirens. A fire truck roared into view. Oh no, Gwendolyn thought, it's not a fire. Nothing is burning. It's raining. There is no fire. It's the goddamn rain.

Amy placed the chair, the square of linoleum, and Auntie Ned's shoes right where she had found them. In the kitchen's rainy gray light, they were remarkable. Dr. Minor's response did not disappoint her.

"Oh, my God," he said when he could speak. "It's astonishing."

"It was just like this," Amy said. "These are her shoes. The ones she was wearing when it happened. I made the coroner give them to me. I wanted them. I knew someone would want to see them."

She gestured to the pair of worn flat-soled orthopedic shoes, pigeon-toed in front of the liquefied chair. The shoes were putty-colored, but the laces were rainbows, variegated strings of startling, bright color.

"They're basically untouched," Amy said. "Just covered in that sticky stuff you talk about in your book. Yellowish. Oily. See it? It was all over the house."

"Uh-huh," he said. He was obviously lost in what he was looking at, imagining what else had been there. "That's usually the case. The conflagration of a human body. Fire. Sizzle. Pop. The smell is quite powerful. Days, for days afterwards the odor permeates."

"Oh, yes," Amy said.

Dr. Minor's eyes met hers. There was something in him, she saw, something he'd been given instead of height.

"Any fire will do that." The deep voice surprised her. Roosevelt was speaking from his corner. She had forgotten him. He had brought the groceries in, two brown paper bags on the kitchen counter. "Any fire smells," he continued.

"Not like this," Dr. Minor said.

"Rancid, spoiled," Amy agreed.

"Depends on what burns," Roosevelt said.

Dr. Minor took a camera out of his trench coat pocket. "May I?" he asked.

"Of course," Amy said.

Gus looked through his lens, focusing, fussing. He took a step and brushed against Amy. She shocked him, the current strong between them. He twitched, jerked away from her.

"Sorry," she said. "The rain, my socks. Sorry."

"I'm sorry," he said, blushing. "Clumsy me."

She looked at him sideways, under her lashes. "I liked your book very much. I wasn't sure what had happened to my poor aunt, but you convinced me."

He blushed again. Amy smiled sweetly.

"It's . . . it's a hard concept," he said and frowned, concentrating, not looking at her. "Hard to get your mind around."

"You made it very clear. Even I could understand it."

Roosevelt knew what Amy was doing, but he didn't know why. To make him jealous? He wanted to laugh, but his cheeks were hot, his throat closing in. His gaze turned reflexively to his heavyweight professional hammer.

It was Dr. Minor who laughed, twittering, tweeting. Roosevelt watched him, knew that he was caught, the desire snorting out his nose, fluttering his beard. Roosevelt watched him try to concentrate on his knowledge of the unreal, the bizarre, turning his back on the flesh-and-blood woman standing right in front of him.

"Classic," the little doctor said. "You can see the drips from the seat on the square of linoleum. In the center the vinyl burned up, but the edges only melted."

Amy leaned toward him. He jumped away. Roosevelt watched, not knowing why he was watching or what he was supposed to see.

"Inside the body," Dr. Minor was almost whispering now, "the heat, the heat is impossible. So profound, so violent everything disintegrates. Organs, cartilage, even bones. But it's very localized. Anything outside is barely affected."

"Her shoes," Amy chimed in, happy, excited, "with her feet still in them and her legs up to the knees, of course, were right there."

Dr. Minor's admiration was intense. "You saw it?"

"I had to ID the body—or what was left of it." Amy glowed at him, for him.

The doctor was warming up. His cheeks were pink, his sparse beard trembled, his forehead glowed. Roosevelt looked at his hands, holding the camera, fiddling with the strap. They were short, fat, a child's drawing of hands, no space between the fingers.

"Have you ever seen it?" Roosevelt asked. He was pleased to see them both jump at the sound of his voice. He was still here. "Have you ever seen it happen?"

"It's never been witnessed. Never." Dr. Minor found his professional voice. "Only a few have survived. A very few. A woman lost her breast"—he blushed—"and suffered second-degree burns along her ribs and abdomen. One man had his hand burned off. But that's extraordinary."

Roosevelt flexed his burned hand. The blister objected. "It's always old people," he said. "Old people, drinkers, smokers, Alzheimer's. They don't know what they're doing."

"Not so. Not so at all. It has happened to infants. In their cribs. All alone at naptime. Pink, white, brand-new, and then—gone. A pile of dirty ash, a puddle of yellow slime on the soft sheet, next to the stuffed brown bear."

Roosevelt saw Amy's face go white, the gasp stifled. He didn't want this doctor upsetting her.

"You have a baby," he said.

"I know." Dr. Minor nodded. "I think about it every day."

"And a wife," Roosevelt continued. "What does she think?"

Amy wasn't listening. She was staring at Dr. Minor. He was staring back.

Roosevelt raised his voice. "Babies don't explode."

"Implode," Amy said.

"I don't believe it."

"I do," Amy said to Dr. Minor. "I do."

Gwendolyn's knee was bleeding, the leg of her white pants dirty and torn. The paramedics fussed over her, wiping and bathing her with soft white squares, pushing her wet hair out of her face, shining their little flashlight into her eyes, first one and then the other. She told them she was not important, but there was no one else for them to help.

"It's the rain," she told them. "I hate the rain."

Gus took pictures. Lots of pictures. Of the chair. Of the shoes, the floor. Of her. More of her than necessary, Amy thought, but that was to be expected. He hopped around the kitchen, awkward and excited. His trench coat flapped; he got it caught on the table, twisted in the curtains.

"It's a terrible fire," he said. "Frantic. It has an extreme need to consume."

"Fires don't have needs," said Roosevelt.

Stick. Stick in the mud. Amy saw him brown and straight, up to his knees in thick, sweet excrement.

"Yes," the doctor argued, "this one does. A burning hunger."

"Yeah, right."

"And it begins within the victim." Dr. Minor's eyes were moist, his voice far away. "The fire grows from within themselves. From within their own need. Their need for completion, fullness. The stronger their need, the stronger the fire."

"What?" Amy asked. His book had not talked about this. "The victim starts it herself?"

Gus nodded, proudly. "Yes. My newest research."

"Come on," Roosevelt said. "No one would choose to die by burning to death."

"It's instantaneous," the doctor said.

"How do you know?"

Amy stopped listening to them argue. Then it wasn't spontaneous at all, she thought.

Auntie Ned sat at the kitchen table with a yellow pad of Post-it notes in front of her. She had things she wanted to say. She had no one to say them to except Amy. And Amy had heard them all before, many, many times.

Auntie Ned picked up her pen. *"Fuck them all to hell,"* she wrote in her best formal hand. She admired the swirls on her capital *F*, the loops in *all* and *hell*. She didn't write these for fun. She meant them. They were things she needed to say. And no one to say them to.

The front door opened. Amy arrived.

"Hello girlie-girl," Auntie Ned called. Cheerful, butter-yellow like the table, like the little pad. "What are you doing here?"

Amy stopped in the kitchen door and Auntie Ned saw her nose was red from crying, her eyes swollen with tears. She opened her arms and Amy curled her long body into them, sobbed against the collapsed breasts, the old-lady tummy.

"What, baby?" Auntie Ned asked, asked the girl who had everything. "What?"

"I'm scared," Amy cried. "I'm afraid."

"Then it's not spontaneous at all." Amy repeated her thought to Dr. Minor.

"Not really. No." He nodded at her, his oversized head bobbing, agitated. "Unconscious, perhaps, but somehow expected."

"Why her?" Amy wasn't really asking the doctor. Auntie Ned, she thought, was this a choice? "Why her?"

"Isn't that how you would choose to die? Not a lengthy hospital stay. And as a suicide, relatively painless."

"So if I wanted to, I could just blow up, right now, right here." Roosevelt. Belligerent. Annoyed.

"No, not necessarily. Not everyone has the power." Gus seemed determined to convince him. "There are some people, some people who generate more heat. Who always give you a shock when you touch them. Who literally can make your hair stand on end."

"That's static electricity," Roosevelt said. "That's different."

"I don't think so," Dr. Minor said. "I've been working on this. Some people are living live wires."

Amy looked at Roosevelt. He was covered in an unattractive stain of skepticism. She could see it in his eyes, his flat mouth, the protective curve of his shoulders. It bothered her. He caught her looking at him. She forced herself to smile. His face softened, his eyes opened wider. She saw his hands relax. Nice hands. For a man.

Last night with Gwendolyn. All the restraint, the repeated lack of consummation with Roosevelt in that dark motel by the beach, had left her breathless, desperate, demanding of her sister. Gwendolyn's soft stomach, the hair below her belly button, the downy smoothness of Gwendolyn's long brown thigh against her cheek; she had wanted to go on for hours.

Amy realized her face was betraying her. It was okay, Roosevelt thought she was thinking of him. He closed his eyes as if he was imagining it too, let his tongue circle his lips. Amy turned away. It was ugly, a man's desire, self-centered, fringed with violence. Even the words of male sex, "hard," "big," "thrust," "penetrate," were not loving words, gentle words. They were not the words of women.

But she hadn't made Gwendolyn happy.

"Stop it," Gwendolyn whispered at the restaurant.

Amy ground her lips into Gwendolyn's long neck. The couple across the room, older, married, out for dinner without the kids, couldn't help but watch. Amy ran her fingers down Gwendolyn's long bare arm, let them stray across her breasts.

"Amy," Gwendolyn said, louder, "I said cut it out."

Gwendolyn was embarrassed by her at the restaurant and at home she was overwhelmed.

"Calm down," she said. "It's okay. You don't have to."

Amy couldn't stop, her sister's pleasure so much more important than her own. Without Gwendolyn's gratification, Amy had none. She kissed, licked, and sucked, ignoring Gwendolyn's hand pushing on her head, pushing her away. She wouldn't be pushed away. But when Gwendolyn finally surrendered, Amy was unimportant.

Gwendolyn's orgasm was far away, not connected to her, to Amy, at that moment. Gwendolyn was thinking of something else.

And then she blew up the toaster in the middle of the night and cried about her toaster oven, all her nice things. Gwendolyn's things. Gwendolyn's longing for the common middle ground, the house in the suburbs, the two kids and the dog. It seemed like everybody wanted something, something Amy couldn't give.

But Roosevelt could. And Amy could give Roosevelt to Gwendolyn. Soon.

Gus had sweat on his upper lip and the bridge of his nose.

"Why don't I take your coat?" she asked.

"That would be very nice," he said. "It's warm in here, don't you think?"

"The rain. It's stuffy."

Gus took his coat off, fumbling with the sleeve, pulling it inside out and then struggling to get it right again.

"Let me," Amy said. "I'll just put it out here on the couch."

She carried the coat to the living room. She lifted it to her nose, just for a second. She could smell the breath mints in the pocket and the sour, diesel-fuel airplane smell. He would help, she thought as she went back to the kitchen.

Roosevelt was leaning against the counter. He tapped his fingers on the Formica. She saw him look at the clock on the wall. She pulled a package of Oreo cookies from the grocery bag and opened them. She loved Oreos. If she was going to eat cookies, those were the ones. She could taste the chemicals mingling with fat and sugar. She offered one to Dr. Minor, but not to Roosevelt.

Dr. Minor took a cookie and smiled at her. He was taking notes. He measured the hole in the piece of linoleum, smelled Auntie Ned's shoes. Roosevelt snickered.

"What can Dr. Minor say to convince you?" Amy turned back to Roosevelt.

"Nothing."

She heard his hostility. The rhythmic thumping of his fingers was getting annoying. He kept glancing over at the kitchen clock. She smiled at Gus.

Gus sat down to write. With his legs hidden under the table, he seemed almost normal. His face was a little odd. His nose was too small above his mouth and his forehead protruded. But the beard evened him out somehow.

"Help me, Gus, can't you? I don't understand." She made her voice wistful, pathetic.

I'll try," he said. "I certainly feel inspired, just being here."

"I bet you do," Roosevelt said. "I have to go."

Amy looked at him. A doctor's appointment, the dentist, why else would he leave her? "Where are you going?"

"I have a job interview."

Amy couldn't think, couldn't speak for a moment. "What job?" she finally said. "You're not finished here."

"This is a big opportunity. Cabinets. Twenty-four kitchens. A whole complex."

"You can't just walk out."

"I'm going to do your floor at night."

"No, you're not."

She was aware of Gus's puzzled expression. He was trying to figure out who Roosevelt really was, who he was to Amy. Amy felt perspiration on her upper lip. He couldn't do this.

"Walk out that door and don't come back," she said. To herself she sounded like a character in an old movie, the ones Gwendolyn liked, the ones where the man never really left.

But Roosevelt hadn't seen any of those films. "Amy," he said, "I have to. It's a big, big job for me. I can do both."

She looked at him, lifted her chin, tossed her hair back.

"Amy," he said again.

She realized she couldn't challenge him. She had to be soft, helpless. He needed to be needed.

"Can't you do it later? In a couple of weeks?" she asked quietly. "I . . . I don't know what I'd do . . ." She looked once at Dr. Minor. He was frowning at his notebook, pretending not to listen. She let her face soften, her eyes get sad and wistful. "I thought yesterday meant something to you," she said, her voice low.

"It did!"

It was the right tactic. He was terrified suddenly to lose her, anxious to make amends.

"Of course it did." He bent to her. "But this has nothing to do with it. I'll still be here. I'll come back every night."

"No," she said. "Gwendolyn will be here."

"I thought you'd be happy for me."

"There'll be other jobs," she said. "I need you now."

Roosevelt heard Amy say the words he had been telling himself over and over last night and all day today. There would be other jobs. If he worked here only at night, Gwendolyn would be around; he would be tired and dirty; they wouldn't have any time alone. If he left her now, things between them might change. And he didn't want them to. She looked so sad, so forlorn, so betrayed. He couldn't stand that. He couldn't let her down.

But Stan was expecting him. If he started now, he would just make it to Stan's office on time. He didn't want to call Stan, to lie to him. He had to go. He would just hear about the job and then he could decide. He and Amy could talk it over together.

"It's too late for me to call and cancel," Roosevelt said. "I have to go. Stan, the guy who offered me the job, he's a good guy. You'll like him. I need to listen to his offer, at least."

Amy could not believe it. He was leaving. He really was. He had said no to her direct request.

She turned away from him and smiled at Dr. Gustave Minor. "Where were we?" she asked.

"I'll come right back," Roosevelt said to her. "It won't take long."

She ignored him. The sweat had broken out on her temples and under the hair on the back of her neck.

" 'Bye," Roosevelt said.

"Good-bye," the doctor answered politely.

Amy refused to say anything. Roosevelt stood there, hovered

over them. He seemed to her an apparition, less than a whole person, floating, already gone.

"Amy?" he said. "Amy?"

"What do you want me to say?"

"Should I come back?"

"Suit yourself."

"I'll be back in an hour and a half. Two at the most."

She shrugged.

He fluttered away.

She heard the front door open, and suddenly realized maybe she had done this badly. She wanted him to turn the job down. He had to; there wasn't any choice. She got up and ran out of the kitchen, through the living room, out the front door.

"Wait," she called.

He stopped, turned to her on the front walk. She could see his face light up, the only bright place in the rain-shadowed day.

"Wait," she said. "I'm sorry. I . . ." She looked away shyly. "I wanted to spend the afternoon together . . . you know."

"You, me, and ole Gus?"

"He'll be gone. By the time you get back, he'll be gone."

"Good."

She kissed him, knowing it would surprise him. His hands held her waist for a just a moment. When she stepped away they reached out to her. Good. Good. Good. This had been the right thing to do.

"I'll be waiting," she said.

"I'll hurry," he said.

He got into his truck and pulled away slowly, hating to go. She watched him. He watched her watching, standing there in the gray rain, in his rearview mirror. Roosevelt swallowed. He felt a tug in his belly and below, the feeling he used to get after swimming when he would take off his wet trunks and his mother would dry him with a soft, thick towel. An urge, a desire, an unspecified wish that his mother used to satisfy with ice cream.

The drizzle continued, the winter weather of Los Angeles. The lawns were green. Bright weeds sprouted through the sidewalks, at the fence corners, around the tires of the discarded cars left in empty lots. And here and there a dead Christmas tree, cast out on the side of the road or deposited in a shopping cart. Brown needles, dry and spiky, branches bare, grasping a few remaining strands of tinsel like the hair that was left after chemotherapy. It happened every year here; the Christmas trees lingered forsaken until March, sometimes April. It was as if they were dropped off from another place, somewhere where it snowed and people drank hot cocoa after ice skating. This land of summer was just the place for old trees to be abandoned.

Dr. Gustave Minor sat at the kitchen table. He made a list of people to call. He knew experts. He knew others who would want to see this. Los Angeles was thick with those interested in the unusual. He ate another Oreo. He usually stayed away from food intended for children. He wondered what Amy was doing outside. He tried not to think about her blond hair against the carpenter's strong chest. He tried not to think of Roosevelt at all, the tall guy with the big hammer and the sullen freckled face.

Dr. Minor recognized the onset of depression. He tried to think of his wife, his baby boy, his work. Instead, he thought of his first love. His mother had introduced them; she was blond, pretty, short but not a dwarf. They had sex on her family couch. His feet intertwined with her knees, only two cushions down, but his penis, erect, was average size. She was satisfied. He was in love. She dumped him before their next date.

He sighed. He was too late at this house. Too late to see the real evidence of the dead. Too late to offer comfort and condolences to the living. He would do his work, the team would come, but without any lasting evidence it would only add to the examples of possibilities.

He had talked to firemen, arson investigators, detectives, physicists, doctors of all specialties. None of them believed. None of them could imagine the human body igniting from the inside, cremating itself, turning flesh and bone into the ultimate funeral pyre. But Gus knew firsthand the oddities of the human body, the occasional unpredictable outcome of normal events.

Chapter Twelve

Gwendolyn was so happy to pull into the bakery parking lot. She had cried the whole way there, the water in her eyes competing with the rain on her windshield, the puddles on the streets, the sloshing in her stomach.

The police had finally come. The truck driver had been "subdued," thrown to the ground and handcuffed, his face pressed to the wet asphalt. She had been kneeling by her car. She could see the gravel pushed up his nose and in the corner of his mouth as they put a knee on his neck to keep him down. The smaller man wasn't moving. His blood mixed with the rainwater, thinning, the color disintegrating on the dark, wet street. There wouldn't be a stain.

She was lucky, the policeman told her twice, that she wasn't involved, that she hadn't been hit, that she wasn't hurt.

Hurt in the accident? she wanted to know. Hit by a car? The Asian man was dead. She watched the ambulance come, his body carried away in a black zipper bag like a suitcase hanging in the first-class closet on an airplane. Straight, thick, contents valuable but unknown.

She wanted to move on, go to work, but she was the only witness. She tried to explain she had not seen the accident. She didn't know who was at fault, but she assumed it was the small brown car and the small yellow man driving it. She assumed that was why the big red truck driver was so angry. But it was only an assumption, she said. She had been more worried about the guy behind her, worried he wouldn't stop in time, worried he'd slide, slip, strike her from the rear in the rain. She told them over and over, she hated the rain, she needed to get to work, she hated the rain.

She cried.

A policeman, middle-aged and mustached, pulled her car over to the side for her, sat in it with her for a moment, looked into her eyes.

"I bet you have a nice house in the Valley," she said, "the suburbs."

"Yes," he said and laughed. "But it rains there too."

She wanted to go home with him. She wanted to lie down on the brown corduroy couch in his family room and watch daytime TV. Later, she would go to the wide, clean neighborhood grocery store. Everyone would look like her, matching sweatsuits, sneakers from the mall. She'd do her shopping and then make a meatloaf, or a pot of hearty vegetable soup for such a rainy day. He would come home. They would watch the news while they ate. And more TV after dinner.

"Will you be okay?" he asked. "Want me to call someone for you?"

"I hate the rain," she said again. "I need to go to work."

So she was grateful to get to the bakery. She stepped inside the front door and stopped, inhaling the smell of rising yeast and warm sugar, feeling her shoulders relax. Tony? Where was Tony? She needed a friendly face.

She walked toward the back. She heard voices from the workroom, Tony's, and someone else's, a woman with an accent.

Tony looked pointedly at his watch as she walked in.

"I saw an accident," she explained. "I was a witness."

And suddenly she was crying again. Tony looked shocked, and then reacted admirably. He put his arms around her, patted her back as he would a child.

"Are you hurt?" he asked.

"No," she sobbed. "But the truck driver killed the other guy. He beat him to death."

Tony pushed her away from him. "God," was all he said, but he looked at Gwendolyn with disgust as if she had done it herself. Kicked the man to death. Felt his heart explode under her hard boot.

The woman he had been talking to reached out one hand and stroked Gwendolyn's forearm. "How completely horrendous," she said. "How horrible for you."

Her accent was thick, but her words clear. Gwendolyn looked into her blue eyes and knew she meant what she said. Gwendolyn tried to smile at her. Tried to stop crying. The woman had short hair, dyed spiky red in the latest style. She was younger than Gwendolyn and smaller, but more muscular. On this cool rainy day, she wore a sleeveless shirt and a short skirt with no stockings. She looked like she loved the rain, didn't mind getting wet. Her body was firm, compact, the muscles in her arms and legs clearly defined. She wasn't wearing a bra, Gwendolyn could tell. No wonder Tony had her in the back room.

"Yes," Gwendolyn said to her. "I couldn't get out of my car. I was stuck. I couldn't do anything."

"Better you didn't," Tony said. "You could have been next."

"People are crazy," the woman said. "They go off, bam! Like that, over anything. Bam!"

"Yes," Gwendolyn said. "It was a little accident. The truck driver just blew up."

"Bam!" the woman said again. She patted Gwendolyn's hand.

Gwendolyn could feel the heat the woman gave off from her warm, tan skin and smell her eucalyptus scent. Was she here for a wedding cake? No diamond ring on her left hand. She didn't look like the type to do a big wedding.

"This is Elsa," Tony said. "Elsa, Gwendolyn. Elsa's here about the job."

Gwendolyn felt she had been gone for days, forever, not just late to work. There was a lifetime she had missed.

"The decorating job," Tony said. "Remember? So you can take some time off."

Then Gwendolyn saw the book in front of her, a portfolio filled with eight-by-ten color photos of incredible cakes.

"Aren't they amazing?" Tony said, but he wasn't seeing the photos, only Elsa's firm thigh.

"You look green. Maybe you should go home," Elsa said. Gwendolyn looked at her face and saw the Asian man staring at her through his car window. One moment he was alive, the next he wasn't.

"I'm fine," Gwendolyn said.

"You are strong." No one had ever called her strong before.

Gwendolyn leafed through the book. The cakes were different. She could tell they were European; the edges were harder, the decorations not as fluffy and overdone as American cakes. She wondered if it hurt to be beaten to death. Did the pain finally stop? Too much, too intense. It was the same thing that had bothered her all along about Auntie Ned's implosion. Did she feel it? Did she realize, have time to understand, that her intestines were going up in flames? Did her legs, her toes remain cool—blissful and chilly—did she concentrate on them? At what point had the little Asian man lost consciousness?

She looked at Elsa's cakes and saw the blood on the street, on the truck driver's knuckles from the nose of the wise little man. His face was like all the faces of the *Five Chinese Brothers* in her favorite childhood picture book. One brother could swallow the ocean. One brother could hold his breath forever. One brother would never burn. They thought he was only one person. They tried to kill him five times, and each time a different brother survived.

The final cake in Elsa's portfolio was less refined. It was representational, not purely decorative. It was a ski mountain with two toy women skiers on the top with their arms around each other. They each wore a candy ribbon and a medal around their necks. Their shadows in the snow, painted in frosting, were astounding.

"Elsa's Norwegian. She won a medal for skiing in the Olympics." Tony said it with pride, misplaced but predictable.

"Only a bronze," Elsa said. "My friend there, she took the gold."

"Congratulations," Gwendolyn said. No wonder she had such amazing muscles, such ease in her own body. She would have been able to stop the truck driver. She could have acted sooner. Behaved better.

"Thank you," Elsa said. "It was a few years back."

"You must have been fifteen." Tony was flirting with her shamelessly. Elsa seemed aware of it, but above it too.

"A little older than that."

"Well, if there was an Olympics for cakes, you'd get the gold. Wouldn't she, Gwen? Aren't these magnificent?"

"Yes," Gwendolyn said, "they really are."

"Oh, thanks . . . It was just a hobby, but now—"

"I told Elsa I thought she should come in, work a day, check the place out." Tony spoke to Gwendolyn as he smiled at Elsa.

"Fine," Gwendolyn said. She felt her throat constrict. Elsa was going to take her place. What would Amy say? She would be angry. Gwendolyn was wearing a sweater and a jacket and still she was shivering, icy cold, her arms contracting, wasting away inside her sleeves.

But Elsa had told her she thought she was strong. She was. She had witnessed a murder and come to work, driven herself through the rain across town to the Fantasy Bakery of Beverly Hills. Elsa said how strong she was. No one had ever said that before.

"Maybe you're too good for us," Gwendolyn said to Elsa.

"What does that mean?" Tony asked, annoyed, insulted.

"I mean," she continued, "the kind of boring, regular orders we get. Could you do a cake that looks like Elvis Presley?"

"He's popular in Norway too."

"Or a child's birthday cake?"

"Or a hot air balloon?" Elsa said and looked over at Gwendolyn's cake. Gwendolyn winced. Her special cake looked flouncy, ridiculous.

"I could," Elsa said. "It would be different, but it could be beautiful."

"Of course it could," Tony jumped in. "I say you come in, try an assignment, and we talk about it then."

"It's good." Elsa shook Tony's hand.

"Great," he said.

Gwendolyn took Elsa's hard, dry hand in her own. The little man was dead. The truck driver's life was over too. Elsa had the job.

Roosevelt was uncomfortable. The trailer was noisy and cramped. Men in hard hats came in and went out, not lowering their voices, not caring that Roosevelt was sitting across from Stan trying to listen, trying not to look at his watch. Stan talked on and on.

"Sounds good," was all Roosevelt could manage. "Sounds good."

"We're craftsmen," Stan was saying. "We have something to give, something they want. It's not a skill, although we're skillful. It's more than just a trade. I'm talking a profession, I'm talking a vocation, a walk of life. I'm talking a calling. You've got that calling."

"Sounds good." Roosevelt hoped that was the right thing to say.

Stan had a really bad case of conjunctivitis in his right eye. "Pinkeye," he explained. "Caught it from my goddamn kids."

His eye kept watering. It was red and swollen, with little globs of pus in the corners. Roosevelt tried not to stare at it.

"Not supposed to scratch it," Stan said, "but it itches so goddamn bad. I'm talking torture."

The meaty fingers of his right hand dug in the inflamed eye and came away moist and, Roosevelt knew, infected. He watched Stan gesture with that hand, point, tap the top of the table, leaving damp fingerprints. Roosevelt knew he was going to get pinkeye. His eyes were beginning to itch already. In the tight, trapped air of the trailer, pinkeye was inevitable. He had to get out of there.

"Listen, Stan," he tried to begin.

"Starts Monday," Stan said. "Meet me here, we can drive down together. Put your tools in my truck."

"Well—"

"Six A.M. Better make it five-thirty the first week. See how the traffic is. Make a good impression. This is just the beginning, Roosevelt. I'm talking trust. I'm talking long-term. I'm talking the future. Get what I mean?"

"Sounds good."

Stan put out the germ-infested hand for Roosevelt to shake.

Roosevelt cringed, took a deep breath, and shook it, briefly but firmly.

"Monday. Five-thirty."

He escaped. He tried not to touch anything in his truck. He drove left-handed, reaching through the steering wheel to use the on-column shift.

At the nearest fast food restaurant, he ran in and washed his hands. The water was so hot he had to bite his lip to keep from screaming. The pain was the worst on the sensitive new skin where his blister was healing. He felt the heat all the way up his arms into his shoulder blades. He hoped it was burning out the poison. The soap was lime green and gritty, but it had that reassuring disinfectant smell. He washed his hands again and again, while other men came in, urinated, barely rinsed their hands once, and left. The world was a filthy place. He cupped the steaming water in his pink palms and splashed his face, trying to leave his eyes open. He felt singed, scorched, but cleansed by the hot water. When he looked up into the mirror, his face was bright red, boiled. He thought of Amy, her naked body, and washed his hands one more time.

"What do you mean, there's no way of knowing?" Amy was furious. This midget, this deformed pygmy, was denying what she knew.

"I know what you think—" he began.

"No, you don't."

"I agree with you—"

She interrupted him. "I need to know the truth." Trying to keep her voice down, trying to stay calm.

"It's late," he said. "I arrived too late."

"I kept all the pieces. You have the evidence. My aunt was special, remarkable, unique in every way."

"I'm sure she was." He nodded, anxious to appease. "I'll make some calls. The team will come tomorrow."

"What team?"

"Investigators, like myself. Specialists in other areas. They can analyze the shoes. Scrape the chair and the kitchen walls."

"You saw the picture."

"I can't say for certain from a picture." He shook his head. "I didn't think you would have done so much work on the house already," he continued. "Usually three weeks, a month later, people are still getting their feet under them—I mean, after a loved one has died."

His disappointment in her made her even angrier. It was his fault. He should have gotten here sooner. Idiot.

"What do you think?" she asked. "What do you think happened to her?"

"Seems like a classic case," he said, but at the last moment he looked away, wouldn't look in her eyes. He was only saying what she wanted to hear.

She wanted to hit him. She wondered what color he would bruise. "What time?" she asked. He looked stupidly blank. "What time will the team be here tomorrow?"

"Eight?"

She would be in bed with Gwendolyn. "Ten."

"Fine."

He put out his hand for her to shake. She took it, the chubby knoblike fingers and squishy palm half the size of her own. She wanted to squeeze, squeeze until it erupted, oozed between her fingers.

"You're hot," he said and then blushed again and eternally. "I mean, your hand is hot. You feel incredibly warm."

"I'm angry. Really angry. I know what happened. It was not a normal death."

"I believe you." Dr. Minor sighed. "But no one else will."

"You have to prove it."

"I promise I'll try."

Why were men always promising to try? Try to come back. Try to stay. Try to take the trash out. She looked at this small, distorted figure standing across from her. He was the same as all the others. She wished he hadn't come. She wished she had told him to get lost, told him to leave her kitchen right away. He was in her way, another variable, another limp vegetable in the soup disguising the good, true flavor of the meat.

But he wouldn't let go of her hand. He wouldn't let her go. He looked at her and she saw in his eyes again that something else, that something special.

"You know, don't you?" He never let go of her hand. "I don't have to prove it to you," he continued. "It's everyone else. One day, if not this case, then the next. I will prove it to the world."

He would, Amy realized; he really would. Sometimes, with her clients on the phone psychic line, she knew their stories, the real story about their future, not just the predictable formula of new jobs and new loves. Most often her premonitions were of trouble, of car accidents, of broken bones and bloody fights. The company discouraged telling bad news. She never mentioned what she saw just over the hill.

"I want this more than you do," Dr. Minor said. "Much, much more."

Amy pressed her face against Auntie Ned's scratchy polyester peasant blouse. She couldn't stop crying. She wouldn't.

"What, baby?" Auntie Ned smoothed her hair, patted her shoulder. "What is it?"

"I can't live without her," Amy confessed. On her knees in Auntie Ned's kitchen, she gave it up, told the truth, prayed for Auntie Ned to fix it. "I can't, I can't."

"Then don't."

"She doesn't want me. She doesn't want it."

"A love like yours?" Auntie Ned knew what Amy was talking about. She knew everything.

Amy looked up into her strong face, the lines a map of her past, her life and Amy's. There were wrinkles there that Amy had seen arrive.

"Who wouldn't want that?" Auntie Ned asked and smiled.

"She wants a normal life."

Auntie Ned snorted, honked at the thought. "Your mother thought that. Is she happy?"

"Wendy thinks she's different. A man, a child, a station wagon. She'll be content."

"You can get her a man. Give her what she wants, as long as you're part of it."

"I told her about that woman I was seeing."

"That was just an experiment."

Amy nodded, agreeing. "It's Gwendolyn. Only Gwendolyn."

"Tell her. Tell her that."

"She won't speak to me. She's not answering her phone."

"Make her come to you."

"Help me?" Amy asked. For the first time in her life, she asked for help. "Please help me."

Auntie Ned burst into flames the very next day.

Amy smiled at Dr. Minor. "I'm sorry I lost my temper," she said. "I loved my Auntie Ned very much."

He nodded. "I can tell you're a woman of very deep feelings."

Amy laughed. "I'll see you tomorrow."

"Ten o'clock." Then Gus frowned. "Will he be here?"

"You mean Roosevelt?"

"The repair man, yes."

They were jealous of each other. Amy was pleased. "I think so," she replied. "I'm sorry about him. I think he's lonely. He's actually very protective of me."

"I can see that."

"You know, I shouldn't say this, but he killed his wife."

"What?"

"They called it 'accidental homicide' or something. He did his time."

"In prison?"

"In a mental institution."

"Are you sure he should be working here?"

"He's harmless." She paused. "To us."

"I hope you're right."

"Dr. Minor," Amy said, "Gus, I'm so glad you've come."

Chapter Thirteen

Nine strokes and then you stop."

"I thought you said—"

"And then another nine."

"Good. We're moving forward. Aren't we?"

As soon as he returned from Stan's, Roosevelt had followed Amy upstairs and into the back bedroom. There were no sheets on the bed, nothing to indicate that anyone used this room. When Amy opened the closet door to get out a blanket, he saw that it was practically empty.

"Isn't this Gwendolyn's room?"

"No."

He could tell she wasn't going to explain and at the moment he really didn't care. The rain outside was harder now, a steady rhythm on the aluminum awning over the back door. Amy undressed him. And then herself. He wasn't allowed to touch her, only watch and be touched.

She told him to lie down on the bed, and then she lay down next to him, a column of air between them. The old mattress undulated and scooped beneath their bodies. He felt the prickly polyester on his skin. The dull green blanket was folded under their heads.

"Nine strokes. Stop. Nine more."

He stared at the translucent skin on the inside of her arms. He was aware of her blood, her blue veins throbbing, moving, living next to him. One hit and a bruise would quickly develop. It wouldn't take much. Life was so dangerous. It was hard to live one day without pain. It took so little for the skin to be broken, sliced open, the veins to spill their juice. The heart would keep pumping and pumping until nothing was left.

He wanted to tell her about Stan, about the job, about Monday, but he hadn't found the right time.

"Listen," she said. "Pay attention."

He tried.

Afterward, he pushed back on his haunches, kneeling in front of her. She slithered off the bed around him and picked up her clothes.

"Only seven more to go," she said.

"I love you," he said. He spoke without thinking. It wasn't something he planned. But it must be true. He did love her. He had to.

"I love you," he said again. It didn't matter how he meant it. He said it, and it would stand there between them.

"Great," she said and left.

That was it? That was all he got? Roosevelt thought he might lose his mind. What would it take to make her happy?

He thought of the work waiting for him downstairs. He thought of Stan and Monday morning and the twenty-four units in Newport Beach and his calling and his profession and his impending conversation with Amy about it all and tonight's Spanish hum in his apartment. He put his pants on.

Gwendolyn tried not to cry on the chocolate cake she was working on. She couldn't seem to stop crying. The cake looked like a brown felt fedora, with a grosgrain band and a pheasant feather on one side. Some movie producer had threatened to "eat his hat" and now his friends were going to make him do it. It was an easy job. Chocolate was forgiving; felt was a simple texture to imitate. The ribbon was a little tougher, but more butter in the frosting made it shine and she had a specific tool for the vertical lines that made grosgrain so distinctive. The guy who had ordered the cake had given her a photo of the producer's actual hat and a close-up of the feather. She had created entire birds; one feather was a cinch.

Who would tell the man's family? Where would they take his little brown car? The handsome policeman with the mustache said she would have to testify at the truck driver's trial. She thought of Roosevelt. He had killed his wife. That's what Amy had told her. He had driven his car into a tree. On purpose. And he was out again. If the truck driver was crazy, how long would it be until he was out of prison? Would they let him drive? Roosevelt was driving. There should be a mark on the car, a sign: DON'T RIDE WITH ME. I'M A MURDERER, or DON'T HIT ME, I MIGHT KILL YOU.

Tony ignored her, came in only once and looked over her shoulder, shrugged, and walked away. He said nothing. He didn't touch her.

She was so tired. When she finished this cake she was going home, no matter what. But she didn't really want to see Amy tonight. She didn't want to go home to Roosevelt and dinner and Amy. Amy. Gwendolyn didn't want to tell Amy about Elsa. She was tired of worrying about Amy's anger. Her whole life she had tried to be what Amy wanted.

"Amy takes such good care of you," their mother had told her time and again. "Be grateful. Be nice. Be a good little sister."

And Auntie Ned, "You can count on Amy. Do what she says. She knows what's best."

Amy swooped in and saved her, usually before Gwendolyn was even aware she needed salvation. Gwendolyn wouldn't have minded falling on her face a couple of times, wearing the wrong dress, dating the wrong guy, fighting just a few of her own battles. But Amy was always there for her. Amy, two years older, continually just out of reach, better at everything, more capable, and so wonderful to her little sister.

"You don't need to worry," Amy always said. "I'll take care of everything."

Gwendolyn's cakes were all she had.

There. The feather looked exactly like the one in the photo. She had done a particularly good job with the quill; it looked hollow, fragile, real.

She walked over and stood in the doorway of Tony's office. He was talking on the phone.

"I'm done," she said. "I'm going home. I'm beat."

He held up a hand, asking her to wait.

She stood there while he finished his conversation, exchanging stupid, obvious insincerities with the customer on the other end.

"Every moment was a pleasure," Tony was saying. "No, no, thank you. I've never seen a more beautiful bridge . . . And the flowers she chose? . . . Yes, inspired. Perfect in every way . . ." He made a face at Gwendolyn. "Lovely . . . Well, thank you again . . . Please, tell your friends . . . Uh-huh, uh-huh, bye-bye." He hung up.

"I'm done with the hat," she said. "I'm leaving."

"Do you want to talk about Elsa?"

Gwendolyn sighed. She didn't. He would anyway.

"Her work is all sharp edges. Too tough for me."

"You mean she's too tough for you," Gwendolyn erupted. "Don't try anything with her like you did with me. She might kill you."

Gwendolyn grabbed the edge of his desk for support. "Tony. I didn't mean that."

"What's the matter with you?"

"The accident, I guess. And I didn't sleep last night."

"You need some time off."

"I was fighting with Amy."

"You shouldn't live with her. I told you that. It's not good for siblings. My brother and I never speak, except at Mom's at Christmas."

"We're not like that." He didn't know the half of it.

"You need your own life," he said. "Amy's too bossy."

She looked at him. "Everybody bosses me around." She turned to go. "Anyway, I think Elsa's wonderful. We should hire her. I'll go to Hawaii, see my mom or something. Maybe I'll never come back."

"I'd like to have you both," Tony said, and then quieter, "Boy, would I ever."

Gwendolyn swung around. "Both of us? At the same time?"

She wasn't smiling and Tony blushed. She had made him

uncomfortable. She had asked him to tell her the truth.

"Isn't that every man's fantasy?" She took a step closer.

Tony shrugged, smirking like a thirteen-year-old caught with his pants open behind a dirty magazine.

Gwendolyn continued, "What about your girlfriend? Would she do it for you? Swing both ways? Let you watch? Go down on you while some woman was eating her?"

Tony's face crinkled in disgust. He closed his eyes against that picture. "Go home," he said. "Get out of here."

Gwendolyn kissed him on the lips, a quick kiss with a lascivious dart of her tongue. He was startled, jumped away from her. She laughed.

" 'Bye," she said and left, still smiling. She didn't feel like crying anymore.

Roosevelt hit his thumb with the hammer. Really hit it this time, not like before with Dr. Minor and Amy. It hurt like hell. It went white and then red and then throbbed. He ran it under cool water. His eyes began to itch. First the right eye, then the left, then both. He blinked, scrunched them up tight, determined not to scratch. He knew conjunctivitis, pinkeye, was coming. He would never get to the Third Reward with pinkeye.

There was a movement behind him. Someone coming in. He swung around, but it was only the kitchen curtains blowing in the rainy breeze. He had been warm coming downstairs, back to work after his ten agonizing minutes with Amy. He had opened the window for some fresh air and to expel the stink of doctors and experts and cold coffee. Sometimes this house gave him the creeps. Sometimes he hated going down in the basement. Sometimes he wondered how Amy and Gwendolyn could stand it. Especially at night. Especially in the kitchen. Especially Gwendolyn.

Amy was so tough. She was so matter-of-fact about her aunt's death; scrubbing the pus-colored grease from the walls, caressing that disgusting pair of slimy shoes. He was in awe, as he was of the way she handled the great slabs of meat at every meal. She held the soft, scarlet flesh in her hands, ignoring the drops of juicy blood spilling on the counter, on the floor, running in rivulets down her white arms.

He heard the front door open and hurried to the corner he was working on. Gwendolyn was home already. Thank God she hadn't arrived twenty minutes earlier. Now he wanted to look busy, like he was working hard, but there really wasn't much to do until he picked up the floor tiles tomorrow. He had done the baseboards. He had measured and cut them, mitered the corners, sanded the rough spots. He wanted to paint them, but he had to wait until the rain stopped. In fact, he planned to paint the whole kitchen. The orange paint was peeling on the ceiling and there were cracks by the windows if you looked closely, and anyway it was so damn ugly. His floor wouldn't look good with it. He figured he could paint it in a day if he worked hard. He liked to paint; the mindless rhythmic motion was soothing and gave him lots of time to think. He could definitely get it done tomorrow, even with some time off for the Third Reward—if it stopped raining.

"You still here?" Gwendolyn asked as she came into the kitchen and threw her purse on the table.

"Looks like it," he said.

"I'm sorry," Gwendolyn said. "I didn't mean it like it sounded."

"Really?" he asked.

"Really."

She leaned against the doorjamb. She looked exhausted, pale. Her eyes were red.

"What's wrong?" he asked. "What happened?"

She wanted to tell him. He could see how glad she was that he had asked, but before she could answer they heard Amy galloping down the stairs, running through the living room. She came into the kitchen, threw her arms around her sister's waist, and lifted her up in the air.

"You're home so early. Hooray!" Amy spun her sister around. "Guess who was here today?" she asked.

"I give up," Gwendolyn answered.

Roosevelt wanted to tell Amy to put her down, something's wrong. But Amy didn't notice.

"You'll never guess," Amy said and spun her sister again.

"I said I give up."

Roosevelt heard the annoyance in Gwendolyn's voice, and something else, something new.

"Then I'll have to tell you." Amy was excited. A self-centered child with a secret. "All the way from Pittsburgh, Pennsylvania—ladies and gentlemen—Dr. Gustave Minor, professor of pyrophenomena, expert in Spontaneous Human Combustion!"

"Oh, Amy."

Roosevelt watched Gwendolyn. She stepped away from Amy, crossed her arms in front of her chest. Roosevelt recognized that pose, the disapproval it suggested and the protection it offered. Obviously Gwendolyn didn't believe in Dr. Minor's specialty either.

"He agreed with me about Auntie Ned," Amy said proudly. "Completely."

"Of course he did," Gwendolyn answered. "That's his job."

"He really meant it." Amy's eyes narrowed for a moment, then she shook her head and began to dance around the kitchen. Roosevelt had never seen Amy dance. She was awkward; the grace usually present in her movement was missing. She jerked; her feet were heavy on the floor.

"He was fascinating," she said as she stretched and turned, no rhythm in her movements. "And he's a midget. Really. This high. I'm telling you, he confirmed all my suspicions. Auntie Ned definitely spontaneously combusted."

"He's a midget?"

"Yes. Or a dwarf. Do you know the difference? He's very smart."

"Do you believe this?"

Roosevelt was startled when Gwendolyn spoke to him. Her eyes locked with his. Come on, she was saying, help me out here.

"No one believes it," Roosevelt said.

Amy's eyes went flat and small. She looked from Gwendolyn to Roosevelt and back again. "Dr. Minor is an expert," she said.

Roosevelt noticed how firmly her feet were suddenly planted on the splintery kitchen floor. Her cheeks were flushed, her anger apparent, her eyes burning into Gwendolyn. Roosevelt moved over and stood in front of Gwendolyn, blocking her from her sister's fiery eyes. He didn't think about it, he just did it, and then realized he had. Amy didn't like it. He stepped away again.

"Do you believe?" Amy asked Gwendolyn. "Do you believe Dr. Minor?"

Gwendolyn looked at Roosevelt. Her eyes were wet, her nose as red as her sister's face. She turned her back on Amy, the first time Roosevelt had ever seen her do that. "People just die," she whispered to him, her voice plaintive but strong. "They do. It's so easy, isn't it?"

Roosevelt took a deep breath. "Can Dr. Minor prove it?" he asked Amy. He thought it was a reasonable question. Amy exploded.

"You asshole!" she screamed. "Who do you think you are? Why should he prove anything to you!"

She grabbed the package of Oreos off the kitchen table and flung them at Roosevelt. He stepped aside and they hit the wall. The thin plastic bag ripped and Oreos flew everywhere. Amy pushed over the kitchen chairs one by one, running around the table until she came to Auntie Ned's final seat.

"It's true," she murmured, as if she was telling a secret to the chair. "It's true, it's true." She knelt, leaned her forehead on the remains of the dissolved vinyl seat, wrapped her arms around the charred chrome, and rocked the chair like a baby.

"You've cut yourself," Gwendolyn said. "Amy. Your arm, it's bleeding."

Roosevelt looked at Amy's arm, her lovely arm. A crimson welt had sprung up on the pure white flesh inside her elbow. Drops of blood appeared in a line along the mark, a row of liquid rubies expanding as he watched.

"You must've cut it on that chair," Gwendolyn said.

"No." Amy shook her head. "Not this chair."

Action is good, Roosevelt thought. It is time to do something. He tore a paper towel from the roll, ran some cold water on it. He crouched beside Amy and reached for her wounded arm.

"No," she said again. "Not this chair. This chair would never hurt me."

"Amy, cut it out," Gwendolyn said.

Roosevelt looked up in surprise at her rational voice. This was a Gwendolyn he had never seen before. Gwendolyn wasn't scared. Not of Amy. She was concerned, but not frightened of her sister, her sister's insane behavior. As Roosevelt was.

He felt the room waver, fade. It wasn't real, any of it. He had never come to work here. He had never met these women. But he had. He had. And they needed him. He blinked, concentrated on Amy's blood being absorbed, turning into bright flowers on the wet paper towel. He hadn't felt his brain retreat like this since the early days in the hospital. He had to tell himself he was here for a purpose, to fix the kitchen, to help Amy. He was supposed to save her.

He lifted the paper towel. It wasn't a cut on her arm, it was an irritation, a fleshy blister. The long scratch was swollen, a tiny mountain range, blood-capped and raw. He closed the damp paper towel over it and looked into Amy's eyes.

Her eyes were vacant, staring over his shoulder. He turned to see where she was looking and crunched an Oreo under his heavy boot. The cookies were everywhere, strangely reminiscent of Halloween, black against the orange walls and golden plywood.

"Are you okay?" he asked her. He would be okay if she answered, if she looked at him, if she stopped staring that way. "Are you okay?" he asked again, and his voice sounded high and feminine.

"Amy." Gwendolyn's voice was deep, grounded. "Snap out of it. I mean it. Or Roosevelt and I are going out to dinner without you."

Roosevelt was amazed. Dinner, out to dinner, what a sensible idea. Gwendolyn sounded wholesome and clearheaded, if a little fed up. Roosevelt smiled at her, gratefully, reverently. She raised her eyebrows, rolled her eyes.

Roosevelt stood up. "I'd love to go out to dinner," he said. "More than anything."

"Me too," Gwendolyn said. "Let's go."

She picked up her purse from the table, ignored the cookies under her feet, stepped over the fallen chair in front of her. "Coming, Ames?"

Amy stood. "Where are we going?" she asked.

Roosevelt laughed. It was a squeak really, but it felt almost like a laugh.

"Vegetarian," said Gwendolyn. "Just to piss you off."

Amy went to the ladies' room. Gwendolyn watched her go. Her sister left and she felt her shoulders relax, her hands stop playing with the silverware.

"Roosevelt?"

He was staring down the hallway after Amy.

"Roosevelt," she said again.

"What's the matter?" He turned to her, looked in her eyes.

"I . . . today . . ." There was so much she wanted to say. She started to cry. The little Asian man hadn't even had time to cry. Maybe his eyes had watered automatically. His body cried for itself.

"I knew something happened," Roosevelt said.

She was grateful he didn't try to comfort her, hold her, get her to stop crying. He watched.

"What is it? Tony?"

"No, no." She pulled herself together, put her mind back in her head, her stomach in its proper place. "It was raining."

"Yes."

"I saw an accident. Right in front of me." There was nothing to do now but say it. "I saw a man get killed."

"He was hit by the car?"

"No. The other driver. It wasn't much of an accident, but the other driver killed him. Beat him, kicked him to death."

"Oh, Gwendolyn. Oh, God."

Still he sat there without touching her. She wasn't crying anymore. Roosevelt's red curls glowed in the dim restaurant light. His chest was wide. She could see where he missed shaving, a darker spot like a stain below his chin.

"Roosevelt," she said.

"Don't tell your sister," he said.

"No. No, of course I won't." She smiled at him.

"She'd go nuts," he said.

Gwendolyn giggled. "Insane."

"She'd want to kill the guy."

"And the police officers."

"She'd never let you drive to work again."

Gwendolyn laughed. Roosevelt laughed with her. It felt good to laugh. It felt good to put her hand on the arm of a man, a handyman, a man who worked with his hands, who worked. For just one moment she leaned her head on his shoulder. He reached up and patted her cheek. They were still laughing at Amy when she came back to the table.

Chapter Fourteen

Amy hated it when she got out of control like that. She had a terrible temper, her mother said. She had a hormone imbalance, her high school PE teacher said. She was a self-indulgent baby, Gwendolyn said.

But Auntie Ned said that she just felt things too deeply, that sometimes her own feelings were too much for her, that she had to explode. Auntie Ned was right. Auntie Ned was the only one who understood.

Amy pushed the covers down off her bare shoulders, poked one naked leg out from under the blanket. She was hot. She lay in bed on her back, feeling prickly and raw, listening to Gwendolyn's ruffled snoring beside her. She could smell the onions Gwendolyn had eaten at dinner, faint, mixed with her usual yeasty odor. Gwendolyn always smelled like a cake baking. Heated, sweet, the batter rising in the oven and the warm odor filling the house with a sense of celebration.

Amy rolled over and put her wounded arm over her naked sister. She snuggled into her neck, her hair, tried to get comfortable. Gwendolyn sighed, but didn't wake up.

It had been a terrible day. First the toaster. Mama Girl and Dr. Minor. Roosevelt's other job. And the sex. She shuddered. Frustrating. No fun. And still so far to go. Roosevelt's job, his job, his new job. And Gwendolyn's new employee, the woman at work, the Olympian. The way Wendy talked about Elsa's skin, her hair, her short skirt and obvious muscles, there was something cold and hard in her voice that Amy didn't recognize.

They had spoken about all these things over dinner. Amy felt shimmery, a mirage at their table. She could see the fear in both their faces as they told her their respective bad news. What would she think? New job on Monday. New girl at work. But she surprised them. She stayed completely calm. She was only an image of herself after all, flat, two-dimensional. She even nodded sympathetically, put an understanding look on her illusive face. They didn't require any more of her, seemed happy even with how little they had.

After they got home from dinner, Roosevelt wanted to stay the night. He offered to sleep on the couch. His concern made her sad, uncomfortable. Nice guy. Idiot. Sometimes the thought of him as permanent in their lives, in Gwendolyn's life, made Amy sick. He could be the first, she thought, looking at his freckled face yellow in the porch light, but not the last, not the only. A temporary solution.

Gwendolyn turned away from the two of them and walked upstairs, taking off her clothes as she went. Amy watched her and couldn't stop her. Didn't say anything. She knew Roosevelt was watching too, that he was fascinated by Gwendolyn's T-shirt dropped on the stairs and her smooth back sectioned off by the white cotton bra. She said nothing when Gwendolyn dropped that too and then gave a half turn back, letting them both catch a glimpse of her round breast and dark nipple.

Then Amy had let Roosevelt hug her, kiss her forehead and her hair. His chest felt good against hers, her head fit snugly between his ear and his shoulder. If she could just stand like this. But his hand moved down her back, hugging her closer to him. He bent and kissed her neck and she felt the urgency. No one ever stood still.

There was never a moment when it stopped, when everything stopped.

Even now, she thought, even lying in this bed without moving, my hair grows and my fingernails, my mind goes forward, my heart gets older. There is no rest, no real rest. We are always going, going, going.

Gwendolyn radiated too much heat. Amy felt cooked. The insides of her elbows and the backs of her knees were sticky with sweat. The rain had stopped but the air was thick and moist, the hot damp of a mosquito-ridden swamp. She moved away from her sister. She pushed the covers off, lay naked, exposed. Finally, she got out of bed, went into the bathroom, and leaned her bare chest and neck against the cool glass of the small window.

Something moved in the backyard. Amy peered down into the moonless dark. It moved again, a black shadow in the wet weeds. She held her breath. Then it stepped onto the patio. An animal. She exhaled. A cat. Just a cat, gray, tiger-striped, stalking something in the grass. She tapped on the window. The cat froze, startled, then ran back in the direction it had come. Amy was sorry. She had kept the cat from its midnight snack, its instinctual act, its fresh kill.

She had to think. She had to figure out what she was going to do about Roosevelt. He was not as pliable as she had first assumed. He had a goddamn mind of his own, after all. This job. Monday. He said he would work for her on Saturday and Sunday. He said if he worked without stopping—and she knew what he meant—he could almost get it done over the weekend. But it wasn't the floor, the kitchen, the squeaky door in the garage. None of those things mattered. A new job would take him back to the other world, away from her, out of this house, Auntie Ned's house.

"Amy."

Amy didn't turn or look. It was Auntie Ned's voice. She heard her in her head, smelled her in the shower curtain's moldy plastic, saw her in the sway of bushes in the backyard. Amy felt the sweat drying under her arms, shrinking her skin. She was angry at Auntie Ned. She missed her and it made her angry.

"Amy."

It was an ache, the missing of her aunt, a hole that couldn't be filled in, a cavity in her chest that would always be empty. Other people in her life had died. Her father had committed suicide three years ago, but she had stopped missing him long before he was actually gone. Her mother, Helen, might as well be dead. Only Auntie Ned would leave a permanent vacancy. Amy wore her clothing, drove her car, slept in her bed, trying to occupy the void with herself. Auntie Ned's death left her feeling desperate and defeated. Death was inevitable. She had always known the words. Now she knew their truth.

Amy shivered. Suddenly she was cold, standing naked on the tile floor, leaning her breasts and face against the window. She looked down at herself. There were goose bumps on her pale flesh, obvious even in the dim light. Her knees looked bony. She could see her ribs, her pelvic bones. She was little more than a skeleton. She needed to go back to bed, wrap her scrawny arms around her bakery-fed sister. Roosevelt would just have to postpone his new job. The apartment complex could wait. Incineration was possible at any moment. She had to get on with things.

She tiptoed back to bed, pressed her chilled skin against her sleeping sister.

"Amy," Gwendolyn whispered without waking.

"I'm here," Amy replied.

Gwendolyn rolled over so she faced her sister and put her arms around Amy without opening her eyes. Amy smelled the sleep in Gwendolyn's hair and cinnamon and sugar. She felt herself nourished, her flesh expanded by Gwendolyn's warmth. Gwendolyn's round fullness entered her, satiated her, and made her hungry for more. She took Gwendolyn's bottom lip between her teeth and pressed down slightly, not to hurt her, but to wake her. Gwendolyn moaned and pushed her belly against Amy's. She threw one leg over Amy's cool thigh and began to pulse, to press and rub herself against her sister. She could come so easily. It was one of the amazing things about Gwendolyn. It took barely more than the desire to do it. Gwendolyn had orgasms in her dreams; she came in her sleep. Amy had sat on the bed next to her and watched, without touching, envious.

Her eyes were still closed and Amy smiled at her younger sister's blank face, features subdued in the soft, woolly dark. She kissed the high cheekbones, the straight nose, the thick black eyelashes that looked like smudges on her tan cheeks. She was beautiful. Amy pulled Gwendolyn tighter, pressed her hand against the small of her back, helped her baby sister along.

Chapter Fifteen

It was cloudy, but the rain had stopped. Gwendolyn was making coffee. Every ordinary ritual this morning, her feet on the cold bathroom floor, the stream of her warm pee, the flavor of toothpaste, reminded her she was alive. And other people were dead.

Gwendolyn switched on the coffeepot, bent her head and breathed in the roasted coffee odor, the smell of morning, new days, fresh starts. She heard Amy come downstairs.

"I'll get the paper," Amy called from the living room.

Gwendolyn heard the front door open. Then Amy's scream, a shriek of fear. Gwendolyn froze. Body bags, men with enormous fists. She ran.

Amy stood at the open door. On the front porch lay three little blobs of something. Gwendolyn had no idea what they were. She bent down.

They were mice, dead mice, crunched, partially flattened, tiny puddles of rust-colored blood and entrails beneath each one.

"I almost stepped on them." Amy was furious. Her bare feet looked so vulnerable in the soft morning light.

"Where did they come from?"

"I know where," said Amy. She looked over to their neighbor's house, the high dilapidated bamboo fence.

"What do you mean?"

Amy shuddered and grunted. She bent down, grabbed the first corpse by the tail and threw it over the fence as hard as she could. Gwendolyn heard the small, sodden thud as it hit the cement patio. Amy picked up the next one and threw it too.

"Wait," Gwendolyn said. "What are you doing?"

"Mama Girl told me we infested her house with mice. Since we moved in," Amy said, "the mice have all come to her house."

"We never had mice, did we? Auntie Ned never had mice."

"I tried to tell her that. They're not ours. But every day now I find dead mice in our trash cans. Traps attached. Cheese. Maggots. The whole thing."

"Gross."

"That's why I haven't let you take out the garbage."

Gwendolyn stopped. She looked at her sister. "I'm a big girl. I can handle it."

"But you don't have to. And I don't mind."

"I don't either."

"I know you hate dead things."

She hated the gravel cutting into her knees, the blood running past her in the rain. "I do not."

"Remember the bird in the garage?"

"I was eight."

"And the dog in the road?"

"I saw that dog get killed," Gwendolyn explained. "He was annihilated, torn apart when that truck hit him. I saw his body split in half, front legs going one way, back legs another."

"You were hysterical."

"His blood splashed on my windshield."

"I didn't think you needed to see this, that's all."

This is nothing. "I can handle this."

"I can deal with the mice."

"Stop, Amy. Stop."

"What? Stop what?"

Stop everything, she wanted to say, stop being my big sister. Stop walking, Amy. Fly.

They both stared down at the third dead mouse.

"Don't throw this one." Gwendolyn's voice was louder than she intended.

Amy looked at her, puzzled, curious. "She's a bitch," she said slowly, pointedly, watching Gwendolyn.

"She's just a crazy old lady." Gwendolyn smiled, tried to laugh. "I'll get the broom, and the dustpan."

"I know what to do," Amy said, grinning in return.

Trouble, Gwendolyn thought. She had seen that malevolent smile too many times.

"I know what to do," Amy said again. "We'll put it in a paper bag, leave it on her front step, and then light it on fire. We'll ring the doorbell and when she comes out—she'll stomp on it to put out the fire."

Gwendolyn went into the kitchen to get the broom. She decided she would go over there later and talk to Mama Girl. She would bake her a cake. Immediately she began planning one that looked like a dead mouse and a trap and a piece of Swiss cheese. She shook her head. Not appropriate.

"Give them to me," Amy said when she returned. "I'll do it."

"I've got it."

"Let me."

"No."

Gwendolyn wouldn't give up the broom and dustpan. She scooped up the mouse quickly.

"Go wash your hands," she said to Amy.

"Are you telling me what to do?"

"Please go wash your hands." Gwendolyn didn't want to fight. There was no point to fighting. They were alive, after all. "Mice carry all kinds of disease."

Amy frowned, but she went inside. Gwendolyn heard the door to the small bathroom under the stairs open and then the water running. A while back, when they first moved in, Gwendolyn had put a gold-foil-wrapped condom on the empty shelf in that medicine chest. It was just for safekeeping, although she couldn't imagine needing it again. Then it was gone. Gwendolyn knew Amy had taken it. She knew Amy was trying, in her own obvious way, to insure that Gwendolyn would have no more sex with men. It was a ridiculous supposition, but it was also a uniquely Amy train of thought.

Gwendolyn wanted to bake a cake. In the middle of the night she had woken suddenly, some time after her nocturnal orgasm. Amy slept on, one long leg hanging off the bed.

"You're damn lucky," the policeman said.

"You're strong," Elsa said.

And she was. She rolled over against her sleeping sister. Nothing would happen here. She closed her arms around Amy. Face-to-face, their breath one breath, the strands of their hair embracing, the cells of their skin trading places. She was still breathing. They were both breathing. The room seemed full of dark clouds, hovering near the ceiling, threatening to fall on them, to suffocate them. But Gwendolyn was awake. She was on guard.

She couldn't sleep. When she closed her eyes, her thoughts were dark red and gruesome. She kept them open until the sun came up.

A cake would make her feel better. A cake just for fun. Something fanciful, lovely. She and Amy could take it to Mama Girl together, happy young sisters, sweet to the neighbors. They could suggest that she feed it to the mice and make friends with her rodent roommates.

Gwendolyn opened the black plastic trash can. The bottom of the container was covered with little dead mice. She dumped the latest one in on top, trying not to look at the decaying maggot-ridden bodies, concentrating instead on the cake she would make. Violets, she thought, in lavenders and pinks. Lilacs. Hydrangeas.

Then she remembered. Roosevelt was working today. Well, he would just have to share the kitchen with her. Poor guy. He had been a mess last night, terrified by Amy's temper tantrum. He was in love. Gwendolyn knew the look, understood his torture, the excruciating, delirious agony that Amy sparked. Gwendolyn knew it well. She also knew that she would never inspire a man to that kind of love. No one would ever kill for her, die for her. No one, except Amy.

Roosevelt ate a piece of toast and stared at his lizard. He had added a rock and some cedar chips from the courtyard of his building to the clear plastic cage. Larry/Lizzy/Sue really could change color. On the rock it was brown. On the plastic leaves it was green. Last night he transferred the crickets from their Chinese food box to a plastic margarine tub he covered with wax paper and held in place with a rubber band. The crickets were quiet. He had thought they would chirp at night, but they didn't. He figured they knew they were in a concentration camp, cricket Auschwitz, waiting for their trip to the Plexiglas chamber.

He was growing attached to his lizard. All day yesterday he had enjoyed knowing it was there, waiting for him while he worked, ate, did other things. Last night he hadn't even turned on the television. He only watched the lizard. He had been so exhausted. Amy had worn him out. Not the sex, but seeing her lose it like that. Then going out to dinner and telling her about Stan. She had been calm, didn't say much to him. Back at the house after dinner, he was cleaning up Oreos when she knelt beside him on the plywood and put her arms around him. She needed him. A lot.

He was picking up the new linoleum tiles this morning. He was excited, couldn't wait to see Amy's pleased reaction. She would love this floor. He wanted to paint the kitchen, not white, but a pale, pale yellow, like her hair in the sun. He would do the trim in a high gloss white; the shine would make the whole kitchen look clean and new. He wanted to scrub the cabinets inside and out. Paint them too. Finally, he would empty and reline each drawer with clean shelf paper. Amy's kitchen would be just like new.

When he arrived at Amy's house with the tiles, Dr. Minor's red rental car was parked in front again. The back end swung out into the street, one front tire squished against the curb. The car looked abandoned, left hastily; the tiny bird-man doctor couldn't wait to get inside.

It was a busy morning in the usually quiet neighborhood. A guy from the duplex next door was carrying a television down to his car. There were two other TVs in the back seat.

"Moving out?" Roosevelt asked.

The man said nothing, obviously didn't want to talk.

The old lady next door was hanging around on the sidewalk in front of her house. She wore rubber gloves and was carrying something on a string.

Across the street, the two Latino brothers and two of their homeboy friends were shaving each others' heads. They were shirtless in the overcast and cool gray air. Their baggy pants hung low on their boy hips, the white waistbands of their underwear like a belt above the khaki. He noticed their tattoos, blue against their brown skin.

"Want a haircut?" the oldest one called to him.

What should he say? "Sure," he said, anxious not to offend them. The oldest boy laughed. The others watched him, their eyes lazy but suspicious, a quiet menace in the morning air.

"Come on over." The big brother gestured with his hand.

"Still be there after work?" Roosevelt asked.

"You workin' today, man? Saturday? That's fucked up."

Roosevelt shrugged. He wouldn't complain to these guys and he couldn't explain he was glad to be there.

He opened the back of his truck to get out the first load of tiles. They were wrapped in brown paper, tall, heavy rectangles. They smelled of plastic and workman sweat. He heard a sliding, a shuffling behind him on the sidewalk. He looked around. The old neighbor lady stood next to him in her nightgown, old sweater, and the rubber gloves. She wore dirty pink bedroom slippers on her feet, the backs bent flat under her heels.

"Look, look, look at this," she said.

Politely, Roosevelt shifted his gaze. She held up the thing she was carrying. It was a mouse, dead, squashed flat. What he had thought was a string was actually the tail. He could see the ochre and olive brains oozing in little blisters from the smashed skull, the popped eye sockets and the big, Mickey Mouse ears. He thought of Susie the lizard waiting at home and Susie's brain. What color would it be? He shook his head to clear it.

"Do you see it?" she asked, holding it up higher, closer to his face.

"Yes," he said. He heard the boys behind him, their laughter high and foreign, the buzz of the electric razor vibrating in his ears.

They had cut his hair with a razor like that in the hospital. They had worn rubber gloves to do it. The hospital was not a sanatorium. No pretty nurses rolled old men in wheelchairs across green lawns to rest in the dappled light of leafy tree branches. The "cats"—as the catatonic patients were known—were left standing or sitting in corners for hours, possibly days. They were used as punching bags by the violent inmates, coatracks by the others. When Roosevelt came to, he had a terrible case of diaper rash; his penis and his testicles were raw and blistered. He hadn't been changed very often, nowhere near often enough.

"What do you suggest, suggest that I do with this?" Her voice was nasal, grating.

Roosevelt held the tall stack of heavy vinyl tiles in his arms. In his truck were all his tools: a pickax, a sledgehammer, saws of different sizes, lengths, blades. But his arms were full.

"Throw it away?" he said.

"That's what I did, I did, I did. That exactly. Exactly that."

He closed the back doors to his truck with his hip. He shifted the weight of the tiles against his chest and began walking inside.

"It came back," the old lady called after him. "It came right back, and one, two, I mean one other besides."

"Try again," he said. Poor old lady. She made him glad his mother hadn't lived long enough to be senile, to worry about mice who traveled postmortem. He would not have been able to live here and leave his mother alone in Missouri.

He set the first package on the front porch. He planned to stack the tiles there, take them one by one as he needed them. He had to paint first, then lay the floor. He was a meticulous painter, but it was inevitable that there would be spots, drips to clean off the new vinyl if he painted afterward. He had the paint in the truck as well, but that would come later, after he had prepped the walls.

He turned to go back to his truck for another load. The old lady was still there, staring at him from the end of the front walk. The boys were across the street. One of the friends whose hair had already been shaved, shaved so close it was just a five o'clock shadow on his skull, sat on the cracked front stoop and watched him.

Roosevelt decided not to go back to the truck right now. He turned his back on the street, split open the brown paper, and took out the top tile. He wanted to get inside. It was too weird out here.

"It's me," he called out as he opened the front door and stepped inside.

He heard Amy laughing in the kitchen and Dr. Minor's responding twitter. He smelled coffee. He closed the door behind him and felt his muscles ease.

"Hello, you," Amy said as he entered the kitchen.

Her smile broke across her face just for him.

"I brought the tile," he said. He held it behind his back, a surprise, a treat.

"You remember Dr. Minor, don't you?" she asked, nodding at the doctor.

Roosevelt looked at him, forgetting how much he disliked him. He was just a midget, a scientist, a lunatic. "Sure. Hey, how are you?"

"I'm fine. Fine, thank you. And you?" He looked at Roosevelt so strangely, a combination of fear and fascination on his face. Short man's complex, Roosevelt decided, in spades.

"Great," Roosevelt said. "Never better."

He handed the single square of tile to Amy.

She looked at it, ran her palm over it, then turned her radiant gaze up into his face. "It's perfect," she said to him. "It's really beautiful."

A jet of molten, liquid pleasure began in his stomach, filled his chest, spread up to his face. Amy was looking into his eyes, telling him he had done well. She was speaking to him alone. He was suddenly aware he was flushed and grinning like the village idiot.

"So," he managed, "Gwendolyn still asleep?"

"She's in the garage. Why?"

"Just wondered," he said.

Gwendolyn undressing on the stairs and flashing her tit at him. Last night in his little apartment, he tried to figure out why she had done that. He pictured her and that one tit again and again. Voluptuous, sexual, but also innocent in the unlit hallway. It was larger than Amy's, and darker. The nipple made him think of chocolate, a single Hershey's Kiss. He finally decided it was a welcoming gesture, a show of faith from Gwendolyn that he was above that kind of thing. He had the best. He could appreciate Gwendolyn's appearance without desiring her at all. Not at all.

"Gus was just telling me about Spontaneous Human Combustion and its connection to tantra," Amy said. "Remember what we were talking about?" Her eyes were golden this morning, like melted sunlight. "The other day—at the beach?"

Roosevelt blushed. Sex. They had been talking about sex. "Excuse me?"

"Excellent stuff," Minor said. "I'm a practitioner myself."

"You what?" Roosevelt was confused, embarrassed by the doctor's open admission. This guy had a wife, after all, and a baby. "How exactly do you do that?"

"I do it for the pain." Minor nodded, smiled. "A form of yoga and meditation. A channeling of my kundalini. For the pain. Pain management."

"Are you in pain?" Amy asked.

"I should not have lived this long." Minor's voice was rich, offering a secret to Amy, a gift of confidence. Roosevelt watched her take it from him with both hands. "Ten years ago," the doctor continued, "I should have been dead then."

"Ten years ago," Amy said.

"Every day is a gift."

Roosevelt could look at Minor and see the organs twisted and struggling inside him, cramped too tightly against his little bones, the heart, the lungs claustrophobic. When would enough be enough?

"I'm so sorry," Amy said. She was fascinated by him. Her eyes were soft, velvety, moist. She put one hand over Dr. Minor's, the other against her T-shirt-covered chest. Minor took this opportunity to stare at Amy's breasts.

Roosevelt felt himself wilt like an overheated flower.

"Of course tantric work helps you," Amy said gently. "Of course it does. It's the ultimate combination of physical force and complete, total consciousness."

"Beautiful," breathed the doctor without moving his eyes.

"So?" Roosevelt clenched his fists, willed himself not to hit the staring doctor, shove him off his self-satisfied miniature ass onto the floor. He looked at Amy. "So?" he said again. "What does this have to do with people burning up in their chairs?"

"Heat," the doctor answered for her. "The body temperature can go up. Up. Up. I've heard of third-degree burns resulting—from the inside out. Obviously, it's just a hop and a skip from there to total human incineration. Or SHC."

The doctor and Amy smiled at each other.

"Resulting from what?" Roosevelt said. This made no sense. He thought tantra was sex, not some metaphysical paranormal nonsense about heat and pain management.

"Meditation. From meditation. The kundalini, the energy, moves through your spine, into each of your chakras. The swamis say this happens," the doctor continued. "I've talked to them. I know. Incredible warmth builds up when your chakras—energy centers—are blocked with worry or unresolved conflicts or guilt."

"Guilt," Roosevelt said.

"I know it sounds odd, but this is true," Minor said and paused for effect. "The only genuine defense against Spontaneous Human Combustion is a clear conscience."

"I want to paint the kitchen," Roosevelt said.

"What?" Amy looked at him.

"I have to paint the kitchen before I lay the tile. I have to lay the tile tomorrow."

Amy shook her head. Roosevelt knew she didn't want to hear what came next. He said it anyway. "I won't be here Monday. I want to finish this today and tomorrow."

"You can't," Amy said.

Roosevelt shrugged.

"No," Amy said, "it's not me. You really can't paint the kitchen today or lay the tile or anything. Gus has a team coming."

For a moment, Roosevelt imagined a midget sporting team from

Paranormal U. in their baggy gym shorts and team jerseys with pocket protectors. He snickered.

"Quite a few of my colleagues live here in the Los Angeles area," Dr. Minor said smugly.

"I'm not surprised," Roosevelt replied. His chin went up. "You have the piece of floor, and the chair, and those shoes." He turned to Amy. "What more do they need?"

"They want to scrape the wall paint. They need to look at the floor joists. Right, Gus?"

"Exactly. I spoke to a number of people yesterday after I left here. We agree this is a fascinating opportunity to study SHC."

"Oh, yeah. Fascinating." Roosevelt knew he was being sarcastic. His mother hated sarcasm.

"I'm sorry, Roosevelt. They want to cut a hole in your new floor."

"Are you kidding?"

"Where it happened," Dr. Minor said, "we need to look at the subflooring. You didn't replace that, did you?"

"There were eleven layers of linoleum. There's nothing to see in the subflooring. No damage. You're wasting your time. And mine."

Roosevelt heard his voice getting high. He was afraid he would be keening in a moment, rocking back and forth like an old woman over a fresh grave, saying over and over, I have to finish today. I have to finish today. It was spoiled, his morning was spoiled. Why couldn't Amy leave her aunt alone? Why not be done with this old dead lady? Auntie Ned didn't like him, he knew that, felt it in the basement, in the dark, even in the bedroom upstairs.

The back door opened and Gwendolyn entered. She carried a box labeled BATHROOM and actually smiled at Roosevelt.

Thank God, Roosevelt thought.

"Find them?" Amy asked.

"I should have packed more carefully."

"You?"

"Or you should have packed for me."

"I offered."

Gwendolyn sighed and put the box on the counter. She had a stray string of fuzz in her hair, something she had picked up in the garage. It looked like an antenna of some sort, identifying her as an alien.

Which she certainly isn't, Roosevelt thought, not in this crowd. He reached out and pulled the fluff from her dark hair. He didn't throw it away in the trash can, just brushed it off his hand and let it drop to the floor.

"Thanks," Gwendolyn said. "How's your lizard?"

"Great." Roosevelt nodded. "I really like it."

She smiled again. She was happy for him, happy to see him.

"I want to paint the kitchen today." He appealed to Gwendolyn's common sense, even though he knew she had no power.

"Good idea to me, but Amy has other plans. As always."

Roosevelt was surprised at the edge in Gwendolyn's voice. Her strength from last night was not diminished. Something was different about her.

"Come here, Roosevelt," Amy said and stood up. "Let's talk about the next few days."

Dr. Gustave Minor sat there with an interested, pointy expression on his face. He swung his feet back and forth above Roosevelt's plywood floor. His eyes blinked and darted from Amy to Roosevelt to Gwendolyn. They rested on Gwendolyn. Roosevelt could see their lecherous point of view. Reluctantly, he followed Amy into the living room.

Immediately she put both arms around his neck and pulled his face down to hers. She kissed him, openmouthed. She gave him a moment to kiss back, to put his arms around her, then she circled his mouth with her tongue. She pushed her pelvis against his, lifted her thigh to rub on just the right spot between his legs. Roosevelt groaned, pulled his mouth from hers.

"I'm gonna spontaneously combust right here," he sighed. "I can't stand this."

She kissed him again. He was well aware this was a tactic. He knew she was convincing him to postpone the paint job in her own, nonverbal way. It was working.

"I mean it, Amy." He held her away from him. "I can't do this much longer."

"I saw you looking at Gwendolyn last night."

"When?" He knew exactly what she was talking about.

"On the stairs. She took her shirt off."

"I don't remember." He hoped she believed him.

"You two were so chummy at the restaurant."

"I was worried about you."

"I'm not enough for you, am I?"

"You're all I think about."

"You're doing it," Amy said to him. "I can feel myself getting stronger, less afraid. I'm almost ready to . . . to . . ."

"What about the seven more Rewards?" he asked. He couldn't resist. He wanted to know.

"Maybe it won't take that long."

"Really?"

She took his hand and put it between her legs, on the thin cotton crotch of her baby-blue pants. "Feel that?" she asked.

She was damp and hot. Actually hot to touch. He looked down. He expected steam.

"See what I mean?" she said.

He closed his eyes. He left his hand there between her legs and moved his first and second fingers as if he was rubbing behind a kitten's ear. She sighed and shifted just a little, back and forth. He could smell her.

"Come upstairs," he said.

"Don't take that new job on Monday," she said.

"I already have."

"I want you, so much."

"I'm here."

"I want you every day. Until we get it done."

She stepped away from him. He saw the sweat on her forehead. Without thinking he lifted his fingers to his nose, breathed in her damp scent. She stood on her tiptoes and took his moist fingers in her mouth. She sucked them up and down, up and down, up and—

"Okay, okay," he said. "Okay. Okay. I'll call Stan. I'll see if I can start in a couple of weeks. Okay."

She released his fingers with a pop. She smiled at him.

"Now, can we please go upstairs?" He was begging, he knew it.

"Later," she said. "Gus's friends should be here any moment."

Gwendolyn had the bowls out and the flour. She was melting butter in a saucepan on the stove. She was worried that Roosevelt and Amy were not really talking in the living room. She knew Amy's usual methods of persuasion. But why did Amy want to persuade him? Why keep him around, have him to dinner, take him to the god-damn beach? Amy didn't even like him, Gwendolyn could tell. She clattered and banged, taking out the metal measuring cups, washing her cake pans. She was afraid to overhear their rustling together, their sighing breaths, their wet murmurs, anything.

"What are you doing?" Dr. Minor asked.

"I'm baking a cake," Gwendolyn said.

"Now?"

Gwendolyn smiled at Dr. Minor. He blushed.

"Is your wife in the phenomena biz too?" she asked.

"Oh no," he said. "She's at home with the baby now, but she's a lawyer."

"Where'd you meet her?"

"Friends set us up."

Gwendolyn imagined the call. "He's really a nice guy. He's a doctor, sort of. Teaches at a college. He's a dwarf, but you don't even notice after a while."

"What . . ." He paused. "What do you do?"

"I'm a cake decorator," she said. "I bake fantasy cakes."

"Fantasy?"

She saw sex in his eyes. It was never very far away with men. "Sometimes that kind of fantasy." She wanted to make him blush again. "I did a penis once. Cream-filled."

He blushed.

She smiled. "Usually I do cakes that look like animals, or flower baskets, or cars."

"Fascinating," he said.

"I love it," she said, but it didn't sound like she loved it. It had been a long time since she had made a cake just for herself. She was going to spend the day doing it. She didn't want to garden or go to the beach. For some reason, her bicycle tires were completely flat.

They had been fine two days ago. She was going to make a long, rectangular cake covered in flowers.

Like a grave, she thought. She looked at Dr. Minor. They would have to use a child's body bag for him. She was sure the ambulance was prepared with black plastic for all sizes.

"So, you're an artist." Dr. Minor brought her back.

"Maybe." Gwendolyn shrugged. "You can decide when the cake's finished."

He looked at his watch. He looked back at her. She heard Roosevelt in the other room say, "Okay, okay." It was a whine, a prayer, a surrendering. Amy had convinced him. He would not be going to a new job on Monday. Amy could be very persuasive. All was quiet now from the living room. Gwendolyn felt a lurch of jealousy, a kink in her stomach. She liked Roosevelt now too, but she didn't want to sleep with him. She didn't care about his big male hands with the long fingers, or the bow of his mouth, the white teeth inside. She had flashed her tit at him last night just to prove it to him, to herself.

Amy returned. Her face was flushed, her lips wet. Gwendolyn didn't want to look at her. Amy walked up and put her arm around Gwendolyn's shoulders.

"You're baking a cake?"

"For Roosevelt," she said.

"Roosevelt?" Amy moved her arm, put it behind her back.

Gwendolyn smiled. "Blue. His favorite color."

"How did you know?"

Gwendolyn didn't answer.

"I said, how did you know?"

Roosevelt came back into the kitchen carrying another package of tiles. Gwendolyn tilted her head, looked at him sideways.

"Blue is your favorite color, isn't it?" she asked him.

"Sure is." He grinned.

Gwendolyn smiled back at him, kept smiling when he looked guiltily at Amy. Two could play at this game.

Amy's lips were pressed flat. She frightened Roosevelt. He retreated to his truck. Gwendolyn banged her pans, slammed the cupboard door. Why couldn't all of these people go away? Dr. Minor. Elsa. Tony. Roosevelt. Even Amy. Especially Amy. If she could just have a break. A day, an afternoon, one hour when she could be truly alone, be satisfied just to be alive. She wanted enough quiet to hear her heart beating, the sigh of every single breath. She wanted the time to feel the cotton T-shirt against her skin, the hair curling on her neck, the roughness of the roof of her mouth.

Gwendolyn wanted to yell at Amy, stop it! Go away! Amy, larger than anyone else, brighter, stronger. Amy, always there before Gwendolyn had a chance to think. There so fast, Gwendolyn was always left behind, always running to catch up. But where were you yesterday? Gwendolyn shouted in her mind. With him. With Roosevelt. And why?

Amy had put on one of Auntie Ned's sweaters. It was too big on her. The buttons were made to look like giant floppy daisies. The front pockets were shaped like flowerpots. Somehow Amy, with her tight blue pants and her bare ankles, could pull it off.

"That sweater is hideous," Gwendolyn said.

Amy stared at her for a moment. Gwendolyn stood her ground, prepared to fight, then saw Amy decide to laugh.

"I know. I love it," she said and turned to the doctor. "When's the gang getting here?"

"Soon," Gus said. "Anytime now."

Chapter Sixteen

In an hour the house was crawling with weirdos. Pyropsychologists, psychic investigators, biofeedback engineers; they were like termites, dangerous, insidious; most of them bearded and wearing cheap blue jeans and old T-shirts with yellow underarms and pictures of tear-eyed aliens. Roosevelt sat on the stairs, not wanting to leave, unsure of his place, but feeling essential.

They scraped the paint in the kitchen and collected it in Tupperware; they measured the distances from stove to chair and window to chair and wrote it down in a tattered spiral notebook; they drilled through his new plywood, examined the core and found nothing. One of them even sniffed the couch. He buried his face deep between the cushions and breathed in.

"Aha!" he announced triumphantly when he emerged, bits of lint stuck to his beard and eyebrows. "The smell. I definitely got the smell."

A skinny college kid in a tie-dyed T-shirt and faded red jeans carried a Geiger counter type of device on a wide rainbow-striped strap around his neck. He looked like a postapocalyptic child with an electronic toy drum; the wand he poked and pointed everywhere a silver drumstick held together with electrician's tape.

"The kitchen's hot," he shouted, and grinned at the others' enthusiastic responses.

Roosevelt reached out from the staircase. He tapped the boy's bony shoulder. "What does that mean?"

"Evidence of psychic phenomenon." Dr. Minor stepped up to answer. He knew everything. He grinned, brushed the hair from his forehead as if he was working hard. "The machine picked up a definite energy buzz."

Roosevelt knew that. He didn't need a machine to feel Auntie Ned's presence. It was a sadness, a lingering regret. She had left, but she wasn't really ready to go. When his mother died, she was gone. Period. A door closed, silence on the other side. But after his wife died, her voice had remained, hovering, accusing, begging him not to do it. Too late, he whispered his reply, too late. It was like a flashbulb going off, the blinding flash! then the light was gone, but the image remained, more painful than before, burned onto his retina. Even closing his eyes could not make it go away.

Too late, he whispered, seeing the car, smashed, totaled, bloodstained. I'm sorry. It's too late. But she would not go. She would not forgive him. She would not shut up. The wail of the tree as it fell over, the scream of the brakes, and her voice, louder and louder until he couldn't hear anything else, not the lawyers, not the doctors, only her voice.

And now he sometimes heard Auntie Ned whispering. There was something she wanted. Something she had left undone.

Gwendolyn came and sat on the stairs next to him. She was waiting for her cake to bake.

Together they watched the crazy SHC bugs and Amy. Amy was the insect queen. She answered questions, asked questions, ordered the creepy crawly scientists around. And these little geeks, these guys who couldn't get a date in high school, with their long greasy hair tucked behind dirty ears, pasty computer-generated skin and black sneakers with the heels worn down on the sides, they followed her, worshiped her with their eyes and their pale hands with the uncut fingernails. She was a goddess, the goddess of oddities, of Spontaneous Human Combustion. When they found out she was a phone psychic, Roosevelt thought a few of them would pass out from sheer joy. She was beautiful and she was one of them.

Gwendolyn watched her sister move with the pack of mad-dog paranormalists. A wave of desire washed over her and hit her low in the sandy beach of her stomach. She had forgotten how much she loved Amy. Suddenly she couldn't remember why she was angry at her. Amy hadn't done anything. Amy loved her and only her. Roosevelt was a flirtation, that was all. It hit her hard and abrupt, the want, the addiction, the complete jones for her sister.

Touch me, she screamed her thought, brush past me and let me feel you. Look at me. That would be enough. Just look at me.

She put her arm through Roosevelt's.

"She's something, isn't she?" she said to him.

Roosevelt looked down at Gwendolyn's arm, afraid to move, afraid she would move. He wanted so badly for someone to know how he felt about Amy. His mother would have understood. He could have put his head in her lap and she would have smoothed away his agony, his uncertainty. She would have told him not to worry.

Gwendolyn patted his knee. "Poor you," she said. "Poor me."

Roosevelt laughed. "A couple of suckers," he said. He knew how Amy kept Gwendolyn wrapped tight and close. "I never had a sister or a brother," he began, then stopped.

"She's different than most."

"That goes without saying."

Gwendolyn looked up and smiled at him. He smiled back. Her blue eyes always surprised him under her dark brows and lashes. She is lovely, he thought and really saw it for the first time. She wore ratty blue jeans and a white T-shirt that accentuated her tan skin and her perfect round breasts. He took a deep breath, let it out slowly. She was a little sister, a good little sister to have. He would take care of her and that would make Amy happy.

"Do you know about her problem?" he had to ask.

"Which problem is that?"

"She—" He faltered, worrying that he was betraying Amy, telling something she didn't want known.

"There isn't anything I don't know about her," Gwendolyn said.

"Then you know she can't have an orgasm."

"What?"

He heard the surprise, couldn't see her face.

"We're working on it," he said. "Did you know?"

Gwendolyn sat up, her back straight, away from him. She didn't know, he realized; he had said too much.

"I'm in love with her." He hoped that would help.

"Since when?" Her voice was far away.

"The day—the day you gave me the lizard."

"Oh, fuck," she said.

"I think she's falling for me too."

The timer rang. The cake was done. Gwendolyn heard it far away, in another house. Why would anyone bake a cake now? She sat on the stairs. She wouldn't get up. She couldn't get up. She stared down at Roosevelt's knee, covered in gray and a spill of white paint like a cloud. Her own knee seemed so small beside it. Inconsequential. Nothing to anyone. Amy should have been happy. Gwendolyn was the one who wanted a man, wanted a hard dick inside her, wanted what was expected. She had given up everything for Amy.

"Hey," Roosevelt said, "the timer went off."

Gwendolyn looked at him. She wasn't angry with him; it wasn't his fault. Amy passed in front of them, smiled at him, not her. Gwendolyn saw his face light up. Like a child at the circus, she thought, or worse: like King Midas being given the golden touch. He was thrilled, he didn't know how the gift being offered would hurt him. Amy didn't really want him. She had something else in her witch's mind. But Gwendolyn knew if she tried to tell Roosevelt, he wouldn't believe her, he wouldn't care.

"I'm sorry," he said. "I thought you knew."

She could smell the cake, past done, close to burning. She could feel the cake covering her eyes, stuffing her throat, wrapped across her mouth. Suffocating. Gwendolyn forced herself to stand up. Roosevelt was watching Amy, lost in what he imagined was their perfect future. She had imagined it too.

"You should go home," she said.

He frowned at her, confused.

"Get out of here," she said and really wanted to tell him to run, run away. His eyebrows lifted. He wondered what she meant. "Really. You don't need to be here. Go to a movie. Go see a friend," she continued more emphatically. "Go to the beach."

That was a mistake. She saw it in his face the minute she said it. That was where it had happened. He thought of the beach, and he thought only of that damn hotel of Amy's, the king-size bed, the ocean view, the man watching golf alone in the office. She and Amy had been there together. She knew all about it.

"I'm not leaving," Roosevelt said. "I'm not going anywhere."

Amy glanced over at her sister and Roosevelt talking on the staircase. She saw Gwendolyn touch his shoulder and Roosevelt look up at her. Gwendolyn gestured at the door, to the outside. Roosevelt shrugged and said something. Then he laughed, but sadly. Amy knew Gwendolyn was telling Roosevelt to leave, that she was worrying over him like he was a stray dog, a foster child in an abusive home. First the lizard, now this. What was up with Gwendolyn? She was different. Had been for a couple of days. Since the rain and Dr. Minor's arrival. Gwendolyn liked Roosevelt better now, and that was good. The time was coming. But something else was wrong. Amy was tired. She felt like she was running, always running to stay one step ahead. If there were rocks in Gwendolyn's path, she would move them. If there were things up ahead that Gwendolyn desired, Amy would be there first to make sure she got them. Roosevelt was something Gwendolyn didn't even know yet that she wanted. When she figured it out, Amy would be ready to supply him. Amy ran and kept running, running, running.

She watched Gwendolyn go to the kitchen to retrieve her stupid cake. She grabbed Dr. Minor's oddly juicy arm. He was happy to be grabbed. He flushed as she held his hand and wrapped her other arm around his shoulders.

"How's it going?" she asked.

"Okay," he squeaked.

"This is so wonderful. Thank you," she said. She knew Roosevelt was watching.

"My pleasure," Gus answered. "It's uh . . . completely my, you know, pleasure."

"Good," Amy said.

Roosevelt's face was red. She could see it glinting like a burnished apple in the corner. She sauntered past him as she went to the kitchen, but didn't look at him.

"Hey," he whispered.

She pretended not to hear.

"Hey," he said again, louder.

She kept walking. She heard him get up and follow her. He stumbled over a researcher and his equipment. She heard him exclaim, "Jesus Christ. Watch out!"

She smiled.

She walked into the kitchen. Gwendolyn was at the stove.

"Hey, baby," Amy said.

Gwendolyn threw the hot cake at her. It was too heavy, fell before it reached her. The pan made an odd thud against the plywood. There were crumbs and clumps of honey-colored cake all over the floor.

"What's the matter with you?"

"Ask him!" Gwendolyn pointed to Roosevelt, just walking in.

Amy turned, saw him, and knew. It didn't take a psychic to figure out what Roosevelt had told Gwendolyn.

"I thought she knew." He was desperate.

And she hated him.

"Give him a big kiss," Gwendolyn hissed.

She would talk to Gwendolyn later. "It's not what you think." She would make Gwendolyn understand, but not in front of Roosevelt. They would laugh about this one day.

"Poor Amy," Gwendolyn continued. "It breaks my heart that you can't have an orgasm. Poor you."

Gwendolyn had never looked more beautiful. She still had the oven mitts on her hands, her hair was a mess, her white T-shirt spotted with cake batter. Little sister.

"I'm having dinner with Gus," Amy said. "Alone."

"Him?" Gwendolyn was incredulous.

"Alone?" Roosevelt echoed Gwendolyn's tone.

United. They were teamed against her, against Gus, against the gift Auntie Ned had given her. She wouldn't feel guilty. She would show them she was right.

"Yes, Roosevelt, alone." She bit off the end of each word. "He and I are interested in the same things."

"And we're not?"

"No."

"Just because I don't believe your aunt got overheated and blew up?"

"You don't believe it, do you?"

"No."

"Neither do I," said Gwendolyn. She slammed the oven door shut. "And even if she did, who cares?"

"I care," said Amy. "And Dr. Minor cares. She was just about my favorite person in the whole world and he cares what happened to her and so do I!"

"Why is this so important to you?" Gwendolyn asked.

Amy realized Gwendolyn would never understand, never know that she had Auntie Ned to thank for all her happiness. And Gwendolyn was going to be happy. Ecstatically happy.

"I care," Roosevelt said. "I'm sorry she died."

Amy wanted to throw up. "What do you know?" she seethed. "She was the only person who ever understood me. The only one."

"Amy," Gwendolyn said, "I thought I . . ." She stopped, turned away. "I'm learning a lot tonight."

Amy could hear the pain in Gwendolyn's voice, but she wouldn't stop. "You don't know how I feel," she said, "how it is. The sorrow, the incredible emptiness."

"I do!" Roosevelt shouted. "I do! Did you ever ask me? Did you ever ask me one thing about myself? I lost my mother. Then my wife died."

"How?"

"In a car."

"An accident?" Amy wouldn't look at Gwendolyn's face.

"Yes. Yes."

"What kind of accident?"

"We hit a tree."

"Were you in the car?"

"I was driving."

"You were driving?"

"Yes. Yes. I killed her, okay? I killed my wife."

Gus was standing in the doorway.

"What the fuck do you want?" Roosevelt shouted, and Amy watched him. She saw his arm go out, the way an arm does when it's not connected to a thought, and sweep a forgotten cup of coffee off the counter in Dr. Minor's direction. The cup shattered on the floor. The thick, clotted coffee and milk splashed the doctor's shoes and pants as he jumped back, away, tried to get clear.

"Shit!" the doctor exclaimed.

"Hey," Gwendolyn said, but she was looking at Amy.

Roosevelt pushed the doctor out of the doorway. He pushed too hard. Dr. Minor wasn't big enough for the push and he stumbled backward and fell. Roosevelt didn't stop. He ran out of the kitchen. They heard the front door open and slam shut. Good, Amy thought. Gone.

"Hey," Gwendolyn said again.

"Don't you dare go after him." Amy turned to her sister. "Don't you even think of it."

"That guy is dangerous," Gus said.

"No—" Gwendolyn began.

"Yes," Amy cut her off. She helped Gus to his feet. "Exactly. Let him go. He's doing what he needs to do."

"What do you want from him?" Gwendolyn was begging to know.

"It's not me. I don't want anything." Amy felt her face shrink, her eyes shut down. She turned away from her sister, took a paper towel, and kneeled before Dr. Minor, cleaning his shoes, his pants legs. "Not me," she said, "you. Only you."

Chapter Seventeen

Dr. Minor was excited. His hands shook in front of the motel mirror as he buttoned a clean shirt. His fingers clicked against the laminated dresser as he picked up his change. This was it, he thought, dinner with her. His wife wouldn't mind. It was work. It was a man's job.

There was an open bottle of wine on the kitchen table. A pizza had been delivered. Amy had showered, changed. Her bare feet twisted around the chair legs.

"Extra meat," she said.

"Excuse me?"

"On the pizza."

Sausage. Pepperoni. Meatballs. Anchovies. He would have indigestion later. The lights were off. They ate by candlelight. She radiated. She glowed. She blinded him.

"A definite case," she said, "don't you think?"

No, he didn't, but he said, "Oh, yes."

"I just don't understand." She sighed. "Why her? Why does it happen to anyone?"

She had asked the right question. This was where he was going. It was the beginning.

"Some people," he said, "some people are literally hotter than others."

"Auntie Ned was always freezing. She ran the heat in August."

"No, no. Internally. Some people have a fire that burns inside."

She was interested, he could tell. She moved her chair closer to his. The candlelight made her hair shimmer.

He continued, "Have you ever met someone who is constantly giving off static electricity? Every time you touch them, you get a shock."

"Yes," she said. She actually blushed. He hadn't thought it possible. "I'm like that."

"I know," he said.

He poured her another glass of wine. And another. He told her his latest research, the mysteries of Spontaneous Human Combustion. He told her about the greasy ash he had inspected, the single piece of clean bone he had found. Mrs. Phineas Murphy. He told her about flesh bubbling and puckering, permanent damage, permanent disfigurement. Ms. Carolyn Culpepper. He told her about the Russian investigations with a man who could rub his hands together and set a piece of paper on fire. Mr. Vladimir Dostovick.

"It isn't spontaneous at all, is it?" she asked. Her hand was now on his, her tongue licking her lips.

"No," he said. "For some people, there's nothing spontaneous about it."

She pulled her chair even closer, leaned toward him, and kissed him.

"Where's your sister?" he asked.

"Out," she replied. "We had a fight."

"I was there, remember?" He waited for her to kiss him again. She didn't. "What about?"

"Roosevelt."

"He's a jerk."

"He scares me." She looked sad, on the edge of tears.

Dr. Minor wanted to put a hand on one of her breasts. Just one hand. Just one breast. "I thought you," he said, "and he—you know—when you were out in the living room."

"No." She looked genuinely disgusted. "He gives me the creeps."

She unbuttoned the cuff of his shirt and ran her warm fingers up his arm. He saw it in her eyes. She was capable of anything.

"You can do it," he said.

"I'm not sure what you're talking about." Her hand wouldn't stop. His arm was trembling.

He had a few tricks of his own. He slipped off his shoe, let it plop to the kitchen floor. He ran one socked foot up her leg, the inside of her thigh. She smiled. His little feet had been successful before.

"You can do it," he said again.

"What?" she whispered.

"You have the power." He was whispering too. "You can send that fire. You can make Roosevelt go away."

"Tell me," she said. Her eyes were wide open, staring into his. He saw sparks. He imagined more. Her hand moved to his chest, began undoing more buttons.

"Make him combust."

"I can do that?" He saw her smile. He knew she could.

"Yes."

"He'd blow up in front of me?"

"You could make anyone spontaneously combust."

Gwendolyn looked at her sister with disgust. Amy saw it on her face, the way her hands hid behind her back.

"You'd sleep with anyone," Gwendolyn said. "Anything."

"It was interesting. I was curious."

"There's a big dog down the street." Gwendolyn spat out the words. "You can try him next."

"His dick is normal size."

"Rub a little dog food on your crotch. He'll be interested."

"Shut up." It was all Amy could think to say. She didn't know why she's had sex with Dr. Minor. It seemed the only thing to do.

"Why? Why?" Gwendolyn was close to tears. "Aren't I enough?"

Gwendolyn had come home in time to see Dr. Minor putting on his shoes. She stood in the front door, arms crossed against her chest like always. He had to ask her to let him pass. Amy laughed; that made her laugh. Good for Gwendolyn. She was really angry.

"You don't own me," Amy said. But she did.

Tears sneaked out of Gwendolyn's eyes, tiptoed down her lovely cheeks. "I understand the midget," she said. "I know your fascination with unusual partners. But Roosevelt. Roosevelt. Why him? He's so goddamn ordinary."

Now was the time. Amy could say, He's for you. You want exactly that, the ordinary. I know you do. But she wouldn't.

"Because," was all she would say.

The phone was ringing. Roosevelt was dreaming of midgets and when he woke up he felt like a giant. His feet looked enormous stretched off the end of the futon, his hands skeletal and gargantuan as he reached for the telephone.

He had stopped in for too much to drink in a Latino bar in Amy's neighborhood. It was named the Auto Bar, implying that drinking and driving were not only allowed but preferred. He had knocked back two shot glasses full of tequila before the first beer chaser even appeared. He remembered the burn in his throat, the fading gray light through the circular porthole on the swinging front door, the brown wood-grained plastic bowl of miniature pretzels in front of him. Nothing else. It was quiet. That was why he had gone in. The bar was crowded on this Saturday afternoon, jumping with dark-haired men and soon-to-be-forgotten paychecks, but none of the noise was for him. He could empty his head of every voice, every sound except his own throat swallowing, his hand rubbing on the smoothly padded bar rail, the clean clatter of his glass on the shiny counter.

"Hello?" he said into the phone. What time was it?

He didn't remember getting home. He hadn't wanted to remember.

A woman was crying over the phone. His head felt huge. His bulging and palpitating body took up the entire room. The shots of tequila had been tumblers for normal-size folks, the pretzels, tiny to him, actually the giant ones sold on New York streets and at baseball games.

"Hello?" he said again. "Who is this?"

The crying continued. He hung up.

His lizard. He had forgotten to feed his lizard. He rolled to his hands and knees. Lifted his head first and then his body. He was standing. In his dream the midgets had been shrinking, growing smaller and more appealing. They were fairies, babies, the cutest of their species.

The phone began to ring again.

Amy sat in his only chair, surrounded by his dirty laundry. Her blond hair shimmered in the dark. What he thought was a pair of his dirty coveralls in her hands was the doctor, Dr. Minor, sitting in her lap. He leaned his big head against Amy's warm chest. He glared at Roosevelt from under his prehistoric brow. He held Amy's hand and told Roosevelt to go away, she belonged to him.

Roosevelt shook his head. He knew by the want, the groan in his belly, the anxiety between his legs, that Amy was not here. No one was. It was all his imagination and the phone was ringing and he was not a giant and he didn't have anything a dwarf would want. Nothing.

He picked up the phone. "Hello?"

"Roosevelt." Amy said his name through her tears, her sobs, her coarse breath. "Oh, Roosevelt."

"Amy."

"I'm sorry," she said. "I didn't know about your wife, the accident. I didn't mean to be such a bitch. I'm sorry."

"It's okay," he said. It was the only thing to say, but not the right thing.

"Can I see you?"

"When?"

"I'll come to you," she said.

"No," he said, too many bad dreams lost in his soiled shag carpet. "No."

"I have to see you." She was crying again. He was normal, normal-size, and he could think to answer her.

"I'll come over," he said.

She didn't answer.

"Is that okay?"

"Yes," Amy said. "Hurry."

He wanted to shower, but didn't. He wanted to find clean clothes, but didn't. He left in the dark.

Outside in his truck he remembered he still had not fed his lizard. It was a dry spell in the rain forest, he thought, or wherever the lizard came from. Some days were like that.

Amy put sheets on the bed in the back bedroom where she and Roosevelt had been before. They were old sheets, psychedelic blotches of Lava lamp color, Auntie Ned's sheets.

Gwendolyn was sleeping. They had not made up before bed. Gwendolyn had ended up crying for Roosevelt. "Don't do this to him," she said.

Amy felt shaky, agitated. Sex with a midget was depressing. Dr. Minor had enjoyed himself. She had watched, waited, couldn't stop thinking about what he had told her, about her power. She wanted to know more. She said "Oh, baby" at the appropriate time.

"I don't want Roosevelt here anymore," Gwendolyn had said. It wasn't a question, it wasn't her usual pleading voice. "Fire him. Make him take that new job."

"You like him more than I do."

"I feel sorry for him."

"I know you like him. Really like him."

"Why are you doing this?"

"Because," Amy said again. Because of you. Because of your stupid plebeian fantasies. Because you're already getting antsy, because you're losing your desire for this, for all of this, for me. She said, "We're all going to be very happy. Everyone will be happy."

Amy put her arms around her sister. She felt their two bodies blend, fuse, meld together as always. But not as always. There was something hard in Gwendolyn, brand-new, a place Amy didn't know.

"What's the matter with you?" Amy asked.

"Nothing."

Gwendolyn pushed away, stood back, alone. Amy felt her skin, her very bones reach for her sister.

But Gwendolyn went to bed, passed out. Snored.

Gwendolyn woke up frightened in the dark.

"Amy?" she called softly.

Amy wasn't there. Gwendolyn lay in bed, listening. Where was she? She waited.

Then, Roosevelt's truck pulled up out front. She knew the sound. His door opened and creaked shut. She heard his key in the lock. She heard his light steps up the stairs and Amy whisper, "In here." She heard the door to the other bedroom close behind him. She could even hear his sigh when he saw the bed, the sheets, the prospects before him.

She didn't want to know, but she lay still under her cold blanket, held her breath and stretched her hearing across the hall, through the other door. She was afraid to know, but wanted to hear the squeak of the box springs, the scrape of the bed's wooden legs on the bare floor, the sliding of the worn and faded sheets against a bare back, a hip, a long thigh. She was afraid to know, but wanted to feel the curly bristle under his arm, the scratch of his toenail against her naked ankle, the sigh of his man's breath on her neck.

He left his clothes on the floor. He stood shivering and shriveled next to the bed.

"Lie down," Amy commanded him. "Lie down."

"Where?" he asked.

"On the bed," she said. "Get under the covers if you want."

He wanted to ask, what next? What were they going to do? But he looked at her perfect, sad face and knew that she wanted to give him something. He was willing to take whatever it was, pain or death, demands he couldn't meet. He was willing, beyond willing now, to owe her, to offer up his past, his future to her. He would take whatever it was with open arms.

"I'm sorry," she had said when he walked in.

"I'm sorry," he had replied.

"Do you still love me?" she asked.

"I do."

"More than anyone else?"

"More than anyone ever."

"Not more than your wife," she said.

"More than anyone. Ever."

"If I asked you, would you do something for me?"

"Anything. Anything."

Then she undressed, and he did, standing on opposite sides of the bed, letting gravity take their clothes and their apologies down and away.

She got in bed, pulled the covers up.

"Lie down," she said. "Here, next to me."

He slid in beside her, careful not to touch her, unsure what she wanted.

"Reward Number Three?" he asked.

"I want more," she said. "Let's skip to Six."

"Six," he said. "Six has always been one of my favorite numbers."

The position was awkward, but he could manage, and once managed it was unbelievable that he hadn't always made love like this. She lay on her back, the leg closest to him lifted. He curled around her and entered from underneath. He could see her face, watch her breasts tremble, the nipples pushing upward.

"Nine strokes," she said.

He didn't want to think about it.

"Nine times six," she said.

His carpenter's multiplication was quick. "Fifty-four?" he asked. "I won't make it."

"Nine and then stop. And then nine and then stop."

"Oh."

"Concentrate," she said. "Think of me."

As if he could think of anything else.

"Remember what you're doing," she said. "It's a sacred act. Help me."

She asked for help. She asked him. Then he knew what to do. He reached a hand down between her legs. He could help her.

"Is this all right?" he asked, his hand moving, his fingers caressing, rubbing.

"Yes."

Her breath was coming faster. He saw sweat appear, little drops of salty wet on her upper lip and the bridge of her nose. He counted nine and stopped. Stopped his hand too and felt her tighten and arch toward him. He was helping.

Nine again. Slowly, but his hand moved quicker. She was warm. She was hot. His wrist resting on her flat abdomen felt the heat inside her, felt it increase as her breath got faster and louder. Her eyes closed.

And he stopped. She groaned.

He began again. The fever in her belly was remarkable. He had to lift his hand, the temperature too high; it burned, it was uncomfortable on the tender flesh of his wrist and arm.

But he kept his fingers going. Seven. Eight. It was working. And the more taken away she became, the more present he was. His own orgasm seemed unimportant and unnecessary. Ridiculous even, when he could offer this much pleasure to her.

He stopped again.

"Don't," she said.

He waited.

"Don't," she said again. Louder.

He smiled. He began, slower than before. She was rocking, tilting, unconsciously helping him as he helped her. This was just the beginning, he thought, their future stretched on and on in front of him.

This wasn't supposed to happen. This was exactly wrong. She had to stop. She knew it. Some little part of her knew that this was going too far, but she didn't want to stop. She really didn't want to. Not yet.

And some other little part of her was surprised.

And some other part of her was scared. There was pain in this much wanting; sadness in this purely physical response. A small voice called her an animal, a dog, a bitch in heat.

But she didn't want him to stop.

Then he did. "Thirty-six," he said.

She grabbed his hand, put it back, pressed it to her.

"Eighteen to go," he whispered, "Eighteen more."

"Do it," she said.

He began again. She kept her eyes closed, pushed herself against his hand and his cock, smelling her own wet smell, feeling the sweat under her arms, sliding down her back. She didn't care anymore. Those other little parts of her, the small voices, were quieter, farther away. They were hard to hear, unimportant. She thought of Auntie Ned, but it didn't matter. She thought of Tony and Elsa and the bakery, but it didn't matter. She thought of Gwendolyn, then didn't. She thought of Roosevelt and keeping him in the palm of her hand, but it was his hand she cared about. His hand that was important.

Gwendolyn heard Amy. She heard her groan, moan, a terrible wail, and then the sobs begin. What had he done to her, Gwendolyn thought. Whatever it was, she would kill him. She would fly across the hall and kill him.

But she didn't move. She knew. She knew what he had done, what had happened to Amy. She knew, personally, the sadness that sometimes enfolded Amy after she had given herself away, given up, surrendered so completely.

Gwendolyn curled into a fetal ball in her bed. The door to the other bedroom opened and Amy's weeping was momentarily louder. The door closed. She heard Roosevelt's footsteps into the bathroom and the water running. He would get a cool washcloth for Amy's face, a drink of water for her, the tissue box. That's the kind of guy he was. If she got up and walked out of her room now, would she see him naked? Would she see the freckles on his back and shoulders, the fine red hairs on his thighs, whatever it was that had made her sister cry?

Roosevelt must be some kind of guy, Gwendolyn thought. No one makes Amy cry. Gwendolyn wondered what he had done. How he had done it. Her sister. He probably thought he had given her her very first orgasm.

Gwendolyn listened to her sister's sobs getting softer. Roosevelt left the bathroom. The bedroom door opened and closed again. The sobs stopped altogether. He was holding her, his arms around her, his face against her hair. Gwendolyn knew what a man's arms felt like, the hard muscle under smooth skin, the attractive, dangerous strength. It had been a long time, but she remembered how it felt to lay her cheek against a broad chest, to fit just under a sandpaper chin, to forget about her sister, her aunt, anything but the movie she and this guy would go to, the dinner they would have, if he liked her, if he called again. Roosevelt held Amy, and Gwendolyn felt it. She felt him smooth back her hair, smelled his male scent, heard the catch in his voice as he whispered. Amy wasn't there, Gwendolyn knew; her brain was already clicking and whirring, explaining away this unexpected event. But Gwendolyn was. She was there, with him, happy to have him. She was ready to forget the whole thing.

Roosevelt looked at the red mark on the skin below her belly button, just above the dark blond curling hair. A round, irritated, angry-looking circle, blotchy on the outer ring, bright in the center. Already beginning to blister.

"Does this hurt?" he asked, and touched it gently with his fingertips and then his lips.

She wasn't crying anymore, but she wouldn't look at him.

"You were so hot—down there." He meant it literally, but she could take it any way at all.

He felt good. He felt incredible. He felt as satiated as if he had erupted with a thousand orgasms. He had done it. He had watched her, shifted himself up onto one elbow as his other hand worked so he could stare at her face. Her eyes closed. Her nostrils opened. Her teeth bit down so hard on her bottom lip that they drew blood. And afterward, when her face crumpled into tears, he kissed the blood away. He thought it was joy she was feeling. He knew it was ecstasy that he felt.

Chapter Eighteen

Dr. Minor was in his underpants. Child size 6–8. In his underpants, down on all fours in his cheap motel room. The stain-resistant royal-blue carpet was rough under his hands and his bare knees. He pressed his forehead to the floor, smelled the industrial-strength cleaner. He prayed.

"Dearest Universal Being, most honored Soul of Souls, make it happen."

A semi truck blasted its deep horn far away. Dr. Minor took it as a sign, got off his knees, climbed onto the bed. It was all too good to be true.

"I'll be staying a few extra days," he told his wife on the phone. He could hear their baby crying.

"How long?" she asked.

"As long as it takes." He wasn't putting up with anything from her. "I'll be back when I'm done."

Now she was crying too. "I'm tired," she said. "He's not sleeping."

He remembered his tall beautiful wife, the way she smiled at him, the way she laughed and circulated at faculty parties. "I'm close," he said to her. "I'm on the brink. Our future will be made."

"I'm glad for you, honey," she said, "I miss you. I love you."

He felt good, he felt ten feet tall.

He unpacked his video camera. He cleaned the lens. He plugged the battery charger into the socket by the sink. He looked at himself in the mirror. He had done it.

"He won't go away," he had told Amy. They were lying naked on her ugly green couch. She had the rosy glow of recent satisfaction. His doing. She had screamed "Oh, baby" at the exact right moment. Simultaneous orgasm was highly unusual, even with his wife.

"He'll hang around and hang around. You need to get rid of him."

"I thought he was harmless," Amy had replied. She wasn't looking at him. She stared at the ceiling. He could feel her sorrow.

"He's waiting to make his move. Rape." The doctor shuddered for effect. "Or worse."

"I have to be sure," she said.

"I'll help you. I'll wait until you call me." And he would. As long as it took. Now that Amy knew she had the power, he knew she would want to use it.

"Thank you," he said to his reflection in the motel mirror and gave a slight nod. "And I want to thank my family, my colleagues and coworkers, and, of course, Amy. Amy Clark, the Queen of Spontaneous Human Combustion. I share this Nobel prize with her." He laughed. "Amy, I hope you're watching this, in jail."

A voice woke Amy.

"Amy."

"What?" She turned to him.

"I didn't say anything," Roosevelt answered, thick and cottony with sleep. He was settled next to her on the unfamiliar bed, not touching her, but by her side, large, solid. She should tell him to go, go home, but she was so tired.

"Amy."

She tried to get up, get out of bed. Her arms were weighted, pinned down, a wrestler's hairless knees on her chest, his dry smell in her throat.

"What are you doing?"

Auntie Ned hissed at her. Amy couldn't move. Her feet had folded into the mattress, disappeared under the sheet. The wrestler shifted his weight, pressed on her stomach, her hips.

"What," Auntie Ned insisted, "are you doing?"

Amy began to cry.

"Crybaby."

"What's the matter?" Roosevelt asked, struggled to his elbow. His face was tender in the gloom. "Hey. What's up?"

"Gwendolyn," she called. "Wendy."

Amy was thirteen when Auntie Ned bought the little house. Amy and eleven-year-old Gwendolyn helped her move in, put the books on the shelves, line the drawers with clean polka-dot shelf paper.

Auntie Ned let them each write a message on a snip of paper and tape it wherever they wanted. Gwendolyn's was THO' YOU MAY ROAM, THERE'S NO PLACE LIKE HOME. Amy wrote, GET IT WHILE YOU CAN.

That night, they ate pizza and drank root beer floats. Auntie Ned invited Helen, but she wouldn't come. She never came.

"There's a boy in my school. I like him." Amy thought Auntie Ned would be pleased with her confession. Her mother was, wanted to buy her a new outfit, new shoes. With Auntie Ned she could tell all of the truth. "He kissed me by the basketball court. We touched tongues. He put a hand on my boob."

"What?" Auntie Ned roared, leaped to her feet, knocked over her chair, surprising Amy, startling Gwendolyn.

"His name is Will, Willy Andrews." Amy stood her ground.

"What do you think you're doing?"

"He's older. He's cute."

"Fuck him!" Auntie Ned screamed.

"I might," Amy said. She knew what it meant. Auntie Ned had explained it, but hadn't said how good it felt. How great it was to kiss a boy.

Auntie Ned slapped her. Caught her hard on the right cheek, part of her ear. Amy yelped, but didn't cry.

"Amy!" Gwendolyn began to cry.

"Look what you've done!" Amy shouted at Auntie Ned.

They faced each other, panting, squared-off lightweights in separate corners. Auntie Ned's long auburn hair, streaked with gray, had fallen out of its twist, down her shoulders, around her face. Her shirt had come unbuttoned. Amy could see one dark nipple. Amy's own little breasts in their brand-new bra strained against her blouse.

"You made her cry," Auntie Ned said and turned to Gwendolyn. "Come here. It's okay, come here."

Gwendolyn sat in her chair, afraid to move. But Amy, still a child, only thirteen, took a step toward Auntie Ned's outstretched arms, her forgiveness. Auntie Ned pulled her in, closer and closer, leaned over, and kissed her on the mouth. Softly, but urgently. Amy closed her eyes and compared. This was better.

"See, Gwendolyn?" Auntie Ned asked. "This is how it should be. This is the right way. You two need to practice."

Chapter Nineteen

"Pretty damn good, huh?" Gwendolyn asked.

"What are you talking about?" Amy pretended she didn't know.

"He made you cry."

"You were listening?"

"You were screaming."

"I was not."

Gwendolyn looked at her with loathing, actual hatred. Suddenly, the burn on Amy's stomach twitched, scratched against her pants painfully.

"Made me miss having a man," Gwendolyn said. "There's nothing like it, is there?"

"Remind me to buy you a dildo for your birthday."

"No, thanks. I can go out and get one of my own."

Amy felt her face flush, her hands tremble. "Better be the kind you put batteries in."

"I want to be just like you."

Gwendolyn walked out. Amy's hands were shaking so badly she couldn't pour her coffee. She needed meat; she was craving a rare hamburger, spicy sausage, thick slabs of pink cow's flesh. She followed her sister.

"Wendy?" she called up the stairs.

"I have to go to work."

"Today? Sunday?"

"I don't want to be here when he comes back."

"Wendy, please." Amy ran up the stairs, two at a time, the way Auntie Ned always took stairs. She opened the bathroom door and found Gwendolyn standing naked at the sink. For her benefit, she knew, to make her crazy.

"I did it for you." Amy's voice trembled like her hands.

"Uh-huh," Gwendolyn said. "You were moaning for me, right? Crying for me."

"It's all for you. He's . . . I mean, I want us to be . . . I just got carried away."

"I'd like to be carried away. By a man."

"Hey." There was a twist, a sharp blow to her chest. "Hey. Listen to me."

But it was action Gwendolyn wanted. Amy thought her arms might come loose, fall off her body, she was shaking so hard. But this was Gwendolyn. Amy kissed her sister's bare shoulder, licked, nibbled, scraped gently with her teeth.

"And I guess this morning you stood out in front of the house smooching for twenty minutes, for me," Gwendolyn said, concentrating on her own face in the mirror, not looking at her sister. Then she pushed past her and went to get dressed.

Amy was left standing alone in the bathroom. Gwendolyn had to understand. It had been a purely physical response. The same would happen with her own hand, or a piece of equipment. It was a mistake, but it was just part of her plan for Gwendolyn's perfect future. She wanted to explain, but Wendy wouldn't listen.

Last night, Amy had wanted to see Roosevelt, but only to test what Dr. Minor had told her. First, she would get him aroused, frustrated, his own body temperature raised. She would practice concentrating. A little spark. Nothing major. It was just a test. It wasn't supposed to end like it did. He was supposed to burn. Not her.

Auntie Ned knew Gwendolyn needed a man, a boyfriend,

someone to mow the lawn. Auntie Ned should understand that Amy was providing one for her, for them. It was what she had intended from the beginning. He was perfect.

"Shut up," Amy told her aunt out loud. "I'm doing it."

Gwendolyn was beginning to fall for Roosevelt. But as she fell for him, she dropped further away from her.

"Wendy!" she called, and ran into the bedroom.

Gwendolyn was pulling on her white clothes, the baker's uniform.

"Be home by three o'clock," Amy said.

"Why?"

"I have a present for you."

"What?" Gwendolyn asked.

"You'll have to wait and see." Amy reached for her sister.

"I have to go." Gwendolyn stepped out of reach.

Amy's hands closed on emptiness. Where are you? Amy wanted to ask. Come back. She heard Gwendolyn's light steps running down the stairs, hurrying away from her.

"Wait," she called, but Gwendolyn was gone.

Roosevelt drove home with the windows rolled up tight and his fingers to his nose, sucking in the scent of her.

The sweet smell of success, he thought, and laughed out loud.

He had done it. He had given her something no one else could. She had sobbed in his arms and then smiled at him. She told him she had never felt that way before. Neither had he. She had exploded beneath him, because of him. She had gone up in fireworks, in a burst of happy flame. He knew the meaning of combustion. The burn on her skin didn't surprise him. He had put it there. And he had felt her pleasure as strongly as she did. It was more important than his own. He felt energized, complete. He would wait a couple of days, she would experience a couple more episodes like last night, and then he would ask her to marry him. He wanted her to be his wife. Gwendolyn could live with them. He would redo Auntie Ned's house the way it should be done. It would be pretty and calm, cream-colored like his mother's house. They would have dinner parties. Stan would come for dinner.

He hopped over the broken lawn chair in his front yard, nodded hello to his fat landlady pulling up whatever looked green from the sagging window boxes. He took the stairs to his apartment two at a time, stretching his legs, feeling capable of anything.

"Susie-Larry-Loretta, I'm home," he called to his lizard. "Are you hungry?"

He walked into his kitchen corner and stopped. A black undulating ribbon squirmed across his kitchen counter. It started in the crack behind the sink, continued down the cabinet front and up the little bookshelf to the lizard's home. At first he didn't know what it was. Then he saw: ants were covering his lizard. It looked like the lizard's skin was black and bubbling, giving birth to some alien life force.

He took a clean cereal bowl from the cupboard and lifted the lizard into it. The lizard was alive; its legs beat the air. The ants swarmed up his arm and it was hard not to drop the bowl and the lizard and shake the ants away. He hurried to the sink and ran water over the lizard's back. The ants washed down the drain. He saw their legs moving frantically, trying to get a grip on liquid nothing. He knew they wouldn't drown; they'd be back, crawling up his drainpipe. The lizard didn't move. The water didn't seem to bother it. The ants on its face were the hardest to get rid of. He took a corner of a paper towel, wet it, and brushed them off, out of the lizard's flat black eyes that didn't close or look away.

Roosevelt could see the lizard's heart beating. The palpitation in its chest was rhythmic, speedy. How easy it would be to put his finger on that spot and stop it. Why kill the ants and save the lizard? One was as foreign to him as the other.

He put his colander upside down over the cereal bowl and cleaned the clear plastic cage with hot, soapy water. He threw away the cedar chips, washed the rock and the plastic leaves. He sprayed insecticide along his counter and into the black slit in the wall above the sink. He sprayed long and hard. He was vicious and thorough. The lizard turned its head once in the cereal bowl.

Roosevelt was angry, sad, disappointed that this had happened to spoil his good feeling. He hated being disappointed. Anger was active, sadness understandable, but disappointment was only useless regret. There was nothing anyone could do to make his disappointment right.

He put the lizard back in its clean cage. He figured his lizard must be really hungry now, after its ordeal. He took the wax paper off the old margarine tub that housed the crickets. They were all dead. They lay on their sides and backs, on top of one another. Their wispy legs stuck in the air like the last few hairs on an old man's spotted scalp. There weren't any ants in there, but the crickets were dead anyway, all on their own, from disease, from hunger, from fear. He didn't know if the lizard ate dead crickets, but he had nothing else to offer. He spooned one into the Plexiglas box. The lizard stayed where he had put it on the clear, smooth plastic floor, the shiny imitation leaves drooping over its head. The cricket fell next to it. It made a little click as it hit the bottom. The lizard didn't move.

Roosevelt took a shower. He changed his clothes, put on his workman's coveralls. There were other things he could do for Amy. Anything, he had told her. He would do anything. He was going to the bakery. He knew Amy hated Gwendolyn's partner, Tony. He knew she was worried that he wouldn't treat Gwendolyn properly, with respect. He thought of Gwendolyn and felt a guilty twitch between his shoulder blades. It was Amy he loved. Gwendolyn was sweet, simple. He could take care of her. That would make Amy proud of him. He would say something to Tony. He would give Tony some shit, scare him, tell him to lay off. That wouldn't be bad. He could do that. He would be glad to tell Amy what he had done.

Gwendolyn wanted to find a man and get even, get laid. She wanted it so badly she practically hollered out her car window at a sixteen-year-old walking past. Even the idea of his skinny little dick sounded good, sounded filling, sounded unbelievably satisfying.

She could find one. She had never picked a man up in a bar or at a party, but she could. She would. She caught a glimpse of a flannel shirt, red hair. Roosevelt. Her hands tightened on the wheel. But it was just a guy, a different guy.

Roosevelt. She knew what to do to get back at Amy. She would tell Roosevelt. Tell him about her and Amy, their strange, sick relationship.

She would tell him.

But then she realized it wouldn't matter. Roosevelt wouldn't care. It would just be another way he could save Amy. Swept up by her, her smell, her touch, her soft lips, the intensity of that love, he would believe anything and not care. Incest was nothing. Men killed themselves for Amy. There was that something in her, always had been, something dangerous and seductive. It made you want to offer your neck to her, beg her to suck your blood, take your life.

Gwendolyn was glad to see Tony's car in his parking spot.

"Tony?" she called as she came in the back door. "Tony?"

"In here, Gwen, in the office."

He wasn't usually here on Sunday. Neither was she. She stood in the doorway. He sat in his desk chair. He was handsome, nothing but man, simple man. She could feel her heart trying to jump out of her chest, run away. Thumpity, thump. A rabbit's hind feet kicking to get free.

"What are you doing here?" he asked.

He smiled. She shrugged, smiled back.

"Want to come over for dinner?" She would bring him home. She would shove him in Amy's face.

"Tonight?"

"Now," she said.

He stood up. He had what she wanted. He came to her, put his arms around her.

"I knew you'd come back," he said.

They kissed. He was a lousy kisser. His hands squeezed her ass. She sighed, but maybe this would quench the odd, foaming thirst in her stomach. She kissed his neck. Too much cologne.

"We're good together," Tony said. "We're meant for each other. It's fate."

Maybe so, Gwendolyn thought, maybe not. Amy knew about fate and future. Gwendolyn didn't care. He was moving so fast, his hands up her shirt, down her pants. Sleeping with Tony would be fucking a dead man, masturbating to a long-gone memory.

The back door opened. Gwendolyn pushed herself away.

"Hello?" It was Elsa's voice.

"Dammit," Tony said.

Thank God, Gwendolyn thought.

Tony sat down in his chair. Gwendolyn turned to the door. Elsa walked into the room. Elsa, the Olympian. What was she doing here on Sunday? She looked fresh and sporty, her strong skier's legs bare in shorts, her arms muscled like a man's. Gwendolyn felt the bubbles in her belly churning faster. There was a tightening, a squeeze.

"Hi," Elsa said, smiling at Gwendolyn, showing her crooked teeth. "I am very glad to see you."

Not as glad as Gwendolyn was to see her.

"I called Elsa in for a second interview," Tony said.

"Yeah, right." Gwendolyn couldn't help herself.

Elsa laughed, rolled her eyes.

"As far as I'm concerned, she's got the job." Tony was embarrassed. "I just wanted to make sure she had a green card, work visa, you know, whatever."

Elsa took Gwendolyn's arm. "Do you want me to work here?" she asked. "I think it is your decision."

Gwendolyn's mouth was dry. She looked down at Elsa's athletic feet in surfer sandals. Her toenails were sky blue. Ridiculous. Beautiful.

"Yes," Gwendolyn said. "We need you."

"Good." Tony nodded. "That's done."

It was. Gwendolyn left with Elsa.

"So," Elsa said in the parking lot, "I know you will tell me about him. About Tony. Is he a womanizer, or what? A big talker, yes, but is that all?"

Gwendolyn smiled back at Elsa and her charming accent. The fluster in her stomach subsided. "You want the truth?"

"Always."

"He'll be all over you," Gwendolyn paused, "like white on rice."

Elsa laughed.

Gwendolyn did too. "But the clients love him."

"I have heard this place is the best."

Gwendolyn nodded reluctantly. "I couldn't do it without him." It was true.

"White on rice." Elsa laughed again. Even her laugh made Gwendolyn think of clear water and sunlight.

"He likes being your partner," Elsa said.

"You could do my job."

"He likes you. I think he likes you a lot."

Elsa leaned against her shiny blue car. Her green eyes stared into Gwendolyn's, asking something, wanting something.

"What?" Gwendolyn was suddenly afraid. Elsa seemed to look and know.

"On the phone, he said you want to go away with your lover. Your boyfriend."

"No."

"A woman, then," Elsa said, not surprised.

Gwendolyn blushed, giving herself, giving too much away.

Elsa nodded, shrugged. "I used to swing both ways."

Gwendolyn was on the swing. Amy was pushing. Amy in control of how high, how far, how dangerous it was for both of them.

"But now I want to be normal." Elsa lifted her hands, palms up. "I want children. I want a man. I want to watch my daughter be a bunny rabbit in the school play and hold hands with my husband."

Gwendolyn turned away. She knew the picture. She had seen it in her own mind many times and pushed it out. Not for her, she told herself. Absurd.

She thought of Amy. She tried to remember her face, but could only see parts of it. The corner of Amy's eye wet and red, the dent of one nostril, the fine lines in her upper lip. She could feel Amy's large hands on her back, but she couldn't picture them, couldn't picture the body she knew as well as her own.

"I tried to bake a cake at home," Gwendolyn said. "I haven't done that in a long, long time. I used to love to bake so much, even on my days off. I threw the cake at her. At her. I threw it. There was cake all over the floor."

Elsa nodded. Elsa understood. Elsa, who would one day sit in a putty-colored folding chair and watch her daughter perform in the school play.

Roosevelt had time. He wasn't supposed to be back at Amy's until three o'clock. He decided to swing by the dog pound on his way across town to the Fantasy Bakery of Beverly Hills. The pound was closed, but he knew how to get in from the back edge of the parking lot and visit the outside dogs. He felt that somehow he needed to atone for the ants all over his lizard, for the dead crickets. All he could do to make amends was a visit to the pound, to the poor pups who were caged and desperate for a friendly word, a chance to bark, to jump, to lick fingers through the chain-link fence.

He parked in the empty lot. He walked around the building along the far side. He scaled the six-foot wall separating dog cages from parking lot, his work boots rasping against the rough cinder-block-and-stucco construction. He stood and got his balance, then he walked along the top of the wall like a child, hands out, one foot in front of the other, pretending either side was hot lava, a pool of piranhas, a thousand-foot fall to hell.

He smelled the dogs before he saw them. Even in the cool January air, the scent of pee and excrement was riveting. No one worked on Sundays. No one hosed down the cages. A dog with a bad stomach was shit out of luck, literally, forced to live in it until Monday.

He hopped down to the other side. There was a sudden chaos of barking, an explosion of interest in him.

"Shhhh, shhh, shh," he said.

There were beagles in the first cage, their barks more like howls than woofs. There were two of them, one old, one young. They had obviously come in together. He walked between the cages. Most of the dogs ran to their fences, pawed at the gates, begged for release. He stopped at each one, said something nice in his softest, most soothing voice.

"Good boy. What a good boy."

"Aren't you pretty?"

"Poor old thing. Not much longer now."

They calmed down as he walked along. They wiggled their tails, thumped them against the plastic water drums in the corners, yawned wide and stretched before getting up to greet him. Only the beagles barked when he left, their hollow wailing following him down the side wall to the puppy cages. He was good with animals. It wasn't his fault about the ants.

He saved the puppies for last. They were the hardest to see and leave, but they were the most likely to be saved. There were two whole litters, blobs of brown and black piled on top of each other. A white pair with their eyes still closed in with their mother, drooping tits, mournful face. In one of the puppy cages a black and white pit bull strutted at the gate. Roosevelt bent to pet him and he snapped at the offered finger. Two other, smaller puppies cowered in the back corner behind the water dish. The pit bull ran the joint. He was arrogant, privileged by his mean disposition.

Roosevelt walked away, other puppies wagging their tails, looking to play. He heard a high-pitched scream and then a rhythmic slapping. He ran back to the pit bull's cage. The pit bull had one of the smaller puppies by the neck. He shook his head and slammed the little one against the cement wall of the cage again and again. Slap. Slap. The sound of meat. The sound of death. Roosevelt shouted at the dog, kicked the bars of the cage with his foot.

"Stop! Stop!"

The pit bull was merciless. Roosevelt looked for something to throw, a stick, a food dish, a broom he could poke through the bars. There was nothing. Nothing. He shouted at the dog until he was hoarse.

The pit bull killed the fluffy puppy and stopped. It dropped the lifeless body and trotted away, to the other side of the cage. It sat down, facing Roosevelt, and panted up at him. Look what I did. What a good boy am I. Roosevelt had never wanted to kill a dog before.

His hands banged nervously on the steering wheel as he headed west. He could get to the bakery, do his business, and back to Amy before the required time. Do his business. His hands beat faster. He shifted lanes, scowled at the drivers on either side of him. Get out of my way. Tony was a pig. An asshole. He was hurting Gwendolyn, scaring her. Amy would be so proud of him. Roosevelt sat up straighter in his car. His wife, Julie, had taken care of every conflict. She fought with bank tellers and salesgirls, made the returns, demanded restitution. Before that, his mother had always shrugged and let it all go. Roosevelt had shrugged with her. But he wasn't going to do that anymore.

Gwendolyn was laughing with Elsa. They were having coffee and croissants at a little shop. Elsa was playing with her roll, pulling the layers apart, bitching about how badly Americans made bread. Gwendolyn missed the company of women. Amy never had friends. Gwendolyn loved women. She was most comfortable in a group of females, at a dress shop, even in a swimming pool locker room.

Amy didn't feel like a woman. She said so herself, complained to Gwendolyn that she was an alien. There were mysteries, Amy said, about women and womanhood that she felt excluded from and unwelcome to know. She would never be let in on the secret, the special handshake. Even Gwendolyn didn't want to tell her, she said.

"What?" Elsa said. "You look sad suddenly."

"My life is a mess."

"Your girlfriend will make up with you."

"I want—" Gwendolyn began, and stopped.

"What do you want?"

"My sister says I want to be like everyone else."

"Is that what you want? To be like everyone else?"

Gwendolyn shook her head. "No. I don't know. I want my sister to be happy."

"Wish I had a sister like you."

Gwendolyn stood up. "I have to go."

"You feel guilty you are here with me."

"No. This was great."

But Gwendolyn was feeling guilty. Not because of Elsa, but because of her own thoughts. They had left a sour, dull feeling in her caffeine-ridden stomach. Amy. Amy. Amy. Gwendolyn didn't want to be with Elsa anymore. She didn't want to hear Elsa's voice of reason and reality. She didn't care if Elsa would or would not get married and have bushels of babies and live in a split-level house. That was Elsa's life, not hers. She loved her sister, more than anything. The accident had really shaken her up, but she was over that now. She would tell Amy. Amy would understand. Everything could go back to normal.

She looked at her watch. She would make it home by three, just in time for the present Amy wanted to give her.

Roosevelt pulled into the bakery lot and parked. He took a deep breath. He saw Tony's new Jaguar, gray like a shark, glossy, expensive. It made him hate him.

He put his keys in his pocket and walked in the back door. The employee door.

"Gwendolyn? Elsa?"

It was Tony's voice, obviously. There was something smug in it, something rich and oily. Tony came out of his office, a smile on his face.

"Couldn't stay away—" he began, and stopped when he saw Roosevelt. "What do you want?"

"Leave her alone," Roosevelt said. He wanted to start with that line, but his voice was barely audible. The words crawled from his mouth, slid down his chin. He hadn't expected Tony's smile, his jeans and sneakers. "Leave her alone," he said again, louder this time, just the way he had practiced on the ride over. "I mean it."

"Leave who alone?" Tony asked.

"You know who."

"You must be Gwendolyn's new boyfriend," Tony said. "Too bad. Have you talked to her today?"

"I'm here to tell you to lay off. Leave her alone."

"I heard you."

"Don't bother her anymore."

"She was just in here with me, all over me. We were almost on the floor. Sorry to break it to you, buddy."

"Amy said—"

"Her sister?"

"Amy told me what you did. She told me about you."

"You listen to her?"

"Don't touch her."

"Amy's a psycho."

"Shut up."

"She's a fucking nutcase dyke."

Roosevelt hit him. He did it. He punched him in the face, once, hard as he could. Sucker-punched him, he guessed. Tony sure didn't see it coming. It felt good, the hard smack of bone and flesh against his knuckles, the jab in his shoulder and his neck from the speed of his arm and the force of the contact. Tony went down, not unconscious, but seeing stars. Roosevelt could see them himself, circling Tony's head.

Okay, he thought, okay. That's that.

Chapter Twenty

Amy had curled up on the couch in Auntie Ned's ugly sweater. She was reading the Sunday funnies when Gwendolyn walked in at six minutes to three. Gwendolyn sat down on the couch beside her. Amy could smell coffee on her breath. There were no streaks or smears, remnants of brightly colored frosting on her pants or shirt. She had not been to work. Amy would deal with that later.

"I missed you," she said.

"I missed you too," Gwendolyn said, but didn't look at her. "I should have told you. Something happened. That rainy day."

Amy didn't have time to talk to Gwendolyn. She didn't have time to listen to Gwendolyn's apologies and explanations. She had to make her shut up and be quiet. Soon it would be done. Gwendolyn wouldn't remember when life had been any other way. Gwendolyn would have her cake and eat it too.

She looked at the clock. Three minutes before three. Roosevelt should be walking in that door.

She kissed her sister's neck. She took the lobe of her ear in her teeth and tugged gently. She saw the color bloom rosy-red on Gwendolyn's cheeks. She knew the effect her lips had on her flesh. It was the one thing she could count on, the one place she knew she could always go.

Gwendolyn opened her eyes, looked at Amy. Amy could see the worry, but also the love, the adoration, the need. Amy kissed her. She let her tongue lap and caress her sister's soft mouth. She still held the comics in her hand. She let them fall and put that hand on Gwendolyn's breast. The nipple stiffened under her palm. Her twisted position on the couch rubbed her pants against the burn on her abdomen. It hurt, but it reminded her of what it was for. Pain was not always the wrong thing.

One minute until three.

She squeezed Gwendolyn's nipple until Gwendolyn moaned. She leaned down and put her mouth where her hand had been, over the soft cotton T-shirt, the nylon bra beneath, sucking, taking.

The front door opened. Roosevelt stumbled in. His face was red, his hair in all directions. He had done something. Amy knew it in the instant she looked up at him. In the instant he realized she was doing something too.

"Come here, Roosevelt," she said.

He didn't move. He looked perplexed, confused, ten years old.

Amy glanced once at her sister. Gwendolyn's eyes were shut tight. There was a gray circle on her T-shirt from Amy's mouth.

"Roosevelt," Amy said again, "come here."

He walked over to the couch. She pulled him down beside her. Now she was in the middle.

"Roosevelt?" She said it softly, then, "Wendy?"

It was as if she was introducing them for the very first time.

Roosevelt burst through the door, anxious to tell Amy what he had done. His knuckles were smarting just like in a detective novel. He had driven so fast over to her house, swerving through traffic, pretending his old panel truck was that snotty Jaguar, daring a cop to stop him. He had exploded into her house, a yell on his lips.

Burst through the door. And stopped. What was going on? What was Amy doing? If it hadn't been for the look on Gwendolyn's face, the ecstasy, the pink in her cheeks, he could have thought it was medicinal, therapeutic, something women did for each other. Maybe. Maybe he would have thought that.

And then Amy looked at him, and he knew.

"Come here," she said to him.

He felt like an idiot. The idiot she had always thought he was. He was. He had never seen it, never even suspected it. When they were sleeping on the couch. The empty closet in the back bedroom. But he was confused. What about last night? What about the heat between them, the furnace he had felt, stoked with his own hand?

"Roosevelt, come here."

He walked over to the couch, but slowly, with reluctance. He wanted his mother. He had loved her so much. Her strength, her humor, the way her red hair had turned slowly silver.

Amy pulled him down onto the couch next to her. He stared past her, couldn't take his eyes from the wet ring circling Gwendolyn's breast. Her eyes were closed.

"Roosevelt?" Amy was offering him something. "Wendy?"

They were sisters. Sisters.

Roosevelt forced himself to look up into Gwendolyn's face. Gwendolyn's starry eyes opened, filled with tears. He could see the drops glitter on her long lashes. It was Amy. Amy had done this to them both. Gwendolyn had tried to tell him so that day on the stairs. Was that only yesterday? Poor you, she had said, poor me. He felt so sad for Gwendolyn.

Gwendolyn had known this would happen. One day, somewhere, someone would know. Strangers had sometimes suspected them of being lesbians, at restaurants, at bars. But she never minded. They weren't lesbians. They just weren't. It was like pretending. Like talking in a British accent when she was a teenager.

No one who knew they were sisters knew, had ever known. And that meant there wasn't anything to know. It was private. It was none of their business. It was nothing.

But now this.

"Roosevelt?" Amy said. "Wendy?"

Gwendolyn kept her eyes closed, the tears inside.

It was too bad it was Roosevelt. She was beginning to like him. She opened her eyes and looked at his face. He stared at the mark of Amy's mouth on her T-shirt. She saw his grief, a twisted suffering and the pain of self-loathing.

He wasn't stupid. She wanted to tell him that. It wasn't his fault. How could he know? Who would suspect?

She watched his eyes travel slowly up from her wet breast, along her collarbone, her neck, her chin, her lips, her nose, until they were staring into her own eyes.

And she saw, remarkably, he was worried for her. He was sad, but not only for himself, for her.

"Roosevelt," she said.

Amy was, for once, silent.

"Gwendolyn," he said.

He leaned past Amy as if she wasn't there. Gwendolyn leaned to him and they kissed. She could not believe she was doing it, but she was. She was kissing him and it was all at once great. Amy had to move back to get out of their way.

Well. If they thought this would upset her, they were wrong. This was perfect, Amy thought, this was just what she wanted. It was.

She saw him sneaking a look at her as he kissed Gwendolyn, trying to figure out what she was feeling. She was not angry, not in the least. The heat she felt came from this bulky sweater, the warm winter sun. She put her hand on his thigh.

He would do it. He would be here for Gwendolyn, and for her.

This was the weirdest thing he had ever done. But he didn't want to stop. Damn, she was a good kisser. Better than Amy, better than her sister. Sisters. He peeked. Amy caught him looking. She didn't look upset. She raised her eyebrows, smiled a little. Sisters.

He felt a hand on his thigh. Gwendolyn's? He concentrated on this terrific kiss. Tongue and teeth, wet, warm, he felt like he was falling into Gwendolyn's mouth.

The hand on his thigh stroked him, moved toward his crotch. He recognized the touch. Amy.

"Whoa," he said and pulled away from them both. "Whoa."

Gwendolyn had always thought that kissing was the most important part of lovemaking, and usually the best part. She searched for a man who could kiss her until she forgot. She wanted him to kiss her until she came. There had been only one of those, long ago, who could make her come just by kissing her. One man and Amy. It always worked with Amy.

But this was a great kiss. One of the all-time great kisses. His tongue was not too gentle. He tasted good, fresh, a little like toothpaste. She felt this kiss down her spine, between her legs. Given time, this kiss might do it. Maybe it was the added presence of Amy, Amy watching and not disapproving. Amy had him first; how could she be jealous? It would be the best of all, Gwendolyn realized, to have a man and her sister.

She put her hand on Amy's back to include her, slid it under the oversized sweater, the little undershirt, ran it up and down her sister's smooth skin.

"Whoa." Roosevelt sat back too abruptly. "Whoa."

Amy knew from her sister's face that it was a good kiss. She knew how Gwendolyn felt about kissing. She liked kissing Roosevelt too. It was surprising, for a simple midwestern boy, what a good kisser he was. Someone had taught him well. She put her hand on Roosevelt's leg to show him she wasn't angry. Then Gwendolyn touched her, under her sweater and shirt, warm hand against her warmer skin. Amy moved her own hand up, higher on Roosevelt's thigh, brushed across his hardening penis, in a way that had worked on him before. She wanted to see what would happen next.

"Whoa," he said, and stopped everything. "Whoa."

He looked at her.

"I didn't want to be left out," she said.

"I don't understand this."

He stood up. She pulled him back down. Then she turned and kissed her sister. Focusing on just this. Putting everything into this kiss.

She looked through her lashes at Roosevelt. He was watching. It was working. Gwendolyn and Roosevelt were both squirming in their pants.

The burn on her stomach was hurting. She wanted to be naked.

She left her sister's lovely mouth and stood up. Gwendolyn looked feverish, confused, drunk with lust. Roosevelt just looked bewildered. He stared from one to the other and back to Amy.

As usual, it was up to her. She had to make the decisions. She always had to make it happen. Suddenly her knees felt weak, her thighs trembled. She ached for a lap to lay her head in, Auntie Ned's cool hands on her cheeks, on the back of her neck.

"Amy."

The whisper. Auntie Ned was there. She was there and she would be as long as Amy did her part. Amy looked down at Gwendolyn. She saw her sister's face glowing with a terrible desire that only she could satisfy. Too much, she thought. Roosevelt looked the same. They were two little white faces looking up at her from the couch, two baby birds, beaks open wide, screaming Feed us! Feed us or we die.

She didn't want to. Maybe it just wasn't worth it.

"Amy." The pressing whisper, reminding her.

Auntie Ned shared this sweater with her, the car, the furniture, the walls of the house, stripped or painted, whatever she might do to them. Auntie Ned wanted her to succeed. Auntie Ned loved her.

Amy took Gwendolyn's hand and Roosevelt's.

She led them upstairs. On the landing, in the dim hallway, she paused. Which room? One she had shared with Roosevelt. One with Gwendolyn. There weren't any sheets on Roosevelt's bed. It didn't matter anymore. She opened the door to the front room, the room she had shared with only her sister, and took them both inside.

Gwendolyn had never felt so loved, so desired, so complete. Loved and loving, giving more than she ever had. She was the conduit that

Amy's and Roosevelt's alternating currents passed through. They sparked off each other and she was ignited.

There were hands in so many places at once. And mouths on hers and on her breasts and between her legs. Any body part that went by she kissed, licked, sucked, tasted, and savored. She had an orgasm within moments of falling naked on the bed, of being covered with bare skin and wet kisses, and came again and again.

She found herself turning more and more to Roosevelt. Somewhere it bothered her. It was just a distant tug, a worrisome pinprick deep in her so-satisfied gut. In her fervent, glowing fever she pushed that worry away. Amy was next to her. This was Amy. But when her hands looked for a body to caress, it was Roosevelt's they reached for. And when her mouth ached to kiss, it was his lips, his tongue she thought of. Then she would find and concentrate on her sister, making up for her embarrassing turn toward the expected, the average, the ordinary.

No wonder this was every man's fantasy. Roosevelt had never felt such bliss. And if there was a nagging squeeze of guilt somewhere, he would think about it later. Or tomorrow. He just felt so appreciative, like he should get down on his knees and pray to these two women, goddesses, the most beautiful, sexual creatures in the world, out of this world. They allowed their glorious selves to be handled by him. He was glad of the techniques he had practiced with Amy. They had been rolling around together for an hour and he was still hard, but not anywhere near an orgasm. This was great. He was in love with both of them.

She was losing her. Gwendolyn was reaching for Roosevelt, turning to him. She was supposed to be the center. They were both supposed to turn to her, to Amy. She was the impetus, the reason for everything. She was the sun that they were supposed to orbit. But they kept forgetting about her. She was left, stranded on the edge of their universe, watching. Gwendolyn hadn't had a man in a long time. Fine, Amy thought, fine. Good, she said, watching

Roosevelt's hands move over Gwendolyn, his lips on the back of her knee, her inner thigh. Watching Gwendolyn twist with pleasure. Great. It was what she intended. Her plan had worked so well.

Chapter Twenty-one

Funny how after sex, even great sex, she always felt so sordid, so used, so gross. Gwendolyn bent her head under the shower. She might stay in there forever. The bathroom was steamy, there was nothing to see. Her own feet disappeared in the fallen fog at the bottom of the tub. She turned the water up higher, hotter.

It had been wild, but afterward they didn't cuddle or laugh. They all lay on their backs, overlapping one another like oily salami slices on a stale mattress cracker. They stared at the ceiling. Roosevelt lifted his arm over his head and she got a sniff of his sour body odor. Just moments before she had put her tongue in his every crevice. Now she shuddered, repulsed, and felt one small curly hair on the back of her tongue.

Only Amy seemed fine. As usual. Sat up. Cleared her throat. Amy. Gwendolyn didn't know if Amy had even enjoyed herself. She had seemed to be an active participant, but her own satisfaction was not apparent to Gwendolyn.

And Amy had done this just for her. It had occurred to her in the midst of everything: Amy had planned this. Amy would not have just let this happen. Roosevelt was the present she had promised. Amy wanted Gwendolyn to have everything she wanted, even if it hurt her, Amy, even if Gwendolyn's pleasure hurt her. It was a remarkable gift, but Gwendolyn had abandoned her sister. She had turned to Roosevelt. She felt queasy admitting it, even to herself.

But when she thought of Roosevelt's eyes, when she thought of the way he looked at her, she felt her breath slow, the nausea subside. It had felt so good. She couldn't help herself. It just happened. And Amy obviously wanted it to happen. She turned her face up to the hot pulse of water, let it beat on her closed eyelids, throb on her throat, on her breasts. She would do it all again with him. She opened her eyes. If Amy said it was all right.

Roosevelt had tried to pay attention to Amy. He tried not to spend too much time with Gwendolyn, but she was so easy. Everything he did, every time he touched her, was a success. She was smooth and giving. She tasted like a cupcake. And she was all over him. Amy had to be aware of that.

He knew Amy had not had an orgasm. He had watched for it, wondering if Amy's "problem" extended to sex with Gwendolyn. She told him she had never come with a man. What about her sister? He stopped caring toward the end. Gwendolyn must have come twenty times. Then it was every man for himself. His orgasm had been amazing, cosmic, worth the wait. He had been inside of Amy, but his hands and mouth were on Gwendolyn.

She had planned this. She didn't want to hate Roosevelt. She wanted him to stay around, make Gwendolyn happy, take out the trash. He was a gift, and wasn't it better to give than receive? Amy trembled, sitting naked on the side of the bed. She had not expected to feel so angry, so hurt. She should have known. She had never shared well.

"You know what she wants," Auntie Ned said. "Give it to her."

"I did," Amy said. "I did."

Amy said something.

"What?" Roosevelt asked.

She put her hand on his thigh. Gwendolyn was in the shower. He and Amy were sitting next to each other on the side of the bed, not touching, waiting for their turns in the shower, waiting for something, he wasn't sure what.

"What happened today?" she asked.

He desperately wanted to know what she thought had just happened. But she meant something else.

"Before," she said. "Before you came over."

That was a long time ago. He ran his hand over his sore knuckles. A long time ago, but if it hadn't been for that, would he have done this? Somehow he thought he would not be sitting here, naked and sticky, if he had not made his trip to the bakery.

"Tell me," Amy said. "It's okay, whatever it is."

"I went to the bakery," he said.

"You did?"

He couldn't see her face. She stared down at her hands, clasped together in her naked lap. "What happened?"

"I punched Tony in the mouth," he said. Now it seemed silly, a ridiculous gesture.

But she smiled at him, actually pleased, happier than she had looked through the marathon on the bed. Every time he had looked at her face, she had been frowning, working, her eyes gone flat and black. Now the line between her eyebrows was gone. Her eyes were open, back to their usual fudge brown. He put his arm around her.

"I hit him," he said. "I went over there to tell him to keep his hands off Gwendolyn. I wanted to impress you." He could admit it. "He pissed me off and I hit him."

"Hard?"

"Knocked him down."

She leaned her head on his shoulder. Her silky hair, messy now, but still soft and thick, brushed against his bare chest. For this moment, she seemed small, dependent.

He sighed. "Cops are probably waiting at my place right now."

She laughed. "Tony's not like that," she said, "He's too Italian, too macho. But don't run into him in a dark alley."

"I'm afraid he'll be mad as hell at Gwendolyn."

"No one's ever mad at Gwendolyn."

Gwendolyn, the little sister. Amy, the older. She looked up at him.

"You did that for me?" Amy asked.

"Yes."

The shower stopped. He heard the curtain slide back, plastic rings on the metal rod. Satiated, exhausted, still he imagined Gwendolyn's clean, wet body stepping out of the shower.

What would they do tonight? he wondered. Have dinner. Watch a movie. Hold hands on the couch. All three of them. And when it was bedtime, where would he go?

He kissed her temple, pulled her closer to him.

"Later," he said. "It can be just you and me."

"No, thanks," she said, and shook him off, stood up. She looked pure, white, and made of something hard and fine, platinum, in the fading afternoon light. "I wanted this to happen."

"Remember," he said. "Remember how I can make you feel."

Gwendolyn walked into the room, covered in a dark plaid bathrobe, her hair in a soft white towel. She grinned at both of them.

"That was crazy, wasn't it?" she said. "I have no idea what we just did."

Roosevelt sighed with relief. Gwendolyn was not Amy. She was not the one who made his bowels squeeze, his breath stop, his blood bubble in his veins, but she had her talents.

"Yeah," was all he said, instantly self-conscious about his naked body, his flaccid self.

"The shower feels great," Gwendolyn said to him. "There's a clean towel on the rod closest to the window."

"Okay," he said. "Sounds good."

He was glad to know what to do next. He got up, gathered his clothes in front of himself. Gwendolyn thoughtfully turned away, opened her dresser for underwear or socks. He scooted past her, avoiding Amy, avoiding them both, and hurried into the ordinary cloud-filled bathroom.

Gwendolyn was anxious to have her sister to herself. She was worried about her. Amy was frozen, a block of carved frosty ice. She hadn't moved or said a thing. As soon as Roosevelt was out of the room, Gwendolyn rushed to her, wrapped her flannel-covered arms around her, kissed her cheek. She tried to be light, giggle in her ear.

"Thank you," she said. "He was just what I wanted."

"He went to the bakery," Amy said.

"What?"

"I thought you were working. Where were you?"

"I ran into Elsa."

"You were with Elsa?" Amy asked.

"Yes."

"Elsa, the muscular Olympian? The remarkable cake decorator? Where? Where did you run into her?"

"Tony asked her to come in. I didn't know she'd be there." It seemed important to say that, important that Amy believe her. "I didn't."

"Where did you go?"

"We had coffee. At that little French place. You've been there."

"The two of you?"

"Yes." Gwendolyn was suddenly exasperated. "So what?" Gwendolyn gritted her teeth. She had been feeling so good, so warm and relaxed. "What happened with Tony?" she asked. "Is he okay?"

"Do you care?"

Gwendolyn went back to getting dressed. She couldn't talk to Amy when she was like this. She was looking for a fight, looking to make Gwendolyn angry. Gwendolyn wouldn't do it.

"He loves you," Amy said.

"Who? Tony?" Gwendolyn grimaced, remembering Tony's hand on her tit, the bulge in his blue jeans.

"No, stupid. Roosevelt."

"Roosevelt loves you."

Amy nodded at the bed, sheets twisted, blanket sliding to the floor. "Now he loves you."

"Amy—" Gwendolyn protested, knew what Amy needed to hear. "It's you. He only did this because it was what you wanted."

She put her arms around her. But Amy's arms stayed where they were, hanging at her sides. Gwendolyn stroked her sister's back. No response. Gwendolyn was suddenly afraid. Afraid of making Amy angrier. Afraid of Amy's jealousy. Afraid of the emptiness in her arms.

"Thank you," she whispered in her sister's ear, against her neck. "Thank you. This will be fun."

Slowly, Amy turned her head and looked into Gwendolyn's eyes. "Fun," she said and finally, finally smiled. "I'm glad you're happy."

"Thank you."

Gwendolyn was dressed and already downstairs. Roosevelt sang the Beach Boys in the shower. Amy would stop shaking and move. She would, in just another minute.

There was a knock on the front door. Not a knock, but a pound, a hit, and more. Pounding on the door, an angry fist. What now? Amy thought. What now?

The shower stopped. Gwendolyn went to the door.

"Who is it?" Amy heard Gwendolyn's hesitant little voice. "Who's there?"

Don't open the door, Amy thought, be careful. But still she didn't move. Her feet were too heavy to lift, gravity too dense.

"Tony!" Gwendolyn shouted.

Amy heard the bathroom door open. She knew Roosevelt was poised at the top of the stairs. She saw him, big like a bear, lumbering on two feet, neck craned forward. Was he wearing a towel, she wondered, around his waist? She saw his fine red pubic hairs tangling in the loops of terry cloth.

"Gwendolyn?" Roosevelt called.

Gwendolyn was talking to Tony. She could hear their angry voices, the murmur, the cadence, but not the words. Then a whine from Gwendolyn, pleading, then a louder, "No!" and distinctly, "Stop it!"

Roosevelt growled, bellowed like the bear he had become. He thundered down the stairs. Amy struggled to pick up one foot. She forced the other foot to follow. She stumbled after him.

Tony had pushed Gwendolyn down on the couch. His hand was up under her dress, his other hand in her hair. Gwendolyn was wiggling, terrified, unhappy. But Amy could not move. It was time to move; it was Tony; it was Gwendolyn, but Amy was stuck on the last step.

Roosevelt did not stop. Tony looked up as the red animal came toward him. Amy saw his slimy Italian bedroom eyes open wide for the first time in his life. He let go of Gwendolyn. He shrank away. Gwendolyn slid off the couch, stood up, turned her back on Tony.

There was a light in the room. It was Gwendolyn's face, shining, luminescent for Roosevelt, only Roosevelt. She wore a pale blue dress, the color of her eyes, she was a liquid star. Her long tan arms reached for him.

"Get out," Roosevelt said.

"Gwendolyn?" Tony appealed to her.

Gwendolyn saw only Roosevelt. Amy could have been another banister, another nail in the wooden steps.

"Get out," Amy said.

Tony thought she was talking to him. "I'm going," he said, "but this asshole better not come around again. I'll kill him."

Amy smiled. What a good idea. Tony left. Gwendolyn went to Roosevelt, pressed her face to his bare bear chest. Roosevelt patted her hair, held her tight.

"Get out of here," Amy said.

"What?" Gwendolyn lifted her small face. It was dark, shadowy, looking at her sister.

"Go to the movies," Amy said. "Why don't the two of you go to the movies? Get out of here."

"Are you sure?"

"You come too," Roosevelt said.

"No," she said. "No."

Chapter Twenty-two

In the movie theater, Gwendolyn held his hand. They laughed at the funny parts. She hid her face against his shoulder when it was scary. There was a couple next to them, and one in front of them and one behind them. The theater was full of people on dates, in love, married and together.

The star of the movie had blond hair and Roosevelt knew they were both thinking of Amy. Sometimes. Sometimes when the star turned, or lowered her head and smiled. Sometimes they were thinking of Amy. But not all the time.

Roosevelt put his lips on Gwendolyn's forehead. She lifted her face and they kissed, smooched, necked like a couple of teenagers. No place else to go. They held hands. They ate popcorn. He was on a date with a girl he was falling for. Falling hard. He forgot she had a sister. He forgot about Amy.

The phone rang in Dr. Minor's motel room. He jumped. The day had been so quiet, so completely still, like a pause before speaking, the hesitation before a leap into midair.

The phone rang and Dr. Minor picked it up.

"Hel-lo?" His voice, out of practice, broke.

"Tomorrow." Amy was matter-of-fact. "Come for dinner."

"Dinner?"

"Bring your camera."

Dr. Minor put his forehead on the carpet. "O Soul of Souls," he prayed, "I am forever your servant."

He would take a shower, put on clean clothes, get ready right now for anything. He got up to close the curtains. The headlights of a car turned on right outside his window. He was just their height; the light blinded him. He did not back away or close his eyes. He knew what it meant. It was the blazing beacon to his future.

Amy stood beside Gwendolyn's precious, brand-new, shiny white toaster oven and waited. The only meat in the house was frozen. She had gone to the freezer in the basement and taken out a large porterhouse, but it was hard, a thick block of icy beef. She put it on the counter and came back in an hour, after showering, after rubbing aloe into the blister on her belly, after stripping the sheets off that bed, that damn bed. The steak was still solid. She picked it up and the white butcher paper slipped out of her hand. She dropped it. It fell, hard, as hard as Roosevelt's hammer, on her big bare toe. She screamed. She couldn't help it, she screamed. She sat down on the plywood floor and held her foot and screamed, howled, yelled, and cursed. She kicked the frozen meat with her other foot and didn't move it. She picked it up and threw it, satisfied by the dent it put in the quality subflooring.

She decided she would eat this steak if it took her all night. No slab of cow was going to get the better of her. No lump of flesh was going to make her starve, make her drool wanting it, thinking of it. She was the one with the brain, after all; she was the superior piece of meat.

So she unwrapped it and put it in the toaster oven on a low heat to defrost. She stood by and waited. Her toe throbbed. She was tired.

"Amy."

Her name, again. Just over her shoulder, just behind her, Auntie

Ned's voice barely above a whisper. She turned, looked around the kitchen. She wanted her to be there.

"Amy."

"What?" Amy said. "What do you want?"

"Amy."

She walked out through the dining room, into the living room. No one was there. Anywhere.

Amy stood in the living room.

"It's not working," she told her aunt. "It was a bad idea. He was a bad choice. I admit it. He was."

She would go meet Gwendolyn at the movie theater. She would tell Roosevelt to go away. She and Gwendolyn would take a trip, go up north, hide in the big trees.

"I can't do this," she said. "I won't."

But she didn't move. She didn't get her keys. She didn't go out the front door. She stood still and waited. Listened. And she heard something. Not her name, but the thick thump of her trash can lid coming down. The sound of industrial-strength rubber hitting rubber.

Amy ran out the front door. Mama Girl was scurrying away as fast as she could in her mismatched flip-flops, one green, one pink.

"Wait a minute," Amy yelled.

Mama Girl pretended not to hear. Her shoulders hunched, her neck shrunk, she ducked her head and kept shuffling forward, toward her rusty front gate.

"Wait!" Amy shouted.

Mama Girl reached her gate, escaped through it. Amy heard it clang shut, the bolt slide and lock.

Amy opened her garbage can and looked inside. Sure enough, Mama Girl had dumped two more dead mice, traps still attached. They had found their final resting place on top of the pizza box left from last night's dinner with a midget paranormalist. One fallen mouse's tail curled around a piece of crust as if embracing it. I would have loved you when I was alive, better than the moldy cheese on this wood-and-wire guillotine.

Amy went to the six-foot-high security gate and shouted through the rusty iron mesh, "Keep your goddamn mice out of my trash can."

"Not my mice," said a little voice.

Amy jumped. Mama Girl was right there, just the other side of the gate. She had not gone back in her house, sheltered and secured.

"Not my mice," Mama Girl said again. "Your aunt sent them, with her fire."

"She didn't have any mice," Amy said.

"She did, she did. Your aunt's mice."

"You're nuts. Do you hear me? Crazy!" Amy was shouting, but she couldn't help it.

"Not my mice," Mama Girl said calmly a last time and went up her walk to her front door. Her flip-flops thwacked against her flat old lady feet.

The piercing screech of the smoke detector exploded from inside Auntie Ned's house. Amy wailed. What was happening? What was it? Who?

She ran inside. The kitchen was filled with smoke. Flames spiked from the brand-new toaster. She had put the steak directly on its little wire grill. The fat had dripped onto the heating coils and caught on fire. The smoke alarm was screaming. She coughed. She pulled open the toaster's door and pulled out the hot meat. It scorched her fingers and she dropped it on the dirty floor. The smoke alarm continued and continued. She scraped a chair across the floor, stood on it to turn it off. Standing underneath it the sound was unbearable; the shriek made her teeth hurt. She fanned at it, pulled at it, finally yanked the whole thing off the ceiling and threw it across the room. It hit the wall and the cry died out in a twisted whine.

Silence.

Wonderful thick silence.

Amy stood motionless on the yellow-and-chrome chair. The steak was oozing a greasy puddle on the floor. The kitchen was filled with smoke. The brand-new bright white toaster oven was black, charred, ruined. The smoke detector lay in two broken pieces of gray plastic across the room.

"What do you want from me?" Amy spoke, teeth clamped together, lips barely moving. "What do you want?"

Dr. Minor reached up and rang the doorbell. His video camera hung over his shoulder. The tripod was in the other hand. He could smell smoke. It worried him. It was not a good smell to a man in his specialty, at a house where the unbelievable had already happened. He rang again, more insistently. Who was dead? Who was alive? Jesus, what if she had already done it and he was too late? If she hadn't waited for him, he would kill her. His knees trembled. He tried the door. It was unlocked.

He followed the smell to the kitchen.

Amy stood in the center of the room, chewing on a raw but charred steak.

"What are you doing here?" she shouted at him.

He was disgusted by the meat in her hands, the smoke in the room, the cow's blood dripped on her shirt, her white jeans, the tops of her feet.

"Amy, darling," he began.

"Don't you darling me," she said.

He didn't want to call her darling anyway. She was odd, sick, terrifying, and a boring lay. "You told me to come," he said.

The door to the basement was open. It was dark down there, but he saw the twisted chrome of Auntie Ned's chair glitter in the faint light from the kitchen.

"Tomorrow. I told you to come tomorrow." Amy put the steak down. There was watery blood on her chin, a black streak on one cheek, her hands were shiny with grease and fat. "Go away."

"I wanted to set up. Make sure everything is just right. You want it to be right, don't you?" It was good she was so upset, so wild. She would need that energy.

"Yes." Amy's voice was odd, quiet. She cocked her head toward the basement. She was listening for someone.

"Is he here?" Dr. Minor asked.

"Roosevelt? No."

"Good."

"He and Wendy are at the movies. The movies."

"He's a loose cannon, a smoking gun. I mean, you never know what he might do."

"He's ruined everything."

"Yes." Dr. Minor was pleased it was going so well. He didn't have to convince her. She was ready. "Yes. I'll get the camera set up. For tomorrow. I'll do it now. You relax. Eat."

Gwendolyn said good night to Roosevelt in his truck. They'd had a good time in the movies, but on the ride home they sat apart, kept the gearshift, the armrests, the idea of going home to Amy between them. He was confused about what to do, whether to come in, where he should be and who with. So was she. So she said good-bye and saw that he was relieved. She kissed him, a perfunctory peck, not long or hard, no tongues, no sighs, no desires exchanged. The house was dark. Amy could be at any window.

"I'll see you tomorrow," he said.

"Thanks for the movie."

He had paid for everything. He had told her he liked her dress. She took off her shoes on the dark front porch, waved good-bye to him before she went in.

The house was cold. Windows were open. Gwendolyn could smell the faint odor of smoke and meat. She wanted to go back to the movies, stay in the movie theater. She was hungry, but the thought of Amy's leftovers was not appealing. She saw the video camera set up in a corner of the living room. The light from the streetlamp outside glinted off one tripod leg. She closed the front door silently.

"How was the movie?"

Amy startled her from the top of the stairs. Amy was naked, her body gray and fuzzy. Gwendolyn was suddenly so tired.

"You would have hated it," she said.

"Come up."

"I am." Gwendolyn came up the stairs. She put a smile on her face. She kissed her sister hello on the cheek.

Amy followed her into the bedroom. There were clean sheets on the bed; the laundry hamper was empty. Amy had wiped all vestiges of this afternoon away. No visible remains. Amy unzipped Gwendolyn's dress without being asked. She turned away when Gwendolyn stepped out of her underwear, shimmied into her warm flannel nightie.

They got in bed. They pulled the covers up. They looked at the ceiling.

"What did you want to tell me this afternoon?" Amy asked. "Before."

"Not now," Gwendolyn said.

"No. It was important. Tell me."

"Tomorrow."

She wanted to close her eyes. Go to sleep. She didn't want to think about Roosevelt, his hands on her skin, his breath in her ear, what they had done, how she had felt, on this bed. The sheets smelled of Amy now. Only Amy. Her sister.

"Tell me," Amy said.

"I want to go to sleep."

"Now." Amy sat up.

Gwendolyn wasn't going anywhere. She rolled over, faced her sister.

"I witnessed a car accident," she said, "the other day, in the rain. The driver in one car beat the other one to death. I wanted to stop him, but I didn't know how."

"He beat him to death? With what?"

"He hit him and knocked him down and kicked him. The little man died. The police want me to be at the trial."

Amy shook her head, put a hand on Gwendolyn's forehead, as if she was checking for fever. "Poor Wendy. You've kept this to yourself."

"No, I told Tony when I got to work late. When Elsa was there. I told them. And Roosevelt."

Stupid idiot. She held her breath. She should not have mentioned his name. Everybody knew, except Amy. Roosevelt knew. Amy had tried to leave no trace of him in this bedroom, but he was there with Gwendolyn. He was there in the bed with them, in her memory of him inside her, his odor in her nostrils and under her fingernails, the taste of him in the back of her throat.

"When?"

"It happened that rainy morning, after our fight about the toaster."

"When did you tell Roosevelt?"

Gwendolyn shrugged.

"When?"

"I don't know."

The light from the window was harsh. Amy's face was shadowed and severe. Her mouth was a black angry stripe, her eyes two furious tunnels going deep in her head. Gwendolyn could see the lines etched on either side of her sister's nose all the way down to the corners of her lips, a darker furrow between her eyebrows. She was aging. They were both getting older.

"That night," Gwendolyn said. Roosevelt would tell her anyway. "I told him that night right after it happened. At the restaurant."

Amy got up and walked out.

"Don't," Gwendolyn called after her. "Come on. I couldn't say anything to you. You were already upset that night. Remember?"

There was no answer. Gwendolyn lay on her back. She wanted to get up. She knew she had better get up. But her limbs were flaccid and heavy, her body without a spine, sucked clean of muscle, tissue, even bone. A blob of jelly, that was all that was left.

"Amy," Gwendolyn called, but faintly. She couldn't keep her eyes open. She would fix it tomorrow.

It had been a long time since he had fed his lizard. It felt like a year had passed since he was home. He drove across town paying attention, remembering the turns, marveling that the same stores and buildings were still standing. So much of him had changed. Still, his lizard would be hungry. He turned down Vine, heading for the all-night pet store. Lucky that little lizard lived in LA. He laughed. A very lucky lizard indeed. Lucky, that's what he would name it. Lucky. Like him.

At the all-night pet store, he bought some more crickets. He got instructions on how to care for them. They needed food and water, too. Of course, he thought, everything needs food and water and air. He watched the puppies trying to sleep in the cages behind the glass. They turned around and around, miserable, uncomfortable, more unhappy than the dogs at the pound. At least the pound dogs had solid cement beneath them, not wire mesh six inches off the ground.

Then it was good to be home, a relief of some kind, dirty and depressing as it was. He didn't think he would be staying there much longer anyway. He didn't know how it would work out between the three of them; he just knew it would. It had to.

He carried the crickets in their little plastic bag into the kitchen. He would get them lettuce and a carrot later.

But his lizard was dead. It had fallen over where it stood, one leg thrust into the air, toes spread stiffly. It was a different color, olive, dusty green, almost brown. Its sides had collapsed. The skin was shriveled, wrinkled, like the cheeks of the shrunken monkey heads in novelty stores. Not the ants, but starved to death, Roosevelt thought. He had starved Lucky to death.

Roosevelt cried. Tears collected in his eyes and spilled onto his cheeks. His nose filled with snot that slid over his upper lip. He sobbed, put his face down on his arms and wept.

Later, he opened his window and spilled the crickets from their plastic bag. He watched the dozen tiny bodies tumble through the air. He was on the second floor, but there were scraggly Hollywood bushes beneath, jade plants and something spiky. The crickets would survive. Or they wouldn't. His bed looked gray and filthy, infested with bad dreams and crusty memories. He didn't want to ever sleep there again. Tonight. Tonight would be the last time.

He shook the dead lizard into a brown paper grocery bag and carried it out of the apartment and down the back stairs. He tossed it into the Dumpster behind his building. The paper bag gave only a faint rustle as it hit.

"Hey." He heard a voice behind him. "Hey," it whispered urgently.

"I didn't mean it," he wailed as he turned.

A homeless man crouched across the alley, behind a stack of corroding boxes. "Got a dollar?" he asked.

Roosevelt backed away, backed all the way to the door of his building, up the stairs. He hurried into his apartment and shut the door.

Chapter Twenty-three

Gwendolyn was going to work. Amy knew that. It was Monday. People went to work on Monday. Roosevelt would be arriving any moment. It was a day like any other.

Amy's right leg was trembling. She had not slept. She had stood over the bed and watched Gwendolyn, sat in the dark and stared out the window, turned on the TV and switched channels, but hadn't slept.

Just before dawn she had gone for a walk, not bothering with clothes, pulling Auntie Ned's funny coat with the fake fur collar over her naked body. The wind blew. The leaves on the trees glittered silver and green. The branches rattled. A car drove by too fast. The driver was a woman with long black hair. A witch flying home from a séance. A teenage girl running from a bad date. A wife who couldn't sleep, who hated her house.

Amy had run home.

The sun was up, the day bright and cloudless when Gwendolyn walked into the kitchen in her bakery clothes. All that white was dingy this morning, the wrong color for her. There were bruised blue shadows in the half-moons under her puffy eyes. Her skin was sallow, apologetic. There was a red crease like a scar on one cheek.

"You look like shit." Amy couldn't resist.

"I've gotta go."

But then the front door opened. Roosevelt called out, "Hi Honey and Honey. I'm home," He laughed.

It wasn't funny, but Gwendolyn smiled. Her shoulders relaxed. The color rose to her face, pink suddenly, blossoming at the sound of his voice.

Amy couldn't bear to have him in the house. Not today. On his knees in the kitchen. On his knees while she was upstairs and he was listening to every step she took, wondering what she was doing, while they both waited for Gwendolyn to get home.

"Not today," she said.

Roosevelt smiled at her, but his face practically split in two for Gwendolyn.

"Hey," he said.

Gwendolyn lifted her face to him, but her eyes went to Amy and she dropped her head, hid her smile.

So Roosevelt turned to her, but she wasn't buying it. Whatever he had, she had had enough.

"Not today," she said again, "Don't work today. I'm making dinner, a fancy dinner for all of us and I need the kitchen. I want it to be a surprise. You can't work today."

"Can I help?" Roosevelt asked, cloying, midwestern.

"No."

"What happened to the floor?" he said. "What spilled?"

They all looked down at the plywood floor and the grease stain in the shape of Australia.

"Where's my toaster?" Gwendolyn asked.

"I broke your toaster and I made a mess," Amy said. Mom and Dad, hands behind their backs, nodded thoughtfully at her. "I cleaned it up. I'll get you a new toaster. Today."

"I'll get it," said Roosevelt.

"Terrific," Amy said. "Why don't you do that?"

Roosevelt came back for dinner with a brand-new toaster oven under one arm and flowers, a huge bunch of exotic blooms, in the other. Amy actually seemed pleased. The house smelled good. Garlic. And meat roasting. Amy was quiet, preoccupied. Gwendolyn was still upstairs, changing after work. He wanted to go up. He wanted to see her, to watch.

But Dr. Minor flittered through the kitchen. Amy had invited the good doctor to dinner, too. Just to annoy him and Gwendolyn, Roosevelt knew. The tiny doctor was more agitated, more fluttery than ever before.

Gwendolyn came down the stairs. She wore that same blue dress. That beautiful dress from the night before, but she had earrings on and a stack of bracelets on one slim wrist. She had been happy at the movies. Now she was nervous, anxious. She watched Amy bustle and fuss. Amy wasn't talking to anyone.

Roosevelt felt a little guilty. Amy was first, had been first, should come first. It was just that Gwendolyn was more his type. He kissed her in the living room, where Amy couldn't see. They kissed some more, mouths open, tongues working, his hand on her breast. He couldn't help it. Tonight, he hoped, he would have her to himself.

"Sit down, everyone," Amy called from the kitchen.

The dining room table was set with china he didn't recognize. There were candles and wine. Roosevelt tried to relax. Dr. Minor would not stop staring at him. Gwendolyn looked at her empty plate. They waited for Amy to bring the food from the kitchen.

She came in, carrying an enormous roast, almost an entire side of beef, cooked rare, oozing thick red blood.

"I had to go to the market," she said. "The meat in the freezer is frozen hard, hard as rocks, hard as the rocks in Roosevelt's head." She laughed. "We should get a microwave."

"Good idea." Roosevelt nodded, ignored her joke.

"We could put your head in the microwave," Amy said as she sat down. "Thaw those rocks."

Dr. Minor twittered at his end of the table.

"Of course we'd have to chop it off first."

"Amy," Gwendolyn said, "that's disgusting."

"No," Roosevelt said, "it's very funny. Thank you for your concern about what's in my head."

He smiled, tried to make it light. Her eyes narrowed, glared at him. He needed to spend time with her, should have insisted she let him stay today and help.

"Tell us about your time in the hospital," Amy said to him.

She sounded like a television mom asking about his day at school. He didn't want her to ask about the hospital now, in front of Gwendolyn and Dr. Minor.

"Please?" Amy asked.

He couldn't say no, wouldn't disappoint her. She had stayed home alone making dinner for all of them.

"It wasn't fun," he said. "But I don't think about it too much."

"And the electric shock therapy? What did it feel like?" Amy asked.

When did she find out he had been juiced?

"They didn't do that." Gwendolyn's eyes were wide. "Did they? It's barbaric."

"It's effective," Roosevelt said.

"Sometimes," chirped Dr. Minor. "Sometimes it doesn't work at all."

Amy smiled at Roosevelt. Roosevelt looked from one sister to the other. It would be all right. He was glad to be sitting at the table with them. Glad Amy had asked him to come over for dinner. He was even glad to see the excessive slice of roast beef on his plate.

Gwendolyn looked beautiful, as beautiful as he had ever seen her. That dress, blue like her eyes, and makeup, something on her dark lashes, her lips. Her hair so dark, her tan skin the color of a caramel in the candlelight. She looked the way she tasted. He knew how she tasted.

And Amy. Sister. Amy was her negative image. Short black dress, hair almost as white as her skin, eyes huge, as deep and dark as a pirate ship lost at the bottom of the sea. He had never seen her wear anything except the childlike pastels. The black was striking. Wicked. When he was eight and saw the movie Snow White at a birthday party, it was the Evil Queen who had given him his first little-boy erection. But then Snow White was so pretty and sweet and could talk to birds. He laughed now, out loud; even at eight he had wanted them both.

"Did it hurt?" Gwendolyn asked.

He sighed. He didn't want to think about the hospital. He didn't want to think about the rubber straps that held him down, the way he gagged on the tongue protector, the fluorescent light in his eyes, even the nurse who spread the conduction lotion on two spots on his forehead. That was what he remembered most. The nurse. Middle-aged, overweight, a bristle on her chin, but her hands so gentle on his head, apologetic, remorseful. Forgive me, they asked. He could see up her nose, the gray hairs, the pores of her skin like the craters in yellow Jarlsberg cheese, and he loved her. She was the first kind touch since his mother died, since his wife left him, since long before the accident. He came to look forward to his treatments, just for her, for her hands on his face. He never even knew her name.

"No," he said to Gwendolyn's sweet, concerned face. "No, it didn't hurt. And here I am."

"Here you are." Dr. Minor snickered.

"Shhh." Amy shut him up.

Amy's stomach was bubbling, boiling, churning urgently. Tonight, tonight, tonight. Her voice, in chorus now with Auntie Ned's whisper, chanted in her head. Tonight. Just a little while from now. Her sister's exquisite baby blues, Roosevelt's disgusting canine eyes, were on her. She sat at the head of the table and devoured her gargantuan piece of meat with gusto, ripping and tearing the flesh in her teeth. She felt the struggle, the cow's last earthly terror; heard the lowing in the slaughterhouse and the cloven hooves clatter against the steel-grated floor. It fed her. Its cries added to her own. Tonight. Tonight. Tonight.

"What's the camera for?" Roosevelt asked.

Gus had set it up in a living room corner, wide-angled to get the best view.

He was prepared. "I'm going to interview Amy," he said.

"Gus and I will do the dishes," Amy said. "Go on, you two, go sit on the couch." It was her best big sister smile. She needed time to prepare. Gus would help her.

"Go sit in the living room," Amy continued. "Get to know each other."

Gwendolyn's eyes were round ringed moons in her face. Amy would answer to them later, fall on her knees and pray to her sister's eyes for absolution from her lunacy. Wendy, she would beg, Wendy.

Gwendolyn left her plate and glass on the table. She stood up stiffly and her chair was noisy. She didn't look at Amy as she went into the living room.

Roosevelt, good boy, took his plate to the sink, gave Amy a kiss on the top of her head, waited for more.

"Go on." She smiled. He started to go. "No," she said, "wait." He turned back. "Thank you," she whispered to him, "for everything."

She watched him freeze and then thaw, melt in front of her. Damn if he didn't get tears in his silly eyes. She went back to the dishes. Reluctantly, he turned away, away from her and toward the waiting Gwendolyn.

The water felt good on her hands. She was warm in the little house, in her bare dress. Auntie Ned's voice was soothing, a comfort really. Things were going along, moving toward their inevitable conclusion.

Dr. Minor's little hands slid up her back.

She jumped, hissed at him, "Stop it, you disgusting little toad."

He smiled, licked his lips. She turned the water up in the sink, hotter. She couldn't feel it. Hotter still.

Suddenly, regret bubbled up in her. And fear. She had made a mess of things. Gwendolyn would miss Roosevelt. At night, in bed, she would think of him. Amy's breasts could not replace his broad chest, her thighs did not have his strength, his girth.

She had watched them at dinner, Gwendolyn and Roosevelt, Roosevelt and Gwendolyn, fuel for her fire, fanning the flames of her anger. Gwendolyn couldn't take her eyes from Roosevelt: She watched his hands bring food to his mouth, his jaw as he chewed, his neck as he swallowed. Roosevelt's face went soft when he looked at Gwendolyn, fuzzy like a baby blanket. But when he turned to her, she saw only anxiety. Roosevelt and Gwendolyn. They laughed together, ignored Dr. Minor, couldn't wait to get back to bed.

Amy had to kill him. She had been wrong. She could admit it.

She was wrong to think she could share her sister. She had never been good at sharing; her playmates went home crying, bruised, battered. She had to get rid of Roosevelt. And Gwendolyn would have to forget. Gwendolyn would turn to her to make her forget. And she could, she could make her lose all memory of him. Her role in Gwendolyn's life would be defined and absolute, once and forever.

Gwendolyn came into the kitchen. Her blue dress wavered behind the steam from the hot water.

"He's not staying," Amy said. She wanted to give her a little warning.

"This was your idea." Gwendolyn's voice had that hard metal ring to it. The new Wendy, the Wendy who didn't tell her sister everything.

"Say good-bye to him." Amy took her sister in her arms, her wet hands on the ass of the blue dress. She didn't care if Dr. Minor was watching, which he was. Amy kissed Gwendolyn's neck, her favorite spot, sucked and bit her. Gwendolyn stood still, accepted the bruise on her neck.

"Say good-bye now," Amy said. "Good-bye. I'm tired of him."

"Amy."

Amy laughed; her mouth was filled with heat. "Him or me. Make your choice. Him or me."

Gwendolyn didn't say anything. Amy waited and Gwendolyn was silent. Amy felt the sweat on her temples. There was no choice to be made. It was a joke.

"You gave him to me," Gwendolyn said.

"He was mine first."

"But then you gave him to me."

Out of the corner of her eye, Amy saw Dr. Minor's odd, wide forehead shining. His eyes were lit, his mouth a red round hole in his fluffy beard.

"Him or me," Amy said again. "Him or me!"

Gwendolyn crossed her arms in front of her chest, squeezed her eyes shut tight. Amy grabbed her sister's hair, pulled it until she opened her eyes. They stared at each other. Amy knew what she would choose. What she had to choose.

"Him or me."

"You," Gwendolyn whispered. "You."

Gwendolyn stepped back. She was sweating. They were both sweating.

"You," she said again.

Dr. Minor's eager face looked up at her, at them. He was drooling. His lips and beard were wet. She backed away. Dreaming, it seemed to Gwendolyn that she was dreaming. Her head was filled with clouds. She opened her mouth and lizards jumped out, mottled, leathery, skinny legs scratching and thrusting, just like the one she gave Roosevelt. Roosevelt. Amy was going to do something. Her sister had a new plan.

She wobbled out of the kitchen, sat down on the ugly green sofa. She hated this sofa. The tufts of upholstery were like sea anemones, waving, undulating beneath her.

Roosevelt came in from the bathroom. His cheeks were polished, squeaky clean. He came to the couch, sat down in the green tide pool next to her. She would tell him to get out of here, quick. Then she could go upstairs, pull the blanket over her head and when she woke up it would all be over.

But the bed didn't belong to her. Nothing did. She lay her head in Roosevelt's lap. His thighs were warm under her cheek; she smelled detergent and a faint odor of paint. She let her fingernails play with the seam on his inner thigh, running along it, scraping. He brushed the hair off her face.

"Roosevelt," she said.

"Yes," he said.

What was she supposed to say next? This was one of those dreams, standing at the front of the class unable to answer the question, realizing she was standing there in her underwear, dirty underwear, torn.

"I . . ." She thought she could begin.

"What?" he said. "You can tell me anything."

"I'm afraid," she said.

"Of what?" he said. "Not me?"

"No."

"Good. Then what?"

"I haven't been with a man in a long time."

"Yes."

"I've never had anyone but Amy."

"I'll take care of you," he said. "I promise."

"Yes," she said to Roosevelt. She should have said run away. Never look back. "Yes," was all she could manage.

She took his hand from her hair, brought it to her lips, and kissed it. She didn't look at his face. In a nightmare it was never safe to look at a person's face.

Amy's breath was sizzling in her throat. She laid her hand on the back of Dr. Minor's neck and he gasped, gurgled and ducked away. She left a red mark, the beginning of a finger-shaped burn. He kept smiling at her, his teeth like yellow Indian corn.

"How are you feeling?" Dr. Minor grinned. "Hot enough for ya?"

"You make me sick." He did. The spicy heat inside her, the churning, bubbling, boiling in her throat, her chest, her stomach, blazed when she looked at him, when she remembered what she had done. "Wendy," she whispered. "Wendy," she reminded herself.

"Your aunt," Dr. Minor cackled, a demented character from a distorted fairy tale. "Did you want her to die?"

"Shut up."

"She left you this house, didn't she?" His breath smelled of blood and flesh. "And some money?"

"Shut up."

"Maybe you killed her," he whispered. "Maybe you sent her the Fire from Heaven. Maybe you did."

"No!" Amy screamed. She thought she saw sparks fly from her fingertips.

"Now," Dr. Minor said. "I'm going to the camera. Now."

Now. She turned off the water and hung up the dish towel. She put her palms on her cheeks. She could feel the heat. Anything she touched she would burn, scorch, leave in ashes. Roosevelt's hammer was still on the floor in the corner, heavy, the head well used, the claw spiked with paint. She touched the hammer and saw it glow red under her fingers.

Roosevelt was sitting on the couch. Dr. Minor put one of his weird little thumbs in the air, giving her the sign. Where was Gwendolyn? Then she saw her sit up. She had been lying on the couch with her head in Roosevelt's lap. They both looked guilty.

And they were.

Roosevelt stood up, blushed, banged his shin on the coffee table.

"Sorry, Roosevelt," she said.

"What about?"

She heard the fear, his urgent need to placate her.

"I'm sorry," she said again. "I just don't think you're the right man for the job."

She had pushed the right button, got the premium sandwich at the Automat. The color rose into his cheeks, across his nose, in a line up his forehead. His chest swelled.

"Yes, I am."

"Not for me."

Gwendolyn stood up. She put her hand on Roosevelt's arm.

"I'll get you a better one," Amy said to her sister, "better for both of us.

"No."

Amy groaned. It was hot. The bottoms of her feet blazed in her little pink sneakers. She thought the rubber soles might melt away. Sweat dripped down her forehead and off the end of her nose. Strands of her hair clung to her neck. It was so hot the air sagged. She could barely breathe.

"Wendy. Go. Go upstairs." She was concentrating. Roosevelt was beginning to steam. She could see it coming off the top of his head. She didn't want her sister to witness Roosevelt's terrible death. "Go!" she said again.

But Gwendolyn wasn't moving. She stayed with Roosevelt. Her blue dress was twisted around her, tucked up on one side. Her hair was tangled. She wasn't wearing any shoes. The sight of her bare, graceful feet filled Amy with reverence and dread.

"Gwendolyn!" she wailed, pleading with her sister to wake up, get away.

Roosevelt looked at Gwendolyn. Looked at Amy.

Amy saw the heat shimmering around him. His face getting redder and redder, expanding. Yet he didn't seem uncomfortable. He was just standing there.

"Do it!" yelled Dr. Minor. "What are you waiting for?"

"I am doing it!" she shouted back. "Can't you see?"

Roosevelt frowned, "What are you talking about?"

"Die," she screamed at him. "I want you to die, you useless piece of meat."

"Amy!" Gwendolyn stared at her sister. "What's the matter with you?"

"Do it," Dr. Minor was chanting.

"Gwendolyn?" Amy took a step toward her little sister, her baby sister.

"Do it!"

Amy blinked, her eyes tearing. She felt herself sliding, melting over to Roosevelt. She put her palms on his chest.

"Jesus, Amy, you're burning up."

"Stop."

"Gwendolyn." Amy swayed against Roosevelt. "This is for you. It's all for you."

"Do it!" the doctor was screeching.

Where was she? Where was Auntie Ned? Amy couldn't hold it up any longer. Not by herself. She would have to let everything fall.

And then Gwendolyn was there, at her side. Her hands were cool on her face, her forehead, her breath as fresh as ice.

"Amy." Her voice crackled, too cold to understand. "Stop it. Don't do this."

"You're hurting me."

But Gwendolyn wouldn't take her hands away. They were frozen to her, attached, burning her with their dry white cold. Amy shook herself free, ran away, halfway up the stairs.

"This is for you," Amy told her.

"No," Gwendolyn said.

She reached out with her frigid fingers, took a step. Roosevelt put his hand out. Roosevelt stopped her. Amy saw Gwendolyn let herself be stopped.

Amy had to close her eyes. The smoke was hurting, evaporating her tears.

"I'm sorry."

Why was Gwendolyn apologizing? Had she spilled her crayons? Torn her best blouse? Not done her homework?

"Amy, I'm sorry."

Amy opened her eyes, looked at her baby sister. She wasn't six years old, or even ten. She was grown up. Old enough to be married, kids of her own, moved out, gone away. Gone away.

"For you," she said, "for you."

Gwendolyn's knees collapsed. Roosevelt reached for her, but missed her, watched her fall to the floor, her back upright, her legs folded under her, her head tilted like a puzzled dog. She fell, stiff blue crumpled on the floor.

Amy gripped the railing. Her face was dark crimson, fevered and fathomless. He saw the perspiration sliding off her, enough to create a puddle at her feet.

"Oh my God!" Dr. Minor shouted from his corner. He swung the camera from Roosevelt to Amy.

Roosevelt remembered the doctor was there. Good, he thought. "Help her," he said.

Amy's tears mixed with the sweat on her face, tears that left red streaks like scars. She was crying blood.

"Help her," Roosevelt said again.

Gus shook his head, too frightened to go near her.

Amy reached both hands to her sister. Steam rose from her palms. Blisters were growing, flowering on her arms and thighs.

"Gwendolyn!"

Roosevelt heard the ache, the craving, the yearning, the temperature in that one word. He knew he was watching Amy die, but he heard her voice and he was jealous. For Gwendolyn, for her, Amy was unafraid. She sank in deeper, dove to the bottom without fear, explored the darkest waters, held her breath for as long as she could, too long, until she couldn't stand it anymore and her lungs burst. For Gwendolyn.

He looked at Gwendolyn. She was more like him. She turned her head, closed her eyes.

He went to her. He pulled her to her feet, put his arm around her shoulders. Amy had misunderstood her own prediction for him, long ago when she told his fortune in that horrible kitchen. She had prophesied redemption. She had promised him it was coming. And now it had. But she had been confused about who would do the saving and who would be saved. Amy's death would release Gwendolyn. But no one could save Amy. He took Gwendolyn out the front door.

Gus kept the camera rolling. It was his specialty after all. It wasn't Roosevelt, but it didn't matter. It was almost better that it was her. She was a witch and she would be burned for her terrible transgressions. She deserved it and he deserved to watch.

Her face was expanding into bright crimson swells of flesh. No nose anymore, cheeks grown into malignant roses, poppies, scarlet chrysanthemums. Her hair began to crinkle, curl on her scalp. She opened her mouth to scream at him and exhaled hot yellow steam, pungent, sweet with Chinese spices.

He couldn't take his eyes away from her.

A cloud, an exhale of smoke. A sudden blinding flash. Her lovely breasts exploded. Opened wide. He saw her heart erupt.

Then he ran. Too much, it was too much. He left the camera rolling and ran out the door. He hid behind Roosevelt and Gwendolyn, crouching on the front walk.

There were fireworks inside. Showers of bloodred sparks spraying out the front door. Each blade of grass was illuminated. The orange-and-black wings of the plastic bird spun wildly in the hot wind.

Gwendolyn wailed, an animal's howl of separation, of departure, of loneliness that would never end. Roosevelt held her, but there wasn't much of her left to hold. She was hollow, a pale blue eggshell with nothing inside.

Mama Girl smelled smoke in her sleep, heard blisters popping in her dreams. She knew something had happened next door. She woke up in the morning and shuffled, bright curling toenails glowing in the dim winter light, to check her traps. Empty. No more mice. Something, something had happened next door.

At nine o'clock, she sent her boyfriend over. The front door was wide open. The smoke alarm was missing from the ceiling. He called the fire department.

The truck came. The new chief had never seen anything like it. He called the arson investigator and homicide, but there wasn't much to report. An unusual odor. A freezer full of meat. A pile of ash on the stairs and two pink sneakers lying there, just like brand-new.

Acknowledgments

I would like to thank the following people for their assistance: Jonathan Jerald for his help with Spontaneous Human Combustion; Ralph Cissne, my tantric connection; Sue Horton, in countless ways; Dave Feinman, Janet Fitch, Dana Gladstone, Claudia Kunin, Fred and Dinah Mills, and my friends in the Silver Lake writer's group for reading and re-reading; and especially my husband and children for their support, encouragement, and amazing patience.

28 DATE DUE **DAYS**

JUN 1 6 2002		
JUN 2 9 2002		
OCT 2 3 2002		
	WITHDRAWN	
		PRINTED IN U.S.A